THE DEADLIEST KILLER OF ALL

Dr. Carey could not relax. There were too many things to consider, too much for him to think about for his nerves to release their tension. He realized—how well he realized—his youth and inexperience, his gullibility and his lack of knowledge. Here he was with sickness all about him and the people of Soltura trusting him, their lives in his hands. The thought awed the young doctor. He was frightened, frightened at the enormity of the task. So far one man had died at Soltura. How many others would die before they got the cure?

TRIGGER VENGEANCE

John Trace

LEISURE BOOKS NEW YORK CITY

A LEISURE BOOK®

December 2008

Published by special arrangement with Golden West Literary Agency.

Dorchester Publishing Co., Inc.
200 Madison Avenue
New York, NY 10016

ISBN 10: 0-8439-6153-8
ISBN 13: 978-0-8439-6153-9

The name "Leisure Books" and the stylized "L" with design are trademarks of Dorchester Publishing Co., Inc.

Printed in the United States of America.

10 9 8 7 6 5 4 3 2 1

Visit us on the web at www.dorchesterpub.com.

TRIGGER VENGEANCE

CHAPTER I

The West

WHEN he was a little boy Eliot Carey's father had taken him to see Buffalo Bill's Wild West Show. The Indians in their paint and feathers, the cowboys, the wild-horse riders and the men who roped the steers, all the fanfare and panoply and glamour, had remained with Eliot. The Wild West and medicine had been the two incentives of Eliot Carey's life. Now, a full-fledged doctor and twenty-eight years old, he stood on the station platform at Feather Springs and the West lay all about him.

It was a flat West. Brown-gray rolling country stretched away on either side. The brown-gray was neatly bisected by the long line of the railroad right of way and behind Eliot was the ugly yellow of the two-story depot. The depot, the siding, a stockyard and the dwindling lines of rails comprised the sole view. In the east, the direction Eliot faced, a dust devil danced a spritely bacchanal. Flat country and

I

a dust devil. Yet out of the east came a faint clean odor that filled the young doctor's lungs with tang and zest. Overhead was a sky so blue as to be unbelievable, a great shimmering expanse, fitting canopy for the vastness beneath it. In Eliot Carey a feeling arose, a feeling as of shackles cast aside, bonds removed. He turned.

At the end of the cinder platform a square-shouldered, red-faced, redheaded man helped a redheaded girl into a buggy. Eliot's trunk reposed upon the platform where the baggageman had dropped it. Eliot's grips surrounded his feet. Beside him, in the shade of the yellow depot, the scrawny station agent bobbed his Adam's apple in his thin neck, spat accurately at a rail and spoke.

"The town's a mile west," said the agent. "It ain't built over to the railroad yet."

"Yet?" Eliot Carey echoed.

"Been buildin' this way for ten years," said the agent. "I been here that long an' they've put up three buildings. They ain't enterprisin' in Feather Springs."

"Isn't there"—Eliot hesitated—"a hack or a stage or some way to get to town? I——"

"Pursley Williams runs a hack," interrupted the agent morosely. "He's drunk, I reckon. He ain't met a train for three days."

"Then——" began Dr Carey.

The agent interrupted once more. "Hey!" the agent called, stepping out of the shadow. "Captain Irish!"

The red-faced, redheaded man had finished placing the girl in the buggy. Her luggage was piled in the body under the seat. The bay team, at the moment of the agent's call, was drawing the buggy past the depot. Now the team stopped and the red-faced man turned his head.

"Got a passenger for town," the agent called, relaxing against a baggage truck once more. "Can you an' Miss Janice take him in?"

The red-faced man called, "Sure" and swung the buggy toward the yellow depot.

"There's a ride," said the agent. "You c'n send a dray over for your trunk."

At the edge of the cinders Eliot looked up toward the man and the girl in the buggy. The man was burned brick red and two blue eyes twinkled in the red expanse of face. The girl's face was heart shaped and lovely.

"You're very kind," Eliot said.

The red-faced man nodded. "Toss your grips on behind and jump on," he directed. "We'll take you to town."

Eliot placed a grip in the body of the buggy, climbed up and, holding his medicine bag on his knees, settled himself. The bay horses snapped the buggy away from the depot, dust billowing up from the wheels.

The depot was a yellow spot in the distance when the driver turned and spoke to his passenger. "What are you selling?" the driver asked.

Eliot Carey thought a moment before replying. "I'm a doctor," he answered.

The driver said, "Oh," and then, after a moment's lapse, "Are you the young fellow that's going to Soltura?"

Eliot said, "Yes."

Again a moment's lapse and then, "I'm Laurence Irish," the driver announced. "My daughter Janice, Doctor——?"

"Eliot"—the buggy struck a stone and bounced—"Carey."

"Glad to know you, Doctor," said the captain. Eliot held onto the sides of his seat. There were more than the one stone in the road.

When the buggy stopped Eliot dismounted. A two-story building blazoned with the sign "Exchange Hotel" was at his right. On either side of the Exchange Hotel were other weather-beaten buildings and opposite were still others, making a single narrow street wherein the dust lay thick.

"Here you are, Doctor," Laurence Irish announced cheerfully. "Here's the hotel."

"I'm very grateful." On the boardwalk in front of the Exchange Dr Carey looked up at the driver and the girl. "Thank you for——"

"Don't mention it." Laurence Irish lifted the lines and the hoofs of the bays puffed dust from the street. Irish looked back over his shoulder. "We'll see you at Soltura, Doctor," he called.

Dr Carey bowed and straightened.

Inside the Exchange Hotel the clerk that assigned Eliot Carey to a room might have come from Haversack, New Jersey. He was sallow faced and wore black sleeve protectors. The pen with which the doctor signed the register was as scratchy as any pen in the post office at Haversack. In his room, his grips on the floor, he looked at a bed with a dingy spread, a dilapidated chair and table and a rickety washstand. A gray pitcher and a grayish bowl adorned the washstand. Originally they had been white. These were the sole toilet facilities. Very slowly Eliot Carey closed the door behind him and walked across to the bed. The springs creaked as he settled himself. From the bed he had a view through the dirty curtainless window of the false front of the building across the street. Black letters on the false front spelled: "RHYNS' GEN'L ST——"

Eliot Carey stared through the dirty window and did not see the sign. Instead he saw the dancing dust devil and smelled the sage. He smiled.

He was roused from his meditation by the clamor of a bell somewhere belowstairs. Interpreting the clanging as a summons to the evening meal, Dr Carey arose slowly from the bed, pulled off his coat and vest and, rolling up his sleeves, poured water from the gray pitcher. When he washed, the grime of the train journey gritted against his skin and, using the gray towel, he left long streaks of black against the grayness. Dust flew from the coat as he shook it and dust came from his trousers as he slapped his hands against them. He was no cleaner than before when, finally, he left his room and descended the stairs.

Supper was in the dining room adjacent to the lobby. A brown-skinned waitress conducted him to a table, announced with pride that this was "The Commercial Table" and recited a singsong litany of food. From that recitation Eliot chose, waited, was served and ate sparingly.

When he left the dining room he repaired to the lobby and seated himself in a rawhide-bottomed chair. Men strolled into the lobby, passing him and glancing at him. Idly the doctor noted them. They seemed ordinary enough but closer inspection showed that this was not true. Wind and sun had browned them deeply, putting crow's-feet wrinkles at the corners of their eyes, and when they looked at the doctor the glance was frank and direct, a swift estimate of the man who sat in the rawhide chair.

Eliot had traveled before. Vienna and the Swiss Alps, the little stone-built foreign towns, the people in peasant dress and with a foreign language were familiar enough to him. Always he had been easy, satisfied, sure of himself. Now he began to experience a new sensation. How, he wondered, did a man comport himself so that these men, these browned, direct-eyed fellows, would accept him as an equal? He wished desperately to know, for he was determined that they should accept him as an equal, that, and soon, the easy greetings they exchanged among themselves would include him in their fellowship. This was his country and Eliot Carey knew it.

From behind him came a soft drawl of voices. The young doctor, relaxed, could not help but overhear.

"They're down in the Silver Dollar," drawled one

voice. "Sid Raupert an' Mark Neville. Mark is dealin' blackjack an' Sid's buckin' the game."

Another voice, soft as the first but deeper, made comment. "I never thought they'd get together. Not after that trouble last spring."

"Sid has been a-talkin'," drawled the first speaker.

A silence followed and then the deeper voice made a statement. "I'm goin' down there," he said.

Eliot could hear the chairs creak as the men rose. Idly he, too, got to his feet. Two broad-shouldered men were going through the door. Curiosity piquing him, Eliot Carey followed them.

Outside the Exchange Hotel Feather Springs was dark. Lights from windows lanced into the darkness and along the street hard leather of boot heels thumped against the planks of the board sidewalk. The air was cool and exhilarating and, glancing skyward, Eliot could see the stars, so close that they seemed to perch upon the tops of the buildings. The raw bones of the buildings were softened by the dusk and faintly but clearly the tinkle of a guitar came to the doctor's ears. He followed the sound of the boot heels, striding off down the walk, his big body lithe in his sack suit. The broad-shouldered men entered a building through a swinging door. Stopping before the door, light streaming out from below it striking his legs, Eliot could hear a hum of voices and the soft clink of glasses. He placed his hand on the door, pushed and went in.

There were men in the room he entered. Two kerosene lights, suspended from the ceiling, illuminated the place. Along the right side of the room ran a polished bar, the back bar mirror and the glasses stacked against it flashing like prisms. Further down the room were tables, three of them. Two were unoccupied and at the third sat two men facing each other. Dr Carey pushed his way between the men at the door, reached the bar and stopped. Although there were two attendants behind the bar, neither moved toward him. Like the others in the room, the attention of the bartenders was fixed upon the card players. Something tight, hard bound like a tourniquet wrapped about the stump of an amputated arm, held barroom and the men in it. As the others, Eliot Carey looked toward the card players.

One man at the table was tall. He was slumped in his chair but even so he loomed large. His face was a smooth melancholy brown mask with wide-spaced blue eyes set in it. The melancholy man held a deck of cards in his hand and there was money stacked upon the table before him.

The other man was small, slightly built, and when he moved it was like the darting of a dragon fly over a pool. His face was thin, narrow, with a nose that jutted out like the beak of a predatory bird. The narrow face was a mask with slits cut in it for eyes and mouth, and, looking at the mouth of the small man, Eliot Carey thought of a freshly healed scar, a thin line of redness puckered at the edges. The small man, too, had money before him and two cards upon the table.

The West

"Hit me," the small man said and made the words a challenge.

Deliberately the larger player slid a card from the deck and placed it face up on the table.

"A deuce." The man beside Eliot spoke the words, whispered them rather. "Mark has been dealin' him little ones."

"Again!" snapped the small man.

Again the dealer slid a card from the deck and placed it face up. Lifting himself to his toes, Eliot could see that this was a face card.

"That breaks me," announced the small man conversationally and pushed a pile of coin toward the dealer.

The dealer disregarded the coin. He reached out for the cards he had dealt, collected them and placed them at the bottom of the deck. His voice was smooth and even as he spoke. "You play in tough luck, Sid," said the dealer.

The small man tipped back his chair, teetered upon it for a moment and then, decisively, let the front legs strike the floor and shoved the chair back. "It ain't all luck," he said thinly and waited.

Beside Eliot Carey a man drew a long breath, the sound sharp in the quiet of the room. The tall dealer made no movement. His left hand held the deck of cards suspended above the green felt of the table and his right, just the fingers touching, rested on the table's edge. For perhaps ten seconds that tableau held, and then, where the dealer's right hand had rested, there was the dull blue and black of a gun.

Trigger Vengeance

The movement had been so swift, so unexpected that Eliot Carey had failed to follow it. The gun lay there, the hand that held it lax. The weapon was not lifted, not pointed, simply was a dully gleaming threat on the green felt.

"I'd call it luck, Sid," said the dealer gently.

Again there was silence. It was broken by the small man's chair rasping against the floor as he pushed it back. The small man got up. "Call it luck then," he said surlily. "I've had enough . . . for tonight."

"Any time, Sid," drawled the dealer softly. "I'll accommodate you any time."

To that there was no answer. The small man left the table, pushing his way toward the door. As he passed Eliot Carey the young doctor saw his eyes. They were small and red and burning. Dr Carey had seen eyes like those once before: the eyes of a bull that had killed a man, goring him to death. When the small man had left the room a babble of voices broke out. Men talked, their voices high and excited. Dr Carey caught words: "Showdown sure. . . ." "Sid is finished." "That done it. . . ." Among the voices came the deep tones of the man who had spoken in the hotel lobby.

"That's just a start," said the deep-voiced man. "Sid's been shamed. That's just a start."

At the card table the tall dealer got up. The gun had disappeared and his face was solemn. Still a light danced in the blue eyes.

"I'm surprised at you boys," chided the tall man.

"You act like you'd expected to see somethin'."

He, too, moved from the table, pausing beside the bar, taking an offered drink and refusing another. Then, the men in the room making way for him, he walked to the door and on out.

When he was gone the talk broke out afresh. Men, moving from the cluster beside the door, lined the bar, took places at the card tables. Dr Carey found himself with a little space on either side and a blond-haired barman facing him. "What 'll it be?" asked the bartender professionally.

"A glass of beer," answered Dr Carey.

When the beer came, cold and foaming, Dr Carey sipped it and asked a question. "Who are those men?"

The blond bartender, mopping up the wet ring left by the doctor's glass, lifted his blue eyes and surveyed his questioner. "New here, ain't you?" said the barman. "That tall fello' is Mark Neville. The little one is Sid Raupert."

"But," said Dr Carey, "I don't understand. . . ."

"They've had trouble," said the bartender briefly. "Is the beer cold enough?"

"Fine," Eliot complimented.

Later, when he had paid for his drink, when he had walked back up the quiet street where still the stars set close and the guitar tinkled faintly far away, when he had climbed the stairs to his room and undressed and blown out his lamp and settled down upon the hard mattress of the bed, Eliot Carey lay awake thinking.

Trigger Vengeance

Through the open window the noises of Feather Springs came softly. Voices murmured. Down below a horse went past, feet plop, plop, plopping in the dust and the saddle squeaking slightly; and somewhere in the distance a cow mourned for the calf of which she had been deprived. Men walked on the board sidewalk, their feet thumping hollowly. In the room next to Dr Carey's a sleeper turned and the bedsprings squeaked, the sound loud through the thin partition.

The West, thought Dr Eliot Carey. The West! He had seen a little of it that night. The country was flat and monotonous. The town was rawboned, unlovely as the naked skeleton of a man. The color, the flamboyancy, the glamour were not visible to the eye, and yet . . .

He had seen the challenge given and accepted. He had seen Death stalk into a room and out again. He had heard the casual drawl of voices, more deadly because of their very casualness.

The West! Tomorrow he must send a drayman for his trunk. Tomorrow he must make arrangements to take the stage to Soltura. He wondered what he would find at Soltura, what it would be like.

Down below a man said: "Good night, Tom. I'll see you tomorrow." A door closed. Dr Eliot Carey rolled over on the hard mattress and, pillowing his head on his arm, went to sleep.

CHAPTER II

Soltura

SOLTURA was not at all what Dr Carey expected. Soltura was a little collection of buildings beside a long swell of ground. There were mountains behind the town, blue-black and frowning. Clem Maybe, the stage driver, said that the mountains were the Robleros. Clem Maybe said a good many things on the long drive from Feather Springs, some of them, Dr Carey shrewdly surmised, untrue. Asking Clem a question was something like turning on a water spigot, with the disadvantage that Clem could not be turned off. Clem discoursed on jack rabbits, antelope, the LS ranch of Captain Irish, his wife's asthma and the drought three years past when, so Clem said, the country had become so dry that all the windmills pumped dust. When, late in the evening, the buckboard that served as a stage reached Soltura Clem Maybe's loquacity had not diminished or dulled.

Trigger Vengeance

"There," said Mr Maybe, pointing with his whip to a big red building, "is Welch an' Company's store. There's their warehouse, Doc. Now see down below? That's where I live. That's Brannigan's saloon, an' that's——" And so Mr Maybe continued, vociferous as a guide on a sight-seeing trip through New York's Chinatown. "An' here's Doc Zeitletz'," announced Mr Maybe in peroration. "Whoa, Hazel. Whoa, Gwendolyn!" The mules that drew the buckboard, Hazel and Gwendolyn, stopped their progress along Soltura's street and, looking to his left, Dr Carey saw the house that Mr Maybe indicated.

It was a rambling white house that Dr Carey saw. There were vines on the porch, brown now, and as the buckboard stopped the door opened and a man appeared in the doorway. Dr Carey dismounted and stood beside the buckboard. The man from the house came down the walk.

He was a small man, white haired and round with good living. His vest was open, exposing an expanse of white shirt and there was a small black string tie awry at his collar. A sweeping white mustache adorned his ruddy face and above pink cheeks his blue eyes twinkled. The small man stopped and surveyed Eliot Carey.

"I brung him, Doc," Clem Maybe announced. "We been——"

"You are Doctor Carey, so?" interrupted the small man. "Come in, Doctor. Come in. Clem, untie the doctor's trunk."

"Sure, Doc," said Clem. "I'll bring in the trunk."

Soltura

Eliot stood indecisively. "You——" he began.

"Zeitletz," said the small man. "Fritz Zeitletz. You have my letter. I have been expecting you. Come in, Doctor." His pudgy hand seized Eliot Carey's arm and, unresisting, the young man allowed himself to be led toward the house.

The interior of the house was clean and brightly painted. Fritz Zeitletz led his companion into a comfortable room, turned and, with both hands on Eliot's arms, surveyed him again. The blue eyes twinkled merrily in the small man's face. "So," said Dr Zeitletz, "you have come. Clem will bring your trunk and put it on the porch. You shall have the north room. The surgery is here." He freed a hand and gestured toward a door. "And you have grown that beard because you are so young and you wanted to be dignified. Not so?" The words came in a flood from the small man's mouth.

Eliot Carey, completely taken aback, could not answer and Dr Zeitletz laughed. "I talk too much and too fast," he said. "I have been waiting eagerly. Sit down, Doctor. Sit down. How was your trip? Not too bad? Do you like the country? You are hungry, so? María. ¡María! ¡Ven acá!"

A white-haired woman with a brown face looked into the room and smiled shyly at Eliot. To her the older doctor spoke swiftly and in Spanish and she withdrew, returning presently with wine in thin glasses and a plate of small cakes.

"Now," said Zeitletz, settling back into a chair, a

glass of wine in one hand and three cakes in the other. "Now, Doctor."

Eliot Carey had caught his breath. Now, supplied with wine and with the cake plate beside him on a table, he also seated himself. "Why," he said slowly, "I had your letter, Doctor. I had always wanted to come to the West. This seemed to be the opportunity and I took it. But I can't understand how you happened to choose me."

A momentary shadow crossed the bright eyes of Fritz Zeitletz. He sipped from the glass of wine, gesticulated with it and spoke.

"I needed a younger man to help me," he said, "so I wrote to my old friend Wabfein at the hospital. Wabfein wrote back telling me about a young man that was in disgrace, a young man who dared to take much upon himself, who says, 'this one has malaria,' when there is no malaria in the country and the older doctors say typhoid or influenza. Wabfein says, 'This young man needs scope or he will hurt somebody's feelings,' so I say, 'Send him to me, Wabfein. Send him out to me.' "

Above the brown Vandyke Eliot Carey's cheeks were rosy. "It *was* malaria," he said hotly. "The diagnosis was positive. Fever mounting for several days with lapses and a chill. The patient had recently come from the South. I prescribed quinine and——"

"Nah . . . nah!" Dr Zeitletz' hand went up in a checking gesture. "Malaria it was. Wabfein said so. He also said that you would butt out your brains against the stone wall of prejudice if you stayed. I wrote you to come and you wrote back that you were coming. Now you are here."

The flush remained on Eliot Carey's cheeks but he laughed. "I'm here," he agreed. "I still don't understand why my going against the ideas of all those others should make you want me."

Fritz Zeitletz sobered suddenly. He leaned forward in his chair, his blue eyes, deep and earnest, fixed upon Eliot. "You studied in Vienna," he said slowly, his voice a caress as he spoke the name. "When you were there and had finished your studies you made a promise."

Eliot Carey's brown eyes were as earnest as Zeitletz' own. "I did," he said. "Of course. The oath of Hippocrates. We all took it. What has that to do——"

Again the checking motion of Zeitletz' hand. "Now I am a patient," he said. "Remember that. There is a thing inside me that will kill me soon."

"You——" Eliot Carey began.

"Cancer. Inoperable," announced Dr Zeitletz as though he spoke of a sliver in his finger. "Someday . . . pouf!" He gestured airily with one plump hand.

"But can't you do something?" said Dr Carey. "Have you had other doctors?"

"Do I not know cancer?" demanded Zeitletz. "As for doing something, I have done it. I have brought you here."

"I don't see——" Eliot said.

Trigger Vengeance

"Listen, Doctor." Again Fritz Zeitletz leaned forward and spoke earnestly. "I have here a great many people that are mine to look after. Can I go away and leave them alone?"

"But you don't know me," Eliot expostulated. "You don't know that I will stay. You don't know that I will fit in. You——"

"You are a doctor, *ja?*" Zeitletz' blue eyes were sparkling once more. "You fight the whole staff of a hospital because you say a man has malaria and they say that you are wrong. You would not leave that fight except that Wabfein tells you about a still better fight that I have here. So you come to see my fight. You will stay and you will fit into the work. Could I wait? This thing inside me will not wait."

"Well——" Eliot Carey said slowly.

Fritz Zeitletz bounced up from his chair. "Now," he said briskly, "we will go and eat the dinner that María has ready for us. Then we will talk a little business and unpack your trunk and you will show me all the new instruments you have brought. You will tell me about Vienna and about what Koch is doing with the little bugs and Von Behring and Pasteur in Paris, and we will argue and have a grand time. Tomorrow you will begin to practice medicine here and join in my nice fight. Come, Doctor."

Eliot Carey laughed. Dr Zeitletz' energy was irresistible. Rising from his chair, he followed the small man out the door and into the dining room.

The meal was good, and when it was finished there were superlative coffee and good cigars. It was over these that the two settled the details of their business. Eliot Carey could not resist the older man. Dr Zeitletz was more than fair. Dr Carey was to stay in this house, he was to board with Zeitletz and his laundry would be done. All expenses, save only the small items of a personal nature, were to be borne by Fritz Zeitletz and he would pay his young assistant eighty dollars a month. In return Dr Carey was to assist, to take calls when Zeitletz could not go, in general to follow the direction of the older man.

"Sometimes," said Dr Zeitletz with a grimace, "this thing I have growing will say to me, 'Stop, Fritz. You must not.' Then you will have to go in my place. We will try it this way awhile, Doctor, and then later we can make another and more just arrangement."

Eliot Carey could not see how a better arrangement could be made and said so frankly but Zeitletz waved that away. "After a while," he said, "you will be doing most of the practice. Then we must plan to pay you better. And now shall we get to that trunk you have so filled? There must be——"

The gray-haired María came into the room and spoke to Dr Zeitletz. He listened, nodded, his face becoming grave.

"We will postpone the trunk, Doctor," he said when María had gone. "I have a call. Will you come with me? If you are not too tired to come. . . ."

"Certainly," said Eliot, rising. "I would like to go with you, Doctor."

"Then come," said Fritz Zeitletz.

Trigger Vengeance

Eliot Carey waited for Zeitletz in the hall while the older man donned coat and hat and collected his bag. When Zeitletz rejoined Eliot the older doctor spoke. "We will not need the buggy," he said. "This is near by. Come, Doctor."

"What is the case?" Eliot asked as he followed Zeitletz through the outer door.

"I forgot that you do not speak Spanish," said Zeitletz, closing the door behind Eliot. "You must learn. María and I will give you lessons. This is a child that is sick and I would like you to see before I tell you what I have decided."

A test, Eliot Carey thought as he walked beside Zeitletz down the walk. Zeitletz had been frank and aboveboard in his talk but he was canny. At the gate Zeitletz paused.

"A child," he said slowly. "It is bad when the *kinder* are sick, Doctor. They are so sick and they go so fast. This one I saw this morning. I thought ——" He broke off and at a rapid pace set out through the darkness.

Twice, following Zeitletz through the night, Eliot Carey stumbled and recovered his footing. Each time Zeitletz paused, patiently waiting for the younger man. Presently the older doctor turned from the road and approached the black bulk of a house. At his knock the door was opened and after a short colloquy the doctors were admitted. Eliot Carey stood beside the door while Zeitletz crossed the single dimly lighted room toward a bed.

Standing beside the door, his eyes becoming ac-

customed to the light, Eliot Carey surveyed his sur-
roundings. The walls about him were made of sun-
dried mud formed into bricks and plastered over.
Above were rafters, smoke stained and gray and
with thin poles laid across them. There was a single
window and a door for openings in the walls, the
lower portion of which had been covered by a thin
cloth, now dingy with dirt. The floor was of earth,
hard packed, and aside from the bed there was but
one piece of furniture in the room: a dilapidated
table. In one corner a small rounded fireplace held
a smoking bed of embers and a single soot-blackened
pot. There were rolls of bedding against the walls
and on the table a lamp with a smoke-blackened
chimney gave off a feeble yellow glow. Not counting
himself and Dr Zeitletz or the patient upon the
bed, there were eight people in the room: an old
man, a younger man, three women and three children. The children were frankly ragged and the
smallest of them had no clothing at all other than
a man's shirt split down the back with a long rent.
The air was heavy, stale and fetid.

"Doctor," said Zeitletz. Eliot Carey crossed the
room and stood beside the bed.

A child lay on the bed, pitifully thin, emaciated until the ribs stood out upon the scrawny body like the
staves of a broken barrel. The baby, he was hardly
more, was naked, the knee and elbow joints swollen
and the abdomen protuberant. As Eliot Carey looked
down, the child gasped a breath, retained it and

then let it go. Zeitletz gestured toward the baby on the bed.

With the thin brown wrist in his hand, Eliot Carey felt the thready pulse. His hand, on the child's forehead, felt the burning of fever. Bent down, his ear against brown skin, he heard the râles in the tiny chest.

"Pneumonia," said Eliot Carey, straightening.

Zeitletz nodded. "And what else?" he asked.

The young doctor hesitated. He looked at the little brown body and then back to the white-haired Zeitletz. "I would say that there had been rickets," Eliot pronounced slowly, "and malnutrition. I don't know——"

"This morning," interrupted Zeitletz bitterly, "this baby had a cold. Tonight he is dying of pneumonia. Rickets, yes. Malnutrition, certainly. Can you raise children on a few beans and a little corn meal and water? Can you?"

The words were fierce, fairly thrown at Eliot Carey. Eliot shook his head. Zeitletz went on, the fierceness gone from his tone but the bitterness lingering.

"With a child that had been fed, with a fat healthy child, I would be giving cough syrup and something for the sniffles. Now I can wait and see the boy die." He moved back toward the bed, standing close beside it, looking down. Somehow Eliot Carey could not move away; he, too, stood looking at the child on the bed.

On the tumbled bedding the boy, pitifully little,

fought for his breath, each inhalation a battle, each
exhalation seemingly the last. Over across the room
the old woman was mumbling a prayer and the
young man had gone out. A breath trembled on the
baby's lips, checked and the laboring chest was still.

"Es todo," said Fritz Zeitletz sharply and turned
away. The younger woman, evidently the boy's
mother, looked with wide, uncomprehending eyes at
the doctors. The old woman, her muttering done,
was fumbling in a wooden box that rested in a corner. She brought a candle stump from the box, lit it
at the fireplace and, her palsied hand shaking the
guttering flame, carried the light to the head of the
bed.

"We can do no more here," said Dr Zeitletz.
"Come, Doctor."

Outside the house the two physicians walked along
in silence. They reached the white-painted cottage
where a lamp shone bright in a window, went up the
walk side by side and into the hall. Zeitletz pulled
off his coat and hung it, with his hat, upon the hall
tree. Eliot Carey placed his own hat there. The two
faced each other.

"The little ones," said Zeitletz and then, shaking
his shoulders as though throwing off a burden,
"Come now, Doctor. Your trunk!"

Later that night, when the trunk had been un-
packed, when Dr Zeitletz had fondled a case of new
and shining instruments, when he had thumbed
through a book or two, exclaiming over the colored
illustrations, when he had peered into the eyepiece

of a microscope and marveled at a collection of slides, when all these things had been done and Eliot Carey was preparing for bed in a clean white bedroom, he heard the older man in the hall. Dr Carey dropped his hands from their occupation of loosening his tie and turned to face the door. Fritz Zeitletz stood there.

"Three years ago," said Zeitletz, "that boy's father had six hundred sheep and a house in Canyon Largo. Good night, Doctor."

Absently Eliot Carey answered, "Good night, Doctor Zeitletz."

CHAPTER III

The Practice of Medicine

THE SURGERY in Dr Zeitletz' home was a small compact room lined with cabinets. Some of the cabinets held instruments, the others contained books. There was a big desk in a corner, a swivel chair before it, a smaller white-painted chair with a headrest standing beside the desk. An operating table occupied the center of the room and beside the operating table was a stand of basins. On another table were adhesive tape, cotton and bandages. A stove occupied a corner and there were two lamps, an overhead light and a portable lamp. Dr Eliot Carey occupied the swivel chair and stared gloomily at a prescription.

In the two weeks that he had spent in Soltura he had filled prescriptions, dispensing them in the little drug room just off the surgery. He had met many people and he had practiced no medicine whatever. To date his business had been that of pharmacist and reception clerk. Soltura seemingly, when a doctor was needed, wanted Dr Zeitletz.

In the two weeks Dr Carey had changed in detail if not in toto. Gone was the brown Vandyke that Zeitlitz so shrewdly surmised had been grown for dignity's sake. The jaw the beard had hidden was square, the mouth firm and decisive. The doctor's nose was dished a little as though it had been broken and was pugnacious enough to confirm the suspicion of breakage. Brown eyes, wide spaced and level, were under firm brown eyebrows and the head was so wide as to make the eyes seem almost close together. Eliot Carey was a thinker and a fighter, if his head meant anything at all.

He scowled at the prescription. It was for Mrs Maybe's asthma and called for four drams of iodide of potassium, among other ingredients. There was no iodide of potassium in the drug room, the box was empty and Dr Carey must substitute iodide of sodium if the prescription was to be filled. Holding the prescription in his hand, he got up from the swivel chair and started across the room. Halfway to the drug room he stopped. There was a sound at the door and, turning, Dr Carey saw that he had a caller.

The man in the doorway was small and held a broad black hat in his hands. Under the doctor's scrutiny he twisted the hat nervously, shifted his weight and looked from side to side as though seeking a way out of the room.

The Practice of Medicine

"Were you looking for Doctor Zeitletz?" asked Eliot Carey.

The man in the door shook his head. "I——" he began. "Say . . . can you give me somethin' to kill a horse?"

Dr Carey dropped the prescription he held. When he had recovered it and straightened he had regained some of his equanimity. "A horse?" he questioned.

The small man determinedly advanced into the surgery. "I got to kill a horse," he stated. "Calico's broke his leg. I tried to shoot him but I cain't do it. Hell, Doc! Every time I tried to pull the trigger he *looked* at me."

Dr Carey retreated to the desk and sat down in the swivel chair. Peremptorily he gestured toward the other chair beside the desk. "Sit down," he ordered.

The small man seated himself gingerly on the edge of the chair. "I come in to get somethin' to kill him," he said defensively. "Somethin' that will put him to sleep an' not hurt him. Can you give me somethin', Doc?"

Eliot Carey's brown eyes narrowed. Was this a stunt? he wondered, a clumsy joke to be played upon him? "Who are you?" Dr Carey asked.

"My name's Mann," answered the caller. "They call me Littlebit. I work out to the LS headquarters."

Eliot digested that information. The LS headquarter ranch was six miles north of town. The LS

27

was cattle and there was an invisible dividing line along the southern edge of the ranch, separating it from the sheep country below. There was no reason for anyone from the LS to try to perpetrate a fraud upon him. Littlebit seemed to catch the doctor's thoughts.

"This ain't no foolishness," Littlebit said earnestly. "Calico's mine. I raised him. Now he's broke his leg an' I want somethin' to put him out of his misery."

Dr Carey came to a decision. He was tired of sitting in the office, tired of filling prescriptions and answering questions, tired of telling patients that Dr Zeitletz was out on a call and would be back after dinner, or after supper, or sometime during the night. A patient was a patient, thought Eliot Carey grimly, even if that patient was a horse.

"Would you kill a man if he broke his leg?" asked Dr Carey.

Littlebit was startled. He surveyed the doctor with questioning blue eyes as he revolved the question in his mind. Then he shook his head. "No," grated Littlebit, "but a horse is different."

"Broken legs are broken legs," suggested Dr Carey.

Again Littlebit thought it over. Eliot urged him. "You seem to think a good deal of the horse," he said and waited.

Littlebit caught at the idea. "Say, Doc——" Littlebit began. "Say . . . you wouldn't . . . Shucks, you wouldn't fool with a horse, would you? Say . . . if you'd fix Calico's leg——"

"Perhaps I can't set it." Dr Carey was beginning to doubt the wisdom of his idea. After all, he had never set a horse's leg.

Littlebit got to his feet. "You ain't foolin' with me, Doc?" he asked anxiously, and then, his voice hardening, "because if you are——"

"I can look at your horse," Eliot Carey interrupted. "If I can't set the leg I can at least put the horse out of his pain."

Littlebit looked down at the doctor seated at the desk. Suddenly he nodded. "You come on," ordered Littlebit Mann. "If you can fix Calico there ain't nothin' I won't do for you. Can you go now, Doc?"

"Why not?" asked Dr Carey. "There's nothing to keep me busy here. You'll have to get a horse for me and——"

"I'll get you a horse." Littlebit was already in motion toward the door. "You get ready, Doc. I'll be right back. An' say, if you can fix Calico——" The small man was gone through the door. Dr Carey, smiling sardonically at himself, got up from the swivel chair and began to prepare his bag.

The bag was packed and Dr Carey had assumed his coat and hat when Littlebit, visibly excited, returned leading a horse from the livery barn. When Dr Carey came out and down the walk toward the front fence Littlebit leaned from his saddle.

"Give me that grip, Doc," ordered Littlebit, extending a hand. "Here's your horse."

Trigger Vengeance

Eliot passed up the grip and in return took the reins of the lead horse. He had as a boy ridden horses when the opportunity offered but this livery stable horse was different. Mounting the livery stable horse was a good deal like getting on a windmill. The horse kept circling away and it was not until Littlebit pushed his own horse in against the other that Eliot Carey got his leg across the saddle. Once the doctor was mounted, Littlebit led off at a trot. He was in a hurry and he had no regard for the doctor's lack of horsemanship.

They went through town toward the north, the doctor bouncing and trying to keep his feet in stirrups too long for him; and Littlebit, graceful on a horse as he was awkward when parted from one, setting a rapid pace half a length ahead.

The six miles to the LS headquarters seemed much longer to Dr Carey. With each jolting step of the last mile he wished that he had not come and resolved that he would not again be so precipitous. The doctor was mightily relieved when at length they reached the lane of trees that led to the long low house that was the LS headquarters.

Littlebit led the way up the lane, skirted around the house and, arriving at the big barn and the clustered corrals behind the house, stopped and dismounted. Dr Carey also stiffly descended from his horse. Littlebit tied both mounts to the corral fence, handed the doctor his grip and pointed. "There's Calico," announced Littlebit.

A black-and-white horse inside the corral came

The Practice of Medicine

hobbling toward them. Looking at the horse, Dr Carey could see that the right foreleg was at an angle and that there was a bulge between fetlock and knee.

"Can you fix that, Doc?" demanded Littlebit.

"We'll see," answered the doctor. "Is he gentle?"

Littlebit was opening the corral gate. "As a kitten," he responded. "Come on, Doc."

Calico stood, his head on Littlebit's shoulder, while Dr Carey cautiously felt of the leg. The horse winced at the touch of the doctor's hand but made no trouble. The break was in the cannon bone and the ends had slipped by each other. Dr Carey, straightening, looked Littlebit in the eye.

"That's a bad break," he said. "We'll have to throw the horse and tie him. Then you'll have to pull on that leg and slide the bone back while I put it in place. It's going to be hard."

"There ain't nobody around to help," Littlebit said. "I reckon——"

"We can do it," Eliot assured. "The first thing is to get him down and tied."

Littlebit stood scratching his head. Calico surveyed his master with big limpid eyes. "All right," said Littlebit. "We'll do it then."

It was much easier to say than to do. With a rope from the fence Littlebit put a loop over Calico's neck. He had to be careful of the injured leg and he had to get Calico down. Both Littlebit and Eliot Carey were sweating when finally Calico lay on his side. Dr Carey knelt on the horse's neck and Littlebit, working carefully, tied the three sound legs together.

"What we need," said Littlebit Mann, "is help."

Dr Carey knew that Littlebit was right but did not voice his thoughts. He held down Calico's head and let the horse rest. Calico ceased struggling and lay motionless.

"Now," announced Dr Carey, "you'll have to pull on that leg."

Littlebit shook his head. "Who'll hold his head down?" he demanded. "He'll get to threshin' around an'——"

"Can I help?" a voice asked from the fence.

Dr Carey and Littlebit turned. Janice Irish, clad in overalls and a blue denim shirt, was perched atop the corral fence looking down at the men and the horse. Neat boots encased her feet and the sun glinted from the red hair that escaped from under her big hat.

It was Littlebit who answered the question. "You sure can, Miss Janice," said Littlebit, relief in his voice. "You can hold his head."

The girl climbed down from the fence and came toward the horse. She smiled at Dr Carey and, as though perfectly familiar with what there was to do, knelt and put a knee on Calico's black-and-white neck. "Now you can go ahead," she directed. "I'll hold his head."

Dr Carey, relieved from his duty, got up. It seemed perfectly natural to have the girl there; she fitted into the picture as authentically as Littlebit Mann or the black-and-white Calico. "I'll need some thin boards for splints," said Eliot Carey. "See if you can find some, Littlebit."

"Sure, Doc," agreed Littlebit. "There's some in the barn." He hurried away at a bowlegged run.

Eliot Carey looked again at the girl. Janice Irish was smiling. Calico, realizing that authority held his head, was quiet. "I didn't know that you were a veterinarian," the girl said.

"I'm not," snapped Dr Carey. "But it seemed a shame to kill a good horse because he had a broken leg."

Littlebit came running back from the barn, pieces of a packing crate in his hands.

Dr Carey, first feeling of Calico's leg, shaped the thin boards with a knife. He wrapped bandage on them for padding, securing it with adhesive tape, put his bag convenient to hand and gave orders.

"Put your foot against his chest and pull on that leg," Dr Carey commended Littlebit. "You"—to Janice Irish—"hold him quiet as you can. I'll feel the break and get it in place."

Both Littlebit and the girl nodded their understanding and Eliot Carey knelt beside Calico. Littlebit got down and, like a flanker holding a calf, got Calico's hoof and braced his foot against the horse's chest.

"Now!" snapped Dr Carey.

Littlebit pulled, Janice Irish squatted on the threshing head, Eliot Carey, big hands sure and deft, held the satin of Calico's cannon. There was a grating sound and then a snap.

Trigger Vengeance

"That's it!" Dr Carey announced. "Now you can ease off, Littlebit. But don't let go. I've got to splint this."

He worked dexterously, placing the splints in position, lashing them there, wrapping yards of bandage tightly in place. When he had finished Littlebit was sweating and there were beads of perspiration on Janice Irish's forehead.

"I think you can let him up now," stated Dr Carey, rising and slapping at his trousers to rid them of the dust. "You'll have to tie him so that he can't get to that bandage with his teeth and so that he will be quiet."

"You can put him in Golden's stall, Littlebit," said Janice Irish. "Turn Golden out. It won't hurt her to run loose awhile."

Littlebit was busying himself with the rope that bound Calico's feet. "Yessem, Miss Janice," said Littlebit.

Calico floundered to his feet. He hobbled out to the end of the rope then turned and looked at the people that had so maltreated him. Janice Irish and Littlebit Mann and Eliot Carey stood and looked pridefully at Calico. They were elated with their accomplishment. Achievement stood out there at the end of Littlebit's rope and looked at them.

"Put him in the barn, Littlebit," Janice Irish directed once more. "Feed him something. Do you think some oats, Doctor?"

"Not too much," said Eliot Carey with authority.

"I'll look after him," assured Littlebit.

The Practice of Medicine

"You'll come to the house, Doctor?" asked Janice Irish. "Littlebit will go back to town with you when he is through with Calico. Won't you come in?"

Littlebit was leading the hobbling Calico across the corral. Eliot Carey found himself following the girl.

The interior of the ranch house was as comfortable as the outside had promised. Janice Irish led the way into a long room bestrewn with Navajo blankets and with leather-covered chairs set about at irregular and intriguing intervals. There was a fireplace with a long divan beside it and bookshelves on the walls. The girl gestured toward the divan, seated herself on a chair and looked at Dr Carey. The doctor found himself ill at ease, prepared to defend himself.

"Why did you come out to set Calico's leg?" the girl demanded, her blue eyes direct and questioning. "You aren't a veterinarian. You certainly didn't think that Littlebit could pay you much."

Eliot Carey answered the question stiffly. "I came because it seemed to me that the horse needed attention."

The girl thought that over. "I've seen you in Soltura," she said suddenly. "Did you know that my father and Doctor Zeitletz are great friends?"

"No."

"Do you know that Doctor Zeitletz is very proud of you? That he has been telling everyone what a fine doctor was coming to assist him?"

Again Eliot answered with one short word. "No."

Trigger Vengeance

"Do you think that coming out here, wasting your time setting a horse's leg will make Doctor Zeitletz feel happy? Do you think that he will like it? Will it help him in his practice?"

"Doctor Zeitletz is too firmly established for the things that I do to affect him," Eliot answered. "I imagine that Doctor Zeitletz would have done the same thing."

Janice Irish came to her feet. The blue eyes were oddly quizzical and she laughed. "When I was eight years old," she said, "I had a pet prairie dog. One of the boys had caught it for me. The little thing took sick and Doctor Zeitletz stayed up all one night with it, and when it died he made a little coffin and helped me bury it. Here is Littlebit, Doctor. He will ride back to town with you."

She crossed the room, long legged, moving easily as a boy, her hand held out to Eliot Carey. The doctor took that extended hand, felt a grip frank as that of a man and let the hand go.

"You must come out to see us, Doctor," said Janice Irish. "Come soon. You have a patient to look after and I know that you and Father will be friends."

"Thank you," Eliot answered awkwardly. "I'll be glad to come."

"Good-by, Doctor," said Janice Irish.

"Good-by," Eliot answered.

Littlebit rode back with Eliot. Littlebit was tongue-tied but he overrode Eliot's insistence that he could return to town alone. They were halfway back

The Practice of Medicine

to Soltura before Littlebit got out what he wanted to say.

"You give me your bill, Doc," Littlebit blurted. "I ain't got a whole lot, but——"

"There isn't any bill," Dr Carey said shortly. "I'm not a veterinarian." He was not thinking about Littlebit or about Calico. He was thinking of Janice Irish and the frank grip of her hand and the half-amused, half-serious expression in her blue eyes. He wondered why the girl had spoken as she had. He wondered why she had talked about Dr Zeitletz and Zeitletz' pride in his new assistant and why she had asked if he thought that setting Calico's leg would make Zeitletz happy.

"But hell, Doc," Littlebit expostulated. "Your time's worth somethin'. You can't just——"

"I'll practice medicine as I please," snapped Dr Carey, not answering Littlebit exactly but rather talking to Janice Irish. "I know what I want to charge for a call."

Littlebit looked his puzzlement. Presently he shrugged. "All right then," said Littlebit Mann. "Suit yourself, Doc. Just the same——"

"There isn't any charge," Eliot said coldly. "Let it go at that."

Littlebit let it go. He delivered the doctor at the house, said good-by to him and took the hired horse back to the livery barn. At the livery Littlebit waxed eloquent and profane as he spoke of Dr Eliot Carey and the thing that Dr Carey had done for Calico. "You can ride the river with that fello'," said Littlebit Mann to Ben Fry, the proprietor of the stable. "Damned if you can't, Ben. An' if any more of these guys around here go talkin' about him bein' stuck up an' such, them an' me's goin' to have an argument."

And so matters rested. Eliot Carey went back to waiting in Dr Zeitletz' surgery, to filling prescriptions and poring over Gray's *Anatomy* and the pharmacopoeia, to peering through his microscope at the slides he had made in Vienna and reading again the publications, in heavy German type, that he had brought.

But while Dr Carey fumed at his impotence and inactivity, word went around Soltura and the country about. Away out in the LS Cienega camp riders squatting on their boot heels against the walls spoke of Calico and Calico's broken leg and gravely delivered an opinion that maybe the new Doc in Soltura would do. Down in the canyons, on the little bottom farms where the patches of farm land were bare now and where chili hung in red strings against adobe walls, the word of Calico and Calico's broken leg was spread, and Ramón and Jesús, Delfino and Manuel, forgathering beside campfires or in sheep wagons, patted their dogs upon the head and spoke of "El Doctor nuevo."

Ten days after Calico's leg had been set Dr Zeitletz and his assistant were in the surgery. There came a knock and the door opened. A tall rawboned rider stood there.

"Come in, Lem, come in," invited Dr Zeitletz. "How are things at the horse camp?"

The Practice of Medicine

Lem remained beside the door. "Laramie," said Lem, "was ridin' a bronc this mornin'. Bronc fell an' kind of smashed Laramie up."

"Wait till I get my bag," ordered Zeitletz, "and I'll be with you."

Lem stood hesitant. "Doc," he stammered and Fritz Zeitletz paused in his hurry across the room, "you won't mind, will you, Doc?" There was apology in Lem's tone. "Laramie kind of wanted the other doc. Laramie's heard that he's hell on broken bones an' such."

Dr Zeitletz' little blue eyes flashed from Lem to Eliot Carey, red faced and worried. For a moment Dr Zeitletz looked at the younger man, and then, boisterously and wholeheartedly, he laughed.

"I don't mind a bit, Lem," he said. "You had better get ready to go, Doctor." And then, as Eliot moved to obey, "Remember, you are hell on broken bones," reminded Fritz Zeitletz.

CHAPTER IV

Ethics and a Murder

THE ACCEPTANCE of Eliot Carey as physician at large to the general ailments of Soltura was a gradual thing. Having attended Laramie Jones, bronc rider for the LS, and strapped Laramie's broken ribs in place, Dr Carey found himself taken by the cowboys of Laurence Irish's ranch as one of their own. But cowboys are healthy persons as a rule, and when they are in need of medical aid it is generally from some hazard of their occupation. There was not a great deal of practice at the LS. In Littlebit Mann Eliot had a constant and vociferous advocate, particularly since Calico's broken leg had healed, leaving the horse without a limp. Still his calls as a physician were limited.

Not so his social calls. Eliot was personable and he was young and he was from the East. An aura of romance hung about him and the upper crust of Soltura, particularly the women, found this intriguing. Eliot, having been introduced to husbands,

Ethics and a Murder

was invited out by wives. He could not plead patients that needed attention and so perforce accepted the invitations. Mrs Maybe, Clem's asthmatic wife, Mrs Benedict, the wife of Welch's bookkeeper, Mrs Jack Brannigan, the saloonkeeper's spouse—each in turn had the doctor in for dinner. But it was not until he received an invitation from the Welches that the final cachet of Soltura's social approval was bestowed. Eliot Carey, dressed in his best, climbed the hill to Welches' home and was received by Mrs Welch in black taffeta and a worried look, by Emma, the Welches' handsome daughter, by Allan himself, small and black haired and dynamic, and by the son of the house, Courtland. Eliot ate a dinner served in state, the food cold because the maid who waited on the table must needs be directed, sotto voce, before each course. He listened politely as Courtland discoursed on horse racing, prize fighting and hunting; he smoked a good cigar with Welch and heard that great man's opinions concerning the Administration, the irresponsibility of labor and the price of lambs, which was low; and he closed his eyes and thought of all the interesting things he might be doing, while Emma played badly upon the great square rosewood piano.

At nine o'clock (dinner had been promptly at six) Eliot made his departure, going home to find that María had left a pot of coffee on the stove and that Fritz Zeitletz had waded through half a pamphlet by Robert Koch. The two men sat up until the cocks were crowing, arguing the matter of avenues of infection, and then went to bed happy.

Trigger Vengeance

Zeitletz was a constant source of joy to Eliot Carey. There was not much in the way of medicine that Dr Zeitletz had not done, and *Zeitletz on Kitchen Surgery*, as Eliot called the older man's recollections, might have been a textbook in improvised medicine with guaranteed results.

By the end of September Eliot Carey had settled into harness, gradually pulling his portion of the load, and at the end of September, too, he was firmly entrenched in Soltura's society.

The society did not bother Eliot Carey but there were other things that did. The chief of these was Janice Irish. Dr Carey had taken the girl's invitation literally. Janice had received him when he called at the LS, announced that her father was at home, conducted the young doctor to Laurence Irish's office and left the men alone. Laurence Irish was a genial, cultured gentleman and he entertained his caller for an hour but Eliot Carey had not come to visit with the captain. The second time he called he found the captain gone and Janice as remote as a red-haired icicle. She had but little to say, would not respond to the various topics that Eliot tossed out for discussion and was so plainly preoccupied that the doctor cut his visit short and left in a huff. Eliot Carey was not used to such treatment from girls. But here was a girl who, plainly, was not interested in him and Eliot rode back to Soltura in bad humor.

October came to Soltura cool and clear as only October can at an altitude of six thousand feet. On the first Saturday in October there was much

Ethics and a Murder

stirring in Dr Zeitletz' house. María cleaned the house from top to bottom, even disturbing the sacred precincts of the surgery, and then retired to the kitchen. Dr Carey, driven from the house by the cleaning, wandered to the main street of the town and dropped into Brannigan's saloon. Jack Brannigan was an Irishman, hearty as his red face and false as the second story of his building which was but clapboards. Still Eliot liked the man and often came into the place.

In Brannigan's he found Tray Barry, Soltura's single representative of the law, engaged in earnest conversation with Brannigan and another. Eliot noted that the third man was familiar and, maneuvering so that he could see, found himself staring at the narrow face of Sid Raupert. Brannigan and Barry were preoccupied with their talk but Raupert favored the young doctor with a long glance from his close-set eyes and half nodded, as a man might to some person that was vaguely familiar. Eliot did not stay in the saloon but went out and on to Welch's store.

The store had interested Eliot Carey since he had first entered it. There was everything imaginable under the roof of the store: rope and hardware, groceries and dry goods. Going into Welch's store was a good deal like reviewing life in a showcase; a man could buy anything from a crib to a coffin.

There was a crowd of natives in the store, four or five families, Eliot surmised, and he loitered beside the door watching the slow shopping and the placid movement of the clerks. The native people did not come to town to buy, so much as to visit. While he stood near the door Eliot was appraised of a disturbance. From the office in the rear came high and excited voices and then, suddenly, the excitement boiled out into the storeroom. Allan Welch, his face highly colored, issued from the office, a young native beside him. The two were arguing and Welch was shaking his finger in the young man's face. A woman detached herself and two children from the shoppers and, joining the two, caught at the man's arm, apparently pleading with him. The young man, broad shouldered and with a strong, swarthy face, shrugged off her hand and spoke hotly to Allan Welch. Welch, about to reply, saw Eliot beside the door and stopped. The other natives were interested and silent onlookers to the scene. Turning abruptly from his companion, Welch came across to Eliot and stopped before him.

"Good morning, Doctor," Welch greeted. "Is there anything I can do for you?"

Eliot smiled. He did not like Allan Welch, not for any particular reason that he could point out but simply because the man seemed almost too pleasant.

"Not a thing, Mr Welch," he answered. "I just dropped in. You seem to be having some trouble."

Welch shrugged. "These native people," he said, "are hard to deal with sometimes. We carry them from year to year, buy their lambs and wool, and you would think that they would be grateful to us. Sometimes, though . . ." He shrugged again.

"Wasn't that Abrán Fernandez?" Eliot asked,

looking now to where the strong-faced man and his family were going out the door. "He came into the office the other day to see Doctor Zeitletz about his wife. I believe Doctor Zeitletz said that was his name."

"That is Abrán, yes," agreed Welch. "If there is nothing I can do for you, Doctor, will you excuse me? We have quite a number of customers." Welch's voice was apologetic.

"Surely," agreed Eliot. "I just dropped in." Welch hurried away, going not to the waiting customers but back to the office, and after a moment Eliot left the store.

He was on his way home, the loafing places of Soltura exhausted, when Dr Carey saw Abrán Fernandez again. Fernandez was sitting on a wagon seat, his face stolid, his wife beside him and the children standing in the box of the wagon. Tray Barry, Soltura's deputy sheriff, was on the ground talking up to Fernandez and there was a threatening scowl on Barry's face.

When he reached home Eliot found a message waiting for him. A call had come in for the doctor to go to Rinconcito, fifteen miles west of Soltura. Dr Zeitletz was out and the Rinconcito call was urgent. From María's gestures Eliot got the idea that he should hurry. He had not as yet acquired enough Spanish to understand the housekeeper completely and María's English was limited. Nevertheless, Dr Carey collected his bags and went back downtown to Fry's livery barn for a team.

Trigger Vengeance

It was nine o'clock when Dr Carey returned to Soltura. He put his rig in the barn, said good night to Ben Fry and walked on toward the house, carrying his bags. Dr Carey was tired. He had had a difficult time at Rinconcito. The call there had been a confinement case, complicated by the fact that there had been twin babies and a dry birth for breech presentations. A native midwife, her ingenuity exhausted, had further added to the doctor's grief. Going up the walk to the door of his home, Eliot Carey resolved that he would do two things: he would learn to speak Spanish and he would educate Soltura and all the country about to shun midwives as one would the plague. When he opened the door he heard voices and, placing his bags in the surgery, he went into the living room. Now the reason for the house cleaning and the extra baking was apparent. Dr Zeitletz and four men were sitting around the dining-room table, their coats off and cards, chips and glasses on the table. Dr Zeitletz had guests.

As Eliot appeared in the doorway Dr Zeitletz bounced up from his chair and came around the table. The other men turned their heads and Laurence Irish, who had been seated at the far side of the table, arose and crossed the room toward the doctor. The other three men were unfamiliar to Eliot but they, too, rose to their feet and Dr Zeitletz made introductions.

"This is my friend Doctor Carey, gentlemen," announced Dr Zeitletz. "Mr Mason, Mr Thomas and Judge Rutledge, Doctor." Each of the men, as Zeit-

Ethics and a Murder

letz spoke a name, shook Eliot's hand and murmured a greeting.

"Come and join us, Doctor," Zeitletz urged. "We were——"

"Doc was takin' our eyeteeth," drawled Mason, a twinkle in his blue eyes. "We come over here every once in a while to let him skin us." Eliot liked the speaker's looks. Mason was a broad-shouldered man of perhaps fifty with a long horse face and weathered as an old oak.

"A sheriff should not talk of being cheated," Zeitletz retorted. "A sheriff is supposed to be a smart man."

The others laughed. Mason said, "Ouch, Doc!" good-humoredly. Eliot looked at the others. Thomas, he knew, was prosecuting attorney for the district and Rutledge was district judge. Thomas was a small alert man with a moon-round face and pince-nez glasses that perched on his insignificant nose. Rutledge was ruddy with good living and a little older than Mason.

"Won't you join us, Doctor?" Zeitletz urged. "Every month or so these sharpers come over to Soltura to eat María's cooking and take money away from me. I need help."

They were old friends, Eliot recognized the fact. They formed a close corporation and while Zeitletz made him welcome, the younger man felt that his presence would not add to their enjoyment. "Thank you," Eliot returned. "I've just come in from Rinconcito. . . ."

Trigger Vengeance

"You are tired and hungry." Dr Zeitletz was contrite. "I know. Did you have much trouble?"

"Not a great deal," Eliot answered. "Amalia Sandoval presented her husband with twins. It took some time. If you gentlemen will excuse me?" He half bowed to the men, turned and went on out.

María was in the kitchen. She had a meal on the kitchen table and she hovered anxiously over Eliot as he ate. The salvation of her two doctors, María believed, lay in eating a great deal. Certainly they got but little rest. Eliot she had adopted, scolding him in Spanish that he could not understand and darning his socks and taking especial pains when she ironed his shirts. Now she carried food from stove to table until the young doctor was surfeited and her offense showed in her face when he could eat no more.

"There's no use, María," Eliot said. "I'm full and that's all there is to it. I couldn't eat another morsel, not a single bite." He grinned at the gray-haired woman and perforce María smiled back at him.

The kitchen was warm and pleasant and Eliot lingered. He watched María wash the dishes and put them away, set things to rights in the kitchen and, finally, don her shawl preparatory to departure. María, pausing at the door said, *"Adios, Señor Doctor,"* and Eliot, stifling a yawn, answered: *"Vaya con Dios, María,"* his accent bringing a smile to her lips. Then María was gone and Eliot was left alone with the lamp and the cat for company.

The cat retired under the stove. The oil was low

in the lamp and, rising, Eliot blew out the light and started up the hall. He would stop and say good night to the card players and then go to bed.

At the door of the living room he paused. There was an argument in progress and the cards lay forgotten on the table. Eliot, standing in the door, looked at the animated faces of the men.

"We'll take a hypothetical case," said Sam Thomas. "Suppose that you, as a doctor, were to attend a known criminal. What would you do, Fritz?"

"I would doctor him," Dr Zeitletz answered.

"You wouldn't turn him over to the law?"

"Criminals are for John to catch." Fritz Zeitletz nodded toward the sheriff. "Not so, John?"

"We try to catch 'em," Mason drawled. "Wouldn't you help us out, Fritz?"

"You would know a criminal," Zeitletz answered. "I would not have to tell you. No, Sam. You have it wrong. I——"

"Now wait a minute," Judge Rutledge interposed, his voice strong, his deep-set eyes flashing from the eager Sam Thomas to Zeitletz and back again. "You've set this thing up wrong, Sam. You ask Fritz if he wouldn't turn in a known criminal to the law. Of course he would. He's a good citizen. Let's put it another way. Suppose, Fritz, that in your capacity as a physician you were to attend a patient who, for some reason or other, informed you that he had committed a criminal act. A murder, we'll say. What would you do? Wouldn't it be your duty as a citizen to inform the proper officials of what you had learned and aid them in bringing the man to justice?"

Stubbornly Dr Zeitletz shook his head. "No," he answered. "That would not be my duty. The confidences of a patient to a physician are inviolate."

"Even a murderer?" asked Thomas shrewdly.

"Anyone!" Fritz Zeitletz swept his hand in a broad all-inclusive gesture.

Eliot Carey listened intently. Perhaps these men were baiting Zeitletz. But no, they were too close friends for that. He had felt their friendship in the very air of the room. They were arguing a point and two different philosophies were clashing. Laurence Irish, catching Eliot's eye, nodded and the young doctor came a step into the room, remaining beside the door. The others did not see him.

"I don't understand your attitude, Fritz," Thomas said.

Fritz Zeitletz made no answer and Laurence Irish spoke. "Here's another doctor, Sam. Maybe he can chip in a little."

Thomas turned so that he could see Eliot, and John Mason also faced toward the door. Rutledge lifted his eyes so that he looked at Eliot, and Fritz Zeitletz, seeing his associate for the first time, nodded.

"You heard what we were saying?" he asked.

"I heard some of it," answered Eliot. "I heard Judge Rutledge state his hypothesis."

"Well then"—Sam Thomas' voice was eager—

Ethics and a Murder

"what would you do under those circumstances, Doctor?"

Eliot Carey answered slowly. "The business of a physician is to heal the sick."

"*Ja!*" Fritz Zeitletz was nodding. "That is a doctor's business exactly!"

Again the men about the table turned their eyes to Zeitletz. Sam Thomas leaned forward. "See here, Fritz," he said. "You're a naturalized citizen of the United States. When you became a citizen you swore to uphold the laws of this country. What about that? You swore an oath, remember!"

For an instant there was silence. Fritz Zeitletz broke it. "I *will* uphold the law," he said slowly. "If necessary I will die to uphold the law. I think any of us here would do that. I swore an oath, yes. But there is an older oath, gentlemen, and that oath I also swore."

Thomas sat back; Rutledge relaxed. Irish was watching Eliot Carey narrowly. John Mason tapped the table top with his long fingers. "You an' Fritz don't see alike, Sam," Mason drawled. "That don't keep you from bein' friends. Differences of opinion is what makes horse races. Let's play some cards. It's your deal, Captain."

Laurence Irish collected the cards in his hand. Eliot Carey, beside the door, spoke to the men in the room. "I just came in to say good night," he said pleasantly. "I am very happy to have met you all."

Voices from the table echoed the sentiment. "Glad

I met you, Doctor." "Good night." "I'll see more of you, Doctor." "Visit me when you come to Feather Springs."

Going back along the hall to his room, Eliot did not think of the voices or the invitations. He was remembering what Fritz Zeitletz had said and the earnest blue eyes of the man as he said it.

"There is an older oath, gentlemen, and that oath I also swore."

As he struck a match to light his lamp Eliot Carey quoted a part of the Hippocratic oath to which Zeitletz had referred. He, too, had sworn it:

. . . Whatsoever things I see or hear concerning the life of men, in my attendance on the sick or even apart therefrom, which ought not to be noised abroad, I will keep silent thereon, counting such things to be as sacred trusts. . . .

Dr Carey went to bed thinking about the thing he had heard. The voices in the living room droned peacefully and now and again a man walked along the hall, bound for the kitchen or returning from that source of supply. Dr Zeitletz had been earnest and sincere in his statement, positive in his philosophy, and as Eliot Carey dozed off he, too, was positive. That was a doctor's business: to heal the sick, to aid those in need of succor, to be a safe depository of secrets so that the mind as well as the body of a patient might find relief.

He was wakened from his slumber by a disturbance in the hall. Eliot found his robe and slippers, groping for them in the dark, and, opening his door, went out. This was Dr Zeitletz' night with his friends. No matter what the call, Dr Carey would take it. As he opened his door he heard the voice of Littlebit Mann. Littlebit was talking to Captain Irish.

"There's a stray buggy come to the ranch, Cap'n," said Littlebit. "Turned up at the gate about an hour ago. Laramie wasn't sleepin' an' he heard the fuss the dogs made an' got me up to go see."

"I don't see why you should report that to me, Littlebit," the deep voice of Laurence Irish made answer. "Don't you know to whom the buggy belongs? Couldn't you——"

"No sir," interrupted Littlebit. " I don't know an' I couldn't find out, Cap'n. You see, the feller in it is dead!"

"Where is the buggy?" demanded John Mason.

"We brought it in," Littlebit answered. "It's outside."

The men followed Littlebit out to the fence. There in the light of a lamp that Judge Rutledge held high they saw a buggy and team. Sam Lutes was holding the lines and in the bottom of the buggy was the whilom driver, shot through the body.

"That's a team I sold to the livery in Feather Springs," Laurence Irish announced. "That's why it came to the ranch."

"Then they'll know this man at the livery barn," announced John Mason. "I guess . . . Fritz, we'll finish our card game some other time.

CHAPTER V

Blizzard Riders

THE FINDING of a dead man in a buggy by the LS gate was a seven-day mystery in Soltura. On the morning following the discovery the corpse was taken to Feather Springs by Sam Thomas and Judge Rutledge. In Feather Springs the livery owner identified the dead man as one Carl Jacks, a sheep buyer who had rented the team and buggy for a period of a month. Further identification was made possible by papers that Jacks had in his pockets. The man had not been robbed but, definitely, he had been murdered. John Mason and Tray Barry, following the dim tracks of the buggy from the LS headquarters, traced the trail to the east. They did not lose it but they could not definitely pick out the spot where the shooting had occurred. Thomas, as district attorney, wrote to the firm that employed Jacks and informed them of their employee's death, receiving within a few days directions concerning the disposal of the body. A coroner's jury met in Feather Springs and returned a verdict that Carl Jacks had come to his death at the hands of a person or persons unknown to the jury. A John Doe warrant was issued and given Mason and for the moment the case rested. These things Dr Zeitletz told Eliot when he returned from Feather Springs whither he had accompanied the body.

John Mason stayed for several days with Dr Zeitletz while he pursued his investigations. But Mason did not find evidence of importance. Jacks had, apparently, talked to no one except the barn man in Feather Springs and a few men in the hotel. He had been close mouthed about his business, as a sheep buyer naturally would be, and Mason found no tangible clues.

Dr Zeitletz and Eliot Carey, although they discussed the killing with the sheriff, had other matters to occupy their time. School had started in Soltura and a small epidemic of typhoid broke out in the school. Typhoid, its treatment and cure and prevention, kept the doctors busy until an early frost settled upon the country. For a week the frosts came nightly and with the frosts the new cases ceased to come in. Neither Dr Carey nor Dr Zeitletz could account for the sudden cessation of the disease, and Eliot Carey, filled with the new science concerning germs and their methods of transportation, had a very pretty scientific problem on his hands. He was puzzled over it but failed to arrive at any conclusion. He had had the water at the school boiled and had taken what sanitary measure he could think of to check the spread of the disease, but at the end of the epidemic he had only one fact to account for its disappearance: frosts had come and the fever had ceased to spread.

Another matter took Dr Carey's attention. Fritz Zeitletz was definitely slipping. The little round man began to sag in his clothing and there were periods when he was in great pain and unable to leave his bed. The cancer in his intestines was beginning to grip him. Dr Carey did what he could to ease the older doctor over the worst of his pain and cursed his lack of knowledge. He had, in his stay in Soltura, become very fond of his preceptor, and seeing Zeitletz in pain, watching the little man fight gallantly against the disease, always cheerful and always game, hurt Dr Carey to the depths and cemented his affection.

With Fritz Zeitletz unable to attend to his practice, more and more work fell upon the younger doctor's shoulders. He worked day and night, not only caring for the practice but watching Zeitletz. Then, following the frosts, Indian summer descended upon Soltura and with it Zeitletz' pain seemed to ease away. The little man was shrunken and yellow as a lemon but he said determinedly that he felt fine and insisted upon getting back into harness. Eliot watched him with worried eyes and protested against too much activity. Dr Zeitletz waved the protests aside.

"My work is all the pleasure I have," he answered Eliot's pleas that he not take so much

Blizzard Riders

"Tell me about it," Janice urged.

Eliot was awkward but the girl's questions were shrewd, and presently he found himself explaining to her, telling her about Pasteur and Koch and Loeffler and Von Behring and the others of those mighty men who were delving into the secrets of disease. Janice Irish listened, head tilted to one side, eyes sparkling.

"But this must bore you," Eliot said suddenly. "I don't know why——"

"It does not bore me and you have been telling me because I asked you questions." Janice refuted the charge. "Tell me, Doctor, what is it you want to do, what do you want to make of yourself?"

Eliot Carey considered that question. "I want to be a good doctor," he said finally. "I want to help people that need help. I want——"

"Of course." The girl's voice was impatient. "I know that. But those others you told me about, they have something real to do. They have a fight on their hands. Wouldn't you like a fight like that?"

"Any doctor fights for his patients," said Eliot stiffly. "Certainly I——"

"I know." Janice waved that aside. "But I mean a big fight, something besides giving cough syrup and pills for a stomach-ache. If I were a doctor I would find something that needed to be changed, some disease that no one could cure or some condition that needed correction, and then I would study and fight until I had conquered it."

There was a trace of bitterness in the doctor's

laugh. "And the colds and the stomach-aches could go uncured," he said. "Perhaps you are right. Perhaps a man should look for a real battle. Still Doctor Zeitletz has devoted his life to Soltura and I can't see that he has wasted it."

"You don't understand me." Janice Irish got to her feet. "I don't mean that a doctor should leave his patients. Perhaps there is a real fight here in Soltura for you if you can find it." She stood looking down at the young man on the divan.

Eliot Carey's big head was lowered, his chin resting on his chest. "Perhaps there is," he said slowly and spoke no more. He was thinking, thinking of the day of his arrival and of what Dr Zeitletz had said about a fight, thinking of the squalor in the little adobe house that first night of his stay in Soltura, thinking about the dirt and the ignorance and the abject poverty that he daily encountered. "Perhaps there is a fight here," Eliot said again.

"I'm sure you will find it if there is." Janice Irish's voice was confident. "Father has just come in, Doctor. I'll call him."

Laurence Irish readily agreed to Eliot's suggestion that he talk with Dr Zeitletz concerning a vacation and Dr Carey drove back to town, the mission of his trip accomplished. All the way back to Soltura he thought about Janice Irish, the way her eyes danced, the easy movement of her lithe rounded body. He thought, too, of what Janice Irish had said and, thinking of that, felt shamed. He had taken things as he found them. He had done his best for his patients in treating their ailments, but he knew that the real reason for more than half the illness in Soltura and in the little settlements of Rinconcito and Logan Wells and in all the country around was ignorance. Ignorance and squalor and poverty. And how can a doctor treat ignorance and poverty? He can do free practice; he can care for those unable to pay as well as those with money; he can buy medicine out of his own pocket—but all those things were but as drops of water striking against the surface of a cliff. They can wear a tiny groove in the cliff but the cliff remains.

Dr Zeitletz responded no more kindly to Laurence Irish's suggestion that he take a vacation than he had to Eliot Carey's. Even a letter from Dr Wabfein, written at Eliot's request, brought but a grunt from Zeitletz. His place was in Soltura, the doctor said. He had lived in Soltura, he had worked in Soltura and he would die in Soltura. As for the rest, what more could Wabfein and those others back East do than was being done? Dr Zeitletz did not take Eliot's insistence kindly and perforce Eliot dropped the matter, at least verbally if not mentally.

So October wore along and reached an end and November came. Lambs went to market, driven the weary way to Feather Springs and the railroad by Welch and Company men. In Canyon Largo and in Rinconcito and at Logan Wells and in Soltura a few new calico dresses blossomed; a few children came to school with new shoes; a few men wore new coats, and a few, a very few, doctor bills were paid. And with November snow fell in the Robleros and, reaching out, blanketed Soltura with its whiteness.

On Wednesday, November twenty-second, Eliot Carey, sitting in the warm surgery, instruments that he had but recently used to treat a felon boiling in the sterilizer, was called to the door by a knock. Opening the door, he peered out into the snow that scurried down from the leaden sky and found a native standing. The man was a stranger to Eliot and his breath announced plainly that he had been drinking.

"Do you want a doctor?" Eliot asked.

He was answered by a flood of Spanish, only part of which Eliot understood, and so, taking his caller by the arm, Eliot led him into the surgery, calling for María to come and interpret. María's English was scanty enough but she was patient, and between her English and the smattering of Spanish that Eliot had acquired young Dr Carey was usually able to learn what was wanted.

María did not answer the call but Dr Zeitletz, in carpet slippers and robe, came from his room and joined the men in the surgery. To Zeitletz the newcomer poured out his tale.

"A confinement case in Manueles Canyon," said Zeitletz when he had asked a few questions and been answered. "This is Julio Chavez. It is his wife that is sick. They have had a midwife but the woman has been at labor for two days and the midwife has given up. I had better go, Eliot."

Dr Zeitletz had long since ceased calling Eliot Carey "Doctor Carey" or "Doctor" when they were alone. Between the two now was the affection and understanding of father and son, and the older man indeed treated Eliot as though he were a son.

Eliot shook his head. "I can't let you go out in this weather, Doctor," he said positively. "It's almost a blizzard. I'll get a team and María can heat the soapstones. This man can go with me and give me directions."

Dr Zeitletz was not satisfied with the arrangement, remonstrating that he was capable of going, that he could understand Spanish and that Eliot could not and that he knew the country. Eliot was firm. He knew that Dr Zeitletz had felt a recurrence of the pain from his cancerous growth and he simply was not going to allow the older man to go out into the storm. Finally Zeitletz gave way and, turning to Chavez, spoke in Spanish. Eliot was already making sure that his obstetrical bag contained the things he would need, and María, having come to the door, had hurried away to put the big soapstones on the stove. They soaked up heat as a blotter soaks water and gave it off gradually, so insuring warm feet on such a day.

Julio Chavez spoke again and Dr Zeitletz, turning to Eliot, interpreted. "He wants to go to the store," said Zeitletz. "You can pick him up there. He has been drinking, Eliot. You must be careful."

"He isn't drunk," Eliot answered. "Tell him I'll find him at the store."

Chavez went on out; Eliot finished checking his bag, pulled on his fur coat, the fur cap that Zeitletz had bought him and stamped into his overshoes. Then, pulling on his gloves, he left the house to go to the livery barn for a team.

At the livery barn Ben Fry was loath to let a team go out. Dr Zeitletz' horses and buggy were kept at the barn but usually Eliot Carey used a hired rig. "This is goin' to be a tough one, Doc," Ben Fry insisted. "You ought to stay home a day like this."

"There's a woman that needs me," Eliot answered shortly. "If you won't let me have a team I'll take Doctor Zeitletz'."

Finally the livery man consented. In the buggy, with a rubber sheet pulled down from the top and fastened to the dashboard, Eliot drove to the house. There he loaded in his two bags and the soapstones wrapped in gunnysacks. Bidding Zeitletz good-by, he drove back to Welch's store.

Julio Chavez was not in the store although he had been there. Dr Carey found the man in Brannigan's. Julio, who plainly had taken another drink or two, was loath to leave the warmth and comfort of the saloon. Still, under Eliot's urging, he came out, tied his saddle horse to the hames of the off-horse of the team and climbed into the buggy. Eliot got in, fastened down the rubberized flap and, peering through the isinglass window set in it, the lines passing through a hole in the sheet, started the team.

"Norte," commanded Julio and Eliot drove north.

For a while after they left the town Julio gave directions. The snow fell steadily and now that they were on the flats the wind had its way with the snow, swirling it up from the ground, sending it scurrying across the prairie. As time progressed Julio's directions become more and more unintelligible. His tongue was thick and his voice muttering. Presently, when Eliot spoke, he received no answer. He looked at Julio and found the man's head lolling limply and his eyes closed. Julio had drunk too much; he had passed completely out.

Eliot Carey knew, in a general way, the location of Manueles Canyon. It was northeast of the town, a narrow twisting crack in the mesa. He believed that he had almost reached the canyon. He knew that he was needed and he was loath to turn back. So he drove on, the horses bucking into the storm. He drove on for half an hour and still had not reached the place where the road broke over the rim and descended into Manueles. And now, for the first time, Dr Carey began to experience doubt. He peered through the snow-rimed window. He unbuttoned the flap and thrust out his head. Blank grayness filled with snow confronted him. There were no landmarks, nothing to guide him. Eliot experienced a momentary sense of fright and then, collecting himself, he rebuttoned the flap and drove on. He could not miss Manueles, he thought. He must strike the rim somewhere and, having struck the rim, he could follow it and so find the road. In the canyon there would be but one way to go. He had his directions, carefully given him by Dr Zeitletz. He could not miss the way. The horses stopped.

Peering through the window, his breath frosting

on the isinglass, Eliot saw that the team had paused at a canyon's edge. This must be Manueles. And now a fresh difficulty presented itself. Which way should he turn? Right or left? If he turned in the wrong direction he would miss the road, would follow along the canyon rim until that rim was gone and then there was a vast open expanse of country with no more markers until the railroad was reached. To add to his dilemma it was growing dark, the short day almost finished.

And now the doctor was frightened. He was lost, a blizzard raged about the buggy and night was falling. Desperately he shook the shoulders of the man beside him. Julio's head rolled limply.

"Wake up!" Dr Carey shouted in desperation. "Wake up. . . . Wake up. . . . Wake up!"

Julio did not even open his eyes.

Once more Eliot Carey peered through the glass and then, taking his chance, turned the team toward the left and drove along the canyon rim. It was all that he could do, save turn back, and the thought of turning back did not enter his mind. If he had turned back, if he had wheeled the buggy around, the team might have taken him safely home. There was a chance that they would drift, with the wind at their backs, but there was a greater likelihood that they would find their way back to the warm stable and the stalls to which they were accustomed. But down in Manueles Canyon there was a woman in labor, a woman that needed a doctor, and Dr Carey did not turn back.

Blizzard Riders

For a time he drove against the storm and then as he peered through the frosted glass into the grayness, as he lowered his head and stared through the little hole rubbed free from frost by his glove he saw motion. Something grayer than the snow, something that was not a rock or a tree loomed up and came toward him. A horseman! Another appeared and then another. They appeared and then, turning, faded back into the snow and grayness again and Eliot Carey, ripping open the flap that confined him to the buggy, thrust out his head and called into the storm.

"Help here. Help!"

The wind moaned at him for an answer.

CHAPTER VI

Chopart's Operation

DR CAREY did not call again. He was frightened but he was more angry. Angry with himself for being frightened, angry at those riders who had appeared and then disappeared into the storm. He started the unwilling team once more, fighting the flap which the wind pulled from his hands. He almost had the flap in place when, once more, a rider appeared in the storm and came steadily on to the buggy. The man came close, stopped and, leaning toward Dr Carey, called to him.

"What's wrong? You want some help?"

"Which way is the road?" Dr Carey screamed into the wind. "The road into the canyon?"

The rider pointed. Eliot had been driving in the wrong direction. "Who are you?" yelled the man on horseback.

"Dr Carey. I'm going to Julio Chavez' house."

Behind the mounted man the other riders now appeared, lurking back of him, their figures indefinite in the snow. The man close to the buggy hesitated momentarily and then called again. "Come on then." He pulled his horse around, giving Dr Carey room to turn the vehicle. Eliot Carey fought down the flap and turned the team.

Now the three riders were ahead of him, progressing through the snow. The team followed willingly enough. They went along the canyon rim, passing by the place where Eliot had first reached it. A hundred yards above that spot the road dropped down toward the canyon.

It was hard going down below the rim. There were drifts across the road. The three riders plunged into the drifts, breaking them for the passage of the buggy. Jaw set grimly, Eliot followed after the riders. At the bottom of the hill it was not so bad. The snow fell straight down, big flakes that came from an unfailing source. The team walked steadily and ahead of the team the riders were simply dim figures in the snow and the dusk. Then riders and buggy left the road and suddenly there was light from a window in a house; a man stood at the team's heads, and Eliot Carey was unbuttoning the flap. He climbed down stiffly from the buggy and spoke to a man who appeared beside him.

"Julio Chavez is in there," said Dr Carey, nodding back toward the buggy. "Better get him in before he freezes to death."

The man said, "Sure, Doc," and Eliot plodded through the snow, reached a door and thrust it open.

Inside the rock-walled house he paused, pulling

off his gloves and unbuttoning his coat, snow showering from it as he threw it open. A friendly fire crackled in the fireplace. His gloves laid aside and his coat off, Eliot took a step toward the hearth and then stopped. The step had exposed to view another room and in that room was a woman half kneeling, her arms lifted as she clung desperately to a rope suspended from a rafter. Beneath the woman the dirt floor was covered with a soiled sheepskin. Behind her the midwife, arms locked around the waist of the woman, was pulling down with agonizing pressure. Dr Carey wheeled from the fire and advanced, as angry as he had ever been in all his life.

"Stop that!" snapped Dr Carey.

As he spoke the midwife released her grip and stumbled to her feet. The patient's numb fingers fell away from the rope and the woman collapsed to the sheepskin. She lay there, face wan, eyes closed, big and bulky with the child she carried. Bending down, Dr Carey gathered the woman up in his arms and carried her to the bed in the corner of the room. He laid her there and, turning, his face white with his anger, sought to find the midwife who had pulled upon the child.

He did not find her. Instead grim tanned faces confronted him. One of these he recognized. One of the men who stood in the doorway was Mark Neville.

"Get me hot water!" commanded Dr Carey. "A lot of it. And bring that bag in here." He turned then to the woman on the bed.

Chopart's Operation

The water came, hot and scalding in a bucket. The obstetrical bag was placed convenient to his hand. Dr Carey pulled off his suit coat, scrubbed his hands in the bucket and ordered more hot water, then turned once more to the woman on the bed. She lay there, supine, inert, only her great dark eyes, open now, telling that she lived.

"Now!" said Eliot Carey.

He fell to work then. Instruments came from the bag and were taken to be boiled at the doctor's gruff order. He noted, absently, that men carried out his commands, men he did not know. The woman on the bed occupied all his attention and all his skill. He labored with her. Presently there was a little plaintive cry in the room and Dr Carey stood up, holding a small naked body by the ankles. He spatted the back of the baby and the cry increased in volume.

"Here," ordered Dr Carey. "Take him!"

A woman was shoved forward, a frightened woman that pushed back against the hands that propelled her. She took the baby and carried him away and Dr Carey turned once more to the mother. Later, when the woman on the bed lay easy, Dr Carey turned and walked out into the other room. The midwife was crouched beside the fireplace, the baby, blanket wrapped, in her arms.

Julio Chavez was slumped against the wall, still dead to the world. Two hard-faced men were standing near by the door and in front of the fire Mark Neville sat upon a chair, his legs stretched out before

Trigger Vengeance

him. Neville's face was gray but his voice was drawling and even.

"How is she, Doc?"

"All right now," answered Dr Carey. "She's resting."

"That's good," Neville drawled. "Anythin' you got to do for her or the kid right away?"

"No," Eliot answered. "The baby should be rubbed with oil."

"She can do that," growled one of the men beside the door, nodding toward the midwife.

"Mebbe so, July," said Neville and then, looking at the doctor, "Can she, Doc?"

"Why . . . yes," Eliot answered. "There is a bottle of olive oil in my bag. What——?"

"I've got kind of a bad foot, Doc." Neville stirred a leg, moving it slowly. "Could you look at it?"

"Why, certainly." Dr Carey advanced toward the fireplace.

When he knelt beside Neville's legs he saw that the right boot was torn and crushed. He looked up into Neville's placid eyes, back to the foot once more and spoke. "Pain you?" he asked.

"I don't feel a thing," Neville assured. "Take the boot off, Doc."

"I'd better cut it," announced Dr Carey and brought his pocket knife from his pocket.

He slit the leather of the boot, laid it free and pulled the boot away. The stocking was a pulpy mass of half-frozen blood. That, too, Dr Carey stripped away and looked at the foot so exposed. The lower half of the foot, from the instep to the toes, was crushed, a purplish pulp of flesh.

"How did this happen?" demanded Eliot Carey, looking at Neville.

"Accident," drawled Neville. "What about it, Doc?"

Dr Carey frowned. "I'll have to take off part of the foot," he said, his voice matter-of-fact.

There was silence following the announcement, and then one of the men by the door growled a curse. "Damn it, no! You ain't!"

"Easy, Wing," warned Mark Neville. "You can't save it, Doc? I'd sort of like to keep my foot."

Firmly Eliot Carey shook his head. "There isn't a chance," he said. "You've waited too long. If I had gotten hold of this right after it happened I might have done something. Now there is some infection and that foot is almost frozen. When did this happen anyway?"

"Last night," Neville answered.

"And you haven't had it attended to? What were you thinking of, man?"

"I wasn't thinking about my foot," Mark Neville laughed grimly. "I was more worried about my neck, Doc. Will the whole foot have to come off?"

"He ain't goin' to . . ."

"I said to be easy, Wing!" There was sharp warning in Neville's tone.

Eliot Carey looked at the man, Wing. Wing was young and he was plainly about at the end of his rope. To Wing Dr Carey gave free medical advice.

Trigger Vengeance

"You had better take a drink and relax," directed Dr Carey. "You'll collapse if you don't." He turned once more to Neville.

"I think," he said frankly, "that the whole foot should come off. That's my honest opinion. However, I can take off the crushed portion and perhaps leave you some foot."

"I be able to use it?"

Again Eliot Carey examined the pulpy flesh with his fingers. His eyes met Neville's again. "I can do Chopart's operation," he said slowly. "That will leave you the heel and some of the foot. It will be useful. You'll be able to ride and—— That is, if the infection doesn't go up your leg and make the whole leg have to come off."

Neville's eyes danced as though he had heard something amusing. "We'll take a chance on that, Doc," he said. "Get at this Chopart business."

Eliot Carey straightened briskly. "I'll need my other bag," he said. "I've instruments in it. I want a lot of hot water. I haven't any chloroform. I'm sorry. I'll have to do this under a local anesthetic." He reached for his bag, brought out a hypodermic and elevated the plunger.

"That put me to sleep?" demanded Mark Neville.

Dr Carey shook his head. "It will ease the pain," he said. "It will make you feel sleepy and——"

"Put it up, Doc," ordered Neville. "I reckon I don't need to feel sleepy right now."

Dr Carey shrugged. "It's your foot," he said.

"Yeah," agreed Neville, "it's my foot."

Chopart's Operation

The man Neville called "July" had gone out. Now he returned carrying the other medical bag. He tendered it to Dr Carey. "You be damned careful, Doc," growled July. "You——"

"I'd suggest that you shut up and get ready to help me," snapped Eliot Carey. "Put some water on to boil."

July looked his surprise and Neville laughed. Wing, having advanced from the door to the fireplace, stood glaring at the young doctor. "Damn you!" snarled Wing. "That foot don't have to come off. I think you know——"

"Drop it, Wing!" ordered Neville. *"I said to drop it!"* He made a little motion with his hand as he spoke. Wing seemed to relax.

"I didn't mean nothin', Mark," said Wing. "Hell, I'm upset. I——"

"If we're going to do this we'd better get at it," warned Dr Carey. "That foot's half frozen now. When it thaws out——" He left the sentence unfinished.

"I'm ready whenever you are," drawled Neville.

Dr Carey, selecting what instruments he needed from the bag, placed them in a pan of water and set them to boil. He had no sutures and so sent July out to get horsehair. This, when it was brought, he also boiled. Neville watched the preparations with interest. July, after his first outbreak, worked as the doctor directed, surlily but efficiently. Wing, little eyes smoldering, watched Eliot Carey's every move. The midwife had retired with the baby, and Dr Carey,

75

looking in on the mother while the instruments were boiling, found that she was asleep. Over against the wall Julio snored.

When all was ready Eliot Carey placed Mark Neville's foot on a clean-scrubbed stool, picked up a scalpel and, after a glance at Neville's gray face, made his incision. He worked deftly, rapidly. Dr Zeitletz had repeatedly told Eliot, had driven it in, that time was the essence in such work. Speed, and the danger of infection was reduced. Speed, and pain was less. Speed and care, and the work went exactly. Dr Carey worked with speed. He dissected through the crushed bones of the foot, leaving a long top flap. The bottom flap he made shorter. He tied off the arteries. He brought the flaps into position, stitching them in place. He applied a dressing, band-aging it in place, and he stood up.

"There you are," he said to Mark Neville, who throughout the operation, holding grimly to the chair, had not flinched or made a sound. "That's it. Now I'll look after those dressings. In a week we'll take out the stitches. You'll have a part of your foot left and I hope that it will be useful."

"Thanks, Doc," said Mark Neville. "What's your tax?"

"What's your charge for guiding me down here?" asked Eliot Carey. "I'll pay that and then tell you what my bill is. Besides, I'm not ready to present a bill. I've got to take you in to Soltura where I can look after that foot for a while. We'll see how you come along."

Chopart's Operation

"Oh, sure, Doc," said Mark Neville, something mocking in his voice. "Sure."

"I wonder if I can make it back to town tonight?" Eliot said, moving toward the door. "I'd like to get in."

He pulled open the door. The rush of wind and steadily falling snow gave him his answer as he closed the door again. "Not tonight," said Eliot Carey.

The men made themselves comfortable in the room around the fireplace. Julio they put to bed, utilizing a pallet in the other room. The mother was still sleeping, and the midwife, whose attentions had so nearly been disastrous, had rubbed the baby with olive oil and put the little thing beside its mother. She herself was crouched on a stool beside the bed, her eyes big and black and lustrous when she looked at Dr Carey. She might be trusted with the child, he thought.

Mark Neville sat before the fireplace, his outstretched legs still resting on the stool. Wing was squatted beside the fire and July had somewhere found a pot. It was on the fire now, a savory odor already steaming from its black maw. Wing stirred nervously as Dr Carey returned, and, glancing toward the man, Eliot could see that he was perched above two pairs of saddlebags, as a hen might hover over a nest of eggs.

"Goin' to have some supper pretty soon, Doc," drawled Neville. "Might as well make yourself comf'table. You ain't going back to Soltura tonight."

"No," agreed Eliot, taking a chair and bringing it

over to the fireplace. "I can't go back to Soltura to-night. The storm won't let me. We'll go in tomorrow."

To that Neville made no comment. He was watching Eliot Carey through slitted narrow eyes. Dr Carey could not but admire the man. Neville had an iron nerve. He was in pain, the doctor knew, and yet the man's gray face held no expression.

"You'd better let me give you something to ease that pain," the doctor said suddenly. "I know it's pretty bad."

"I can't, Doc." Neville glanced toward Wing. "I . . . Well, I'd better not."

Wing came to his feet in one swift motion. "For Christ's sake, Mark," he almost screamed the words, "I've told you I won't——"

"I can't quite trust you, Wing," drawled Neville. "No, thanks, Doc. I reckon I'll get along."

Dr Carey did not understand the byplay. He did not try to understand it. He nodded his acceptance of Neville's decision and remained in his chair. Presently July, with a big iron spoon, began to dish stew from the pot. The midwife came creeping in, attracted by the odor of food, and the woman and the men ate hungrily.

There was no pretense of cleaning up after the meal. July lay down, pillowing his head on the saddlebags that Wing had vacated. Wing, after scowling at July, sat down on the floor and leaned his back against the wall. Eliot, using his overcoat for a cover, made himself as comfortable as he could before the fireplace. Only Mark Neville did not move; he simply sat staring at the flames as they danced above the burning log.

When he dozed off, Dr Carey could not say. Sleep he did, for he wakened to find cold morning light streaming into the rock house. He sat up. The fire was out, only embers remaining. Julio Chavez was stirring, moving restlessly, and Neville and July and Wing were gone. Throwing off his overcoat, Dr Carey got to his feet. There was a little pile of gold pieces on the table, stacked on a piece of paper. The paper bore a scrawled message.

Sorry I can't go with you, Doc. These will pay for the foot and for your overshoes and bandages. I needed them.

There was no signature. Looking down at his feet, Eliot saw that his overshoes were indeed missing.

He roused Julio, a repentant Julio whose head was one vast ache. Together the men kindled a fire, and when it was blazing Dr Carey looked in on his patient. He tipped back the blankets that covered the woman and found that the baby was nursing. The mother looked up at him with big grateful eyes and whispered a single word, "Gracias."

Later, before he harnessed his team and drove back to Soltura through the crisp cold of the snowless morning, Eliot Carey made a thorough examination of child and mother. The baby was fine, fat and well colored. The mother, too, was as well as could be expected. In his uncertain Spanish Dr Carey gave directions to the old midwife. She looked at him with lackluster eyes and answered, *"Sí, sí, Señor Doctor."* Julio, too, nodded his understanding of what Eliot told him and then went out and harnessed the doctor's team.

When he reached Soltura late that afternoon Eliot found Dr Zeitletz worried. The little man listened to what Eliot told him about the delivery of Julio Chavez' child and nodded. "She was trying to pull the baby down," he said, referring to the midwife. "Sometimes I have found that. You had no trouble with the delivery?"

"I had to use instruments," Eliot answered.

"The Flyer was held up over above Feather Springs day before yesterday," said Zeitletz, abruptly changing the subject. "Four men. The express messenger killed one of them as they were getting away. One of the men had his foot crushed in the coupling of the express car. He was pretty badly crippled. They got away with the strongbox but there wasn't much in it."

"When did that happen?" Eliot asked.

"In the evening," Zeitletz answered. "The evening of the day before the storm. The whole country is roused."

"Yes," said Eliot slowly. "I suspect it would be. You say that one had his foot crushed?"

"That is the report," Zeitletz answered. "One was killed and one had his foot crushed."

Eliot thought of a purple, bloody mass of flesh at

the end of a man's leg. "So that's how it happened," he said slowly.

"How what happened?" demanded Dr Zeitletz.

"Nothing," Eliot answered. "I was only thinking aloud."

"You will quit thinking and take a hot bath and drink a toddy," directed Fritz Zeitletz. "What were you thinking of, Doctor, going off on a trip like that without your overshoes! It is a good thing I am here to look after you."

"Yes, it is," Eliot laughed and, crossing the surgery, moved toward the hall. "A very good thing, Doctor."

He wondered if his overshoes were warm. He wondered if a bootless man, a man with only half a foot, might find comfort in the thick felt and rubber of the overshoes. Somehow Dr Carey hoped he would.

CHAPTER VII

Schuetzen Rifle

ON THE DAY before Thanksgiving Jack Brannigan staged a turkey shoot in Soltura. Despite María's demands and protests, Fritz Zeitletz had refused to buy a turkey for the holiday, declaring rather that he would win one at the shoot. Now on Wednesday morning he came into the surgery where Eliot Carey was reading carrying a heavy Schuetzen rifle in his hands.

"Have you ever seen a gun like this before, Eliot?" Zeitletz asked, stopping beside the desk and resting the long curled iron butt plate of the rifle on the desk top.

Laying aside his book, Dr Carey smiled at his friend and reached a hand toward the rifle. "I think I must have its little brother back home," he answered, taking the rifle. "I joined a Schuetzenbund in Vienna while I was there. Every Sunday morning we went out to the range and drank beer and shot our rifles. This is a fine gun, Doctor."

Zeitletz' face was a curious mixture of pride and astonishment. "And you never told me," he chided. "You are a great one for hiding your light under a bushel. Why haven't you mentioned this before?"

"I didn't think you would be interested," Eliot answered. "This is certainly a fine rifle." He had risen from his chair and now he tried the gun, lifting it so that the butt place curled under his armpit, sighting down the long barrel.

"You will shoot today, *ja?*" demanded Zeitletz eagerly. "This gun. I will lend it to you and we will win all the turkeys."

Dr Carey saw that it would please Zeitletz if he said yes and accordingly nodded, making only one reservation. "If I'm not on a call," he said, "I'd like to go with you, Doctor."

Having made answer, he fell again to examining the rifle. Oddly it was not a foreign-made weapon. Instead the gun was a Schoyen-Ballard, .32-.40. There was a palm rest, a beautifully carved stock with high comb and cheekpiece and an aperture sight on the tang. The gun was fitted with blocks for a telescope sight, and, seeing his friend's interest, Dr Zeitletz hurried out, returning with the long tube of the telescope in his hands. This he fitted to the rifle and for half an hour the two men enjoyed themselves arguing, discussing rather, the comparative merits of powders, of muzzle loading versus breech loading, of alloy mixtures for bullets and their proper lubrication. Here was a new field of mutual interest and they explored it together. They were still at it when María came to call them to lunch.

After the meal they smoked cigars in the warmth of the surgery and then, it being time for the shoot to begin, they dressed and, with Eliot carrying the rifle, went out into the clear cold November air.

The shoot was held at the lower end of town. There were turkeys in crates and a crowd at the firing line, while, sixty yards away, the targets were placed against a cut bank. Brannigan was explaining the rules to a group of shooters but he broke off when he saw the two doctors and came toward them.

"Goin' to win all the birds, Doc?" he asked Zeitletz.

Dr Zeitletz shook his head. "One for me, one for Doctor Carey," he answered.

Brannigan laughed and returned to the group of shooters.

The rules, as laid down by Jack Brannigan, called for three offhand shots at sixty yards, the man making the smallest group winning the bird. There must be at least five entries for each bird, the saloon-keeper said, and for those who preferred not to shoot there were dice. A man could throw dice or take his rifle and go to the firing line. The entry fee for each contestant was fifty cents.

In the first group to shoot for a bird was Dr Zeitletz and he proved his confidence in his heavy gun and in his own skill. The three holes torn by the .32-caliber slugs the doctor fired could have been covered by a quarter, and Dr Zeitletz returned to Eliot Carey flushed and triumphant.

While the doctor was firing his three shots, seating the bullets through the breech and carefully slipping in the loaded cases, Eliot Carey stood watching. To him, as he stood, came Littlebit Mann, acting like a small boy that knew a secret. Littlebit touched Eliot's arm and, when the doctor turned, nodded his head. "Want to speak to you, Doc," said Littlebit and drew Eliot aside.

When the two were by themselves Littlebit, first looking all around to make sure that they were unobserved, drew a folded paper from his pocket. "Friend of yours sent you this, Doc," he said, tendering the paper. Eliot unfolded the sheet. There, spread upon the paper, were small bits of horsehair. At first Dr Carey could not imagine their meaning and then, examining the horsehair, he saw that there were surgeon's knots tied in it and that the horsehair had been cut. These were stitches that had been removed and Eliot looked sharply at Littlebit.

"He said he wanted you to know that he took 'em out all right, Doc," announced Littlebit. "He took 'em out an' the foot's comin' all right. An' he sent you this an' said for you to keep it with you."

From the pocket of his coat Littlebit produced a pistol, a heavy-barreled Frontier model and shoved it out to Eliot. "Put it away, Doc," ordered Littlebit nervously. "Don't stand there lookin' at it. Somebody might see you."

Trigger Vengeance

Eliot Carey put the gun in the pocket of his coat. "Why did he send that?" the doctor asked.

"It's his own gun," Littlebit answered. "It's a .32-.20. He said to tell you that he's movin' around for his health, an' he said that Wing was scared that you'd talk too much an' that Wing might be lookin' for you so to keep that gun handy. Can you shoot a six-shooter, Doc?"

"I never have," Eliot answered. "How is your friend, Littlebit?"

"Just fine, Doc, an' he ain't just my friend. He's a friend of yours too."

Further conversation was interrupted. It was time for the younger man to shoot and Dr Zeitletz was calling for Eliot.

When Eliot Carey went up to the firing line he was nervous. He knew that the Schoyen-Ballard he held was a fine instrument, a precision tool, and he knew that most of Soltura and practically all of the surrounding country would be watching to see what he did with it. As he loaded the gun his nervousness passed. He had held his own in rifle matches where he competed with famous shots. And now, as he cuddled his cheek against the cheekpiece of the Ballard and set the trigger, he was cool. The mark came up in front of the sights; Dr Carey steadied and then touched the crisp hair trigger. The Ballard bellowed and Dr Carey lowered the piece. Twice more he fired, and when the targets were compared he felt a flush of pleasure. He had not beaten Dr Zeitletz but the black-rimmed holes in his target were almost as close as those in the group that Zeitletz had fired. Dr Zeitletz pounded him on the back and urged him to compete again but Jack Brannigan vetoed that.

"They say they won't go up against that gun, Doc," announced Brannigan. "If you want to shoot any more you'll have to use somethin' else."

This Dr Zeitletz disdained to do. He and Eliot watched the progress of the shoot for a while and then, each carrying a turkey, went back to the house. There they found John Mason waiting for them and, delivering the turkeys to the enchanted María, went into the living room with the sheriff.

The sheriff, with one of Dr Zeitletz' good cigars in his mouth, perched on a corner of the table and grinned around the cigar. "I don't suppose, Fritz," he said conversationally, "that you've had a man with a badly smashed foot in here to doctor, have you?"

Fritz Zeitletz smiled at his friend. "No, John," he answered.

"I just thought I'd ask," the sheriff drawled. "Mark Neville had his foot smashed when he held up the Flyer. Likely he'll have to get it tended to someplace. That is, unless he does it himself. Neville's got nerve enough to do that, I reckon." The last sentence was musing as the sheriff spoke. Watching Mason, Eliot Carey thought of the strong gray face of Mark Neville, immobile even though the eyes showed his pain. Yes, Mark Neville would have had nerve enough to cut off his own foot.

Trigger Vengeance

"You know that it was Neville that held up the train?" Zeitletz asked.

"Sure," Mason nodded. "He was seen and recognized. There were three others with him. Nobody seems to know who they were for sure but there's a five-hundred-dollar reward out for each of them. The express messenger grabbed his shotgun and downed one man just as they were pulling out. Wouldn't have got him but the fellow that was holding the horses got in a hurry. Well, I just thought I'd ask. Mark Neville has got friends all over this country and he's going to be hard to find." Mason sighed and, slipping down from the table, walked over and took a chair.

"First a murder and then a train robbery," he said, stretching out in the chair. "This country's getting to be tough, Fritz."

"Have you found out anything about Jacks?" Eliot asked.

Mason turned his head toward the doctor. "Not a whole lot," he replied. "We've got a lead, though. Jacks had trouble with a man up north, a fellow named Walters. Walters is supposed to be bad and he was gone from home when Jacks was killed. He's been picked up and questioned but he claims that he was out hunting when the murder happened. We're watching him."

"That's not much to go on," Fritz Zeitletz commented.

"Not a whole lot," Mason agreed. "We did find that Jacks had been over to Abrán Fernandez talking to Abrán about buying his lambs. He'd left Abrán's place in Canyon Largo and Abrán came to town to see Welch. Welch holds a mortgage on the sheep and Abrán had to see Welch before he could sell."

Eliot recalled the occurrence in Welch's store, the dark face of the native, Welch's sharp words and the angry discussion he had seen take place between Abrán Fernandez and Tray Barry.

The sheriff shifted in his chair and Eliot could see the brown butt of a gun hung in a shoulder holster under Mason's left arm.

"How is business with you, Doctor Carey?" Mason asked conversationally.

"He has begun to practice," Zeitletz said dryly, answering for the younger man. "He set the leg of a horse for Littlebit Mann and since then he has maintained quite a reputation for broken bones." The small doctor chuckled and Mason, noting Eliot's flush, changed the subject.

"I've got to see Littlebit," he announced. "He and Mark Neville used to be thicker than thieves. Littlebit is at the Bar T Crossing camp now, Irish tells me. I reckon I'll ride out that way."

"You'll have dinner with us tomorrow?" Zeitletz interposed hastily. "Doctor Carey and I each won a turkey at the shoot and we need company to help us eat them."

Mason exclaimed over that and asked questions which led to Zeitletz' telling of the turkey shoot and the performance of the Schuetzen rifle. That talk brought on reminiscence from the sheriff and it was a full half-hour before Mason got up and announced his intention of departing.

"You said that Littlebit was in town," he commented, turning to Zeitletz, who in the course of the conversation had given that information. "I'll catch him before he pulls out for camp. Save me a ride. And, Fritz, I've been wondering about Tray Barry. I've been told that he's drinking a lot. Keeping at it pretty steady. You know anything about that?"

"I heard that he was drinking," Zeitletz answered. "I don't know much about it."

"I'll see Tray while I'm here," Mason decided. "Welch has been after me to appoint Sid Raupert over here. I think I'll do that. I'll be back, Fritz, and spend the night. Mrs Mason isn't going to like it but that can't be helped this time, I reckon."

The sheriff departed then, a strong, sturdy man with an air of assurance and authority set upon him, and Fritz Zeitletz and Dr Carey were left alone. Zeitletz announced that he was going to lie down awhile and take a nap, and Eliot, picking up the book he had laid aside, said that he would finish reading it.

The doctor had scarcely covered a chapter before there was a knock on the door. Eliot answered the summons and, opening the door, found Emma Welch standing there. The girl was flushed with the cold wind and the rich blood shone through the olive of her cheeks. As he invited his visitor into the house and allowed her to precede him into the surgery

Schuetzen Rifle

Eliot wondered what the occasion for her call might be. Emma crossed directly to the desk and seated herself in the chair beside it while Dr Carey dropped into the swivel chair before the desk.

"You're wondering why I came, aren't you?" Emma Welch's smile showed white even teeth.

Eliot could not but return the smile as he nodded.

"I came to ask you a favor." Emma's muff lay on her lap, one of her hands concealed within the fur. The other hand she placed upon the desk. It lay there, long and slim and, despite its lack of movement, filled with life.

"A pleasant favor, I hope," the doctor suggested.

Emma nodded. "Tomorrow is Thanksgiving Day," she said. "I would like to help someone to be thankful. I want you to take this"—the girl drew a little fold of currency from her muff—"and give it to someone who needs it. Will you do that for me, Doctor Carey?"

Eliot did not take the bills the girl extended. His eyes were questioning as he looked at her. "Why don't you give the money yourself?" he asked.

Emma Welch shrugged. "I suppose I could," she answered, "but really I don't know who needs it the most. I thought that in your practice you would know someone who could use it."

"I could name half a dozen," Eliot said. "If you like I'll give you the names of several families."

Emma dropped the money on the desk. "I wish that you would do it for me, Doctor," she said.

"Won't you?" She smiled again as she spoke and Eliot could not resist the smile.

"Certainly," he agreed, picking up the bills and leafing through them. "There is . . . twenty-five dollars here. I'll gladly do as you ask, Miss Welch. And when I say who this comes from——"

"Don't tell them, please," the girl interrupted. "If you told a native that I had given them money I would have a crowd on my porch every morning. Just give the money and say nothing about where it comes from."

"If you want it that way," Eliot agreed.

The girl rose briskly from the chair. "I'm ever so grateful, Doctor," she said. "Thank you." She walked toward the door and Eliot, rising, followed her. At the door Emma paused.

"You haven't been to see us, Doctor," she chided. "It's not far up the hill."

"I've been busy," Eliot evaded.

"Come when you can," Emma urged. "Mother and I are always at home. Good-by, Doctor, and do come and visit us."

Eliot followed the girl on into the hall. Emma, opening the door, went out on the porch, turned and, flashing her smile once more, again said good-by. Mechanically Eliot answered her. He was wondering concerning the real motive for the visit. Certainly if she wished to bestow benefices Emma Welch could have found a dozen worthy recipients within stone's throw of her own home. The girl went down the steps and along the walk and, following her with his eyes, Eliot saw that a buggy had stopped by the fence and that Janice Irish and her father were alighting from it.

The arriving Irishes and the departing Emma Welch passed on the walk and the girls stopped and exchanged a few words. Then Emma went on and Janice and her father came to the house. Eliot, at the door, held it open for the captain and his daughter, smiling his welcome and calling over his shoulder for Dr Zeitletz.

The little doctor came from his room, shook hands with the captain and kissed Janice on a rosy cheek. Eliot envied the older man.

"We can't stay but a minute." Captain Irish answered Zeitletz' hospitable invitation. "I wanted to see you, Fritz, and Janice has an invitation for you."

"We want you both for dinner tomorrow," Janice said.

Dr Zeitletz shook his head. "We can't come," he answered. "I'm sorry, Janice."

The girl did not ask for a reason but turned to Eliot. "Will you show me your surgery while Father talks to Doctor Zeitletz?" she asked. "The doctor has been telling me about the changes you have made and he says that you have a microscope. May I look through it?" She was eager as a four-year-old child in a candy shop.

Eliot could hardly keep from laughing at her eagerness. "Certainly," he agreed. "I'll be glad to show you. It's right in here."

Coat collar opened so that her face was framed

by the rich fur, Janice preceded Eliot into the surgery, stopping just beyond the door and looking at the room. "It's much cleaner"—she pronounced judgment—"and it smells differently. What is the smell, Doctor?" The girl wrinkled her straight little nose.

"Iodoform," Eliot answered, laughing. "I'm something of a fanatic on cleanliness and sanitation. Here's the microscope, Miss Irish."

He took the instrument from its case, selected a slide and placed the glass slip on the table of the microscope. Bending, he adjusted the focus and stepped back so that the girl might look through the eyepiece. "That is anthrax," Eliot explained. "Those dark-colored rods you see."

Janice lifted her head. "Anthrax?"

"It's sometimes called woolsorter's disease," Eliot explained. "These are diphtheria bacilli. The little faint blue ones with the blue bands across them." He placed another slide beneath the nosepiece of the microscope. Janice Irish brushed back a curling tendril of red hair and again applied her eye to the eyepiece.

One by one the doctor showed the girl his treasures, explaining as he did so. In the hall the captain's deep voice rumbled and Fritz Zeitletz' lighter voice made answer.

"Are you coming, Janice?" the captain called.

The girl lifted her head and smiled at Eliot Carey. "I must go," she said. "Father wants to get back to the ranch and I have some baskets to deliver before

Schuetzen Rifle

we go back. Thanksgiving is a festive occasion, don't you think, Doctor? We have so much to be thankful for."

"We have indeed," Eliot said warmly. "I'm afraid I've bored you with my talk, Miss Irish, but I get enthusiastic and——"

"You didn't bore me at all," the girl interrupted. "I've enjoyed it. I asked to be shown your microscope, remember? I think it's fascinating."

Eliot wished that Janice Irish might find the microscope's owner as fascinating as the microscope but forbore saying so. Janice made a picture as she stood framed in the doorway. "Good-by, Doctor," she said. "I'm sorry that you and Uncle Fritz can't come to dinner tomorrow."

"So am I," Eliot agreed. "Very sorry."

Later, when the girl and her father were gone, Eliot Carey and Fritz Zeitletz turned away from the front door and walked together along the hall. Zeitletz shook his head. "There is a girl, Eliot," he said impressively. "Every Thanksgiving, every Christmas, she makes baskets of food and brings them to needy families. Is it any wonder that I love her?"

"No," agreed Eliot. "It isn't."

Zeitletz placed a hand upon his assistant's arm and the men stopped their slow walk. Eliot Carey was immersed in his thoughts. He was comparing Janice Irish with Emma Welch. Both were beautiful, both were desirable. Emma Welch had brought him money to give to some needy person. Janice Irish had brought in baskets of food to be given to someone who otherwise would be without a Thanksgiving dinner. Eliot wondered if Emma would have cooked over a hot stove and prepared a basket and brought it in. He wondered. . . .

"A fine girl, Eliot," continued Dr Zeitletz. "It will take a fine man to be worthy of her."

Eliot Carey nodded soberly.

CHAPTER VIII

"Brannigan's Back Room"

THANKSGIVING DINNER with Dr Zeitletz was an event that Eliot Carey, long as he might live, would never forget. The day was memorable in many ways. He had a letter from his mother back in her placid New Jersey home, and when he sat down to the table he found that there was another guest besides John Mason. Father Revelet—a little dried-up wisp of a man with a face that made Eliot think of the saints pictured in cathedral windows—joined Mason, Zeitletz and Dr Carey. Eliot had met the priest casually but had not come in close contact with him, learning of him only through hearsay. Now, as the men sipped good wine and ate the meal María had prepared, Eliot really learned something of the priest. There was an inner light in Father Revelet that shone through his eyes, almost glowing through his parchmentlike, nearly transparent skin. Father Revelet, Eliot decided, was that rare thing, a thoroughly good man.

Trigger Vengeance

When the meal was finished and the four men, surfeited with food, relaxed in their chairs, Mason, Zeitletz and Eliot to smoke and Father Revelet to smile upon them benignly, Eliot learned why it was that Thanksgiving was a particular feast day with the little doctor. Zeitletz tapped cigar ashes on the edge of his plate, smiled at Eliot and John Mason and spoke to the priest.

"This is our twentieth Thanksgiving, Father," he said. "Remember the first one?"

Father Revelet nodded. "You were younger then," he said. "As I was. We had newly come to Soltura."

Zeitletz nodded. "I was fresh out of Austria," he said. "I remember well. I could not understand this new country with its freedom. I thought that Thanksgiving Day would be my feast day to celebrate my freedom in my own home. It has been that ever since."

"And our first feast day we celebrated with mutton stew and red chili," the priest laughed. "And you were called from the table to attend a birth, and I to shrive a dying man." His face sobered suddenly as he completed his sentence. There was silence in the room while priest and doctor mused, wandering in the past.

"That was long ago," the priest said.

"Long ago," Zeitletz echoed.

"I was a button coming up from Texas twenty years ago," drawled John Mason. "An' you"—he grinned at Eliot—"most likely were a kid snitching extra grub from your grandmother's table."

"Brannigan's Back Room"

All the men laughed and the talk went around the table, each adding his bit. It was three o'clock when, finally, they left the board, Father Revelet to go to prepare for evening Mass, John Mason to walk through the town and Zeitletz to go to his room to rest. Eliot chose to accompany Mason and the two men, doctor and officer, donned their overcoats and left the house.

"Doc," Mason said, with a nod toward the house as they went down the walk, "had it pretty tough for a while after he came here. You don't know how lucky you are, young fello'. Doc Zeitletz is the salt of the earth."

"I know he is," Eliot agreed, his voice sober. "We'll miss him."

Mason's eyes were sharp as he scrutinized the younger man. "You know why he sent for you then," the sheriff observed. "Doc talked it over with me an' Sam Thomas. I'm glad you're fitting in, Son."

The two walked on in silence. Below Welch's store, where the clustered adobes housed the native population of Soltura, Mason spoke again.

"How long do you reckon?" he said and then, seeing the question in Eliot's eyes, "I mean for Doc."

"I don't know," Eliot answered slowly.

A little further along the way, walking single file now because of the narrowness of the track through the snow, Mason, who was in the lead, halted. Coming down the street was a wagon drawn by two long-eared burros and piled high with household goods. A man and a woman and children rode in the wagon.

"Fernandez!" snapped Mason and then more slowly, "I heard that Welch was goin' to put him out."

Eliot recognized the man on the wagon as Abrán Fernandez. He and Mason faced the street, watching the wagon as it pulled to a halt before the house. "Welch had a mortgage on Abrán's sheep," Mason said, half to Eliot, half to himself. "I reckon he foreclosed. Abrán was a little too up-and-coming to suit Welch."

"You mean he put the man out of his home in this weather?" Eliot asked incredulously.

The sheriff nodded. Eliot repressed the hot words that rose to his tongue.

Mason walked ahead and Eliot followed him, falling in beside the officer when the path widened.

"And that's the way that people get rich," Mason said suddenly. "I've worked for a living all my life. If that's what it takes to have money I don't want any!"

Eliot thought of the money in his pocket, the money that Emma Welch had given him. Welch and Company had ruined Fernandez and twenty-five dollars would not be much in the way of amends, but it struck the young doctor that it would be simple justice for Abrán to have the money.

"If you'll excuse me, Sheriff," Eliot said suddenly. "I just thought of something I should do."

Mason glanced curiously at his companion and then nodded agreement. "Sure," he said. "I'll walk along. See you tonight, Doc."

He strode off along the path and Eliot, waiting

until the sheriff had disappeared around the corner of a building, waded through the snow and crossed the street.

Abrán Fernandez was lifting a chair from the wagon when Eliot came up. The native, a solid, powerfully built man, placed the chair on the ground and looked inquiringly at the doctor. Eliot was at a loss as to how to begin.

"Doctor?" Abrán said slowly.

That was the opening. "*¿Habla inglés?*" Eliot questioned.

"Sure." Abrán's voice was heavy and the words came one at a time as though he translated Spanish to English as he spoke. "I can talk some."

"Good!" Eliot spoke rapidly. "Here's something for you and I hope that you have a good Thanksgiving." As he spoke the doctor took the little fold of bills from his pocket and held them out.

Abrán blinked uncomprehendingly and then half lifted his hand toward the bills. "For me?" he questioned.

"Of course for you," Eliot agreed. "Take it."

"You give?" asked Abrán.

It would be good, Eliot thought, if Abrán knew that the man who had turned him out was the donor of the money. Abrán would appreciate the grim humor of the thing, even as Eliot appreciated it.

"No," he said. "This is Miss Welch's money."

At the mention of the name Abrán Fernandez' face darkened with a scowl. "No," he said forcefully and lowered the half-lifted hand.

Trigger Vengeance

"Please take it," Eliot urged. He could see the face of Abrán's wife as she timidly peeped around the edge of the door. There were children's faces peering from behind the woman.

"No!" rasped Abrán again and with a sudden motion struck the money from Eliot's hand. It fell to the snow. For a moment Abrán faced the doctor and then, stooping, lifted the chair and, carrying it, his back, broad and strong, turned toward Eliot, went into the house.

Eliot watched Abrán go. He had made a mistake, he realized. Perhaps he should have said that he himself was giving the money. He stooped and, picking up the scattered greenbacks, refolded them and returned them to his pocket. Then slowly he walked off toward Dr Zeitletz' house.

Back at home the young doctor was moodily silent when Zeitletz, roused from his nap, joined Eliot in the surgery. Zeitletz tried in vain to arouse the spirits of the younger man and, failing, became sober himself.

"What is the trouble, boy?" he asked, touching Eliot's arm.

"I've made a mistake," Eliot answered. "I thought I was doing the right thing and I spoiled it."

"Sooo?" Zeitletz rumbled. "We all do those things. What was it?"

"Nothing of importance, I suppose," Eliot answered. "I saw something today, Doctor. Abrán Fernandez is moving into town. Mr Mason told me that Fernandez had been dispossessed by Welch. It seemed almost inhuman to me. To think that a man would turn another out——"

Eliot stopped suddenly. He had never seen such an expression on a man's face as that which flashed across Zeitletz'.

"Inhuman!" Dr Zeitletz snapped. "Inhuman? I could tell you things——" Pain flooded across the bright blue eyes. Zeitletz sagged. Eliot Carey, reaching out his long arms, caught and supported the little man. He half led, half carried Fritz Zeitletz to his room, put him on the bed and hurried out into the surgery. Later, when morphine had mercifully eased the older doctor, Dr Carey stood beside the bed looking down at his friend. Dr Zeitletz, undressed now and covered, lay with his eyelids lowered so that his eyes were hidden. His voice was almost dreamy as he spoke.

"Three years ago, Eliot," said Zeitletz with an effort, "there came a drought. Welch and Company were benefactors then. They gave credit and carried the sheepmen through the drought. That fall the lambs did not bring much money and the store extended more credit. They took mortgages to protect themselves and that was business. Then in the spring the store bought the wool and the price was low and there was more credit, and presently, to protect the store, there were mortgages on the sheep. And now the lamb buyers and the wool buyers do not come to Soltura. Welch and Company buy the lambs and the wool at their own prices and apply the money to the accounts at the store. You saw today——"

Trigger Vengeance

The words lapsed. The morphine had taken hold and Dr Zeitletz dozed. Eliot Carey, reaching behind him, pulled a chair close to the bed and, sitting down, stared at the man that lay there. He was not thinking about what he had heard. He was thinking of Fritz Zeitletz and of how lonely it would be when Fritz Zeitletz was gone.

How lonely it would be!

For three days Dr Zeitletz remained in his bed, Eliot hovering over him like a mother hen with but one chick. Then, despite Eliot's protests, Dr Zeitletz got up, wan and weak but determined. He would not go back to bed and insisted that he was all right and there was nothing that Eliot Carey could do about the matter.

The first day that Dr Zeitletz was out of bed a call came in from Logan Wells. Dr Carey, answering that call, found an acute appendicitis awaiting him. The appendix had ruptured, and Dr Carey removed it, operating on a kitchen table with a frightened woman and a man that turned pale but stayed on the job to assist him. Carey removed the fluid from the abdomen as best he could and put in a drain. He could not leave the patient at once but stayed and watched the case. For twenty-four hours he hung on, fighting for the man's life. Then, feeling that he was winning, he relaxed, only to be called before he had napped an hour to attend a man who had been badly cut by barbed wire. That ordeal was barely passed when again the appendicitis patient needed his attention, and the evening of the second

"Brannigan's Back Room"

day Dr Carey took his way back to Soltura, a tired but very happy man. His operative intervention in the case of the appendectomy had been successful and the man with the wire cut was coming along with no sign of infection. Dr Carey had left strict orders as to the care of both patients and felt reasonably sure that his directions would be carried out, for in both instances the patient's attendants understood English.

When he had reached Soltura and turned his team over to the ministrations of Fry at the livery barn Dr Carey walked on home. He whistled as he came up the walk to the house and pushed open the door. He was elated. This was his first kitchen-table operation and it had been successful! Not only had he diagnosed the case properly but he had operated, and while McBurney had made his publication in 1889, appendectomies were not yet as common as they were to become later. Eliot Carey felt that he had something of importance to tell Zeitletz.

But Dr Zeitletz was not in the house. María, meeting Eliot at the door, told him that Dr Zeitletz had been called in the afternoon and had not returned. Eliot frowned.

Where had Dr Zeitletz gone? he demanded.

María did not know but the doctor had not taken a team and was, therefore, somewhere in the town. Tired as he was, Eliot was about to institute a search when Dr Zeitletz came up the walk.

Dr Zeitletz was glad enough when his assistant departed for Logan Wells. He loved Eliot Carey as a son and it was not easy to hide from the younger man the almost constant paint that gnawed at his vitals. There were mornings when Zeitletz administered a sedative to himself so that he might carry on through the day, and only the iron determination of the little man enabled him to go at all. With Eliot gone he could relax a little, but when Eliot was present Dr Zeitletz forced cheerfulness into his eyes and gamely stayed on the job. He knew, could not help but know, that he had not long to live. There would come a time soon when it would be impossible for him to leave his bed. But until that time Dr Zeitletz intended to keep going, not only because it was his duty but because he wished to train his young assistant and to plant his roots firmly in Soltura.

The first day of Eliot's absence passed uneventfully for Zeitletz, but the second day was not so calm. He had three patients at the office in the morning and just after lunch Jack Brannigan came to the house and asked Zeitletz to accompany him.

"It's Tray Barry," explained Brannigan. "He's been drinkin' steady for a month and Thanksgiving Day he started a real one. He's got the d.t.s, Doc, an' I wish you'd come down. I got him in my old room behind the saloon."

Zeitletz, equipping himself with his bag and a supply of sedatives, left the house with a word to María and went downtown with the saloon man. He found Tray Barry just as Brannigan had described. Barry lay in a tangle of blankets in the room behind the saloon, his eyes wide and glassy and his muscles twitching. When Brannigan, followed by Zeitletz, entered the room the man sprang up and it was all that Brannigan could do to put him back to bed.

For a time there was trouble in that small semi-heated room. Tray Barry's heart was wild and fast and irregular and would not stand an opiate. Dr Zeitletz called for a glass of water and administered a bromide. The sedative did not take hold and Tray Barry continued to twitch and mutter. He could answer a question readily enough but immediately relapsed into his busy restlessness. Zeitletz knew that he must administer another sedative and again sent Brannigan for water.

While the saloonkeeper was gone Barry lay twitching on the bed. His wildly rolling eyes and trembling lips spoke of a hidden fear. "Don't you, Sid," he half whispered. "Don't you! There ain't no need to shoot!"

Brannigan came back and again Dr Zeitletz mixed a sedative and administered it. "I'll watch him, Brannigan," Zeitletz said. "You've been on duty for quite a while. I'll look after him."

Brannigan nodded his relief. "I'll be right out in front," he said, moving toward the door. "You call me if you need help, Doc. He's been talkin' wild an' out of his head right along. Mebbe he'll try to hurt himself."

"I don't think so," Zeitletz answered. "I'll call you if I need you, Jack."

Brannigan went out, closing the door softly behind him, and Zeitletz sat down beside Barry, waiting for the bromide to take effect. The mutterings of the man on the bed, unintelligible at first, became coherent words.

"There ain't no need for you to get riled up, Sid," Tray Barry mumbled. "He wasn't nothin' but a lousy sheepman. I told him to get out. I told him nobody but Welch bought lambs around here. He deserved killin'."

The words were garbled for a time and then once more were distinguishable. "I ain't goin' to tell, Sid. I was with you, wasn't I? Hell, I ain't goin' to squeal on you."

Dr Zeitletz' hand trembled. Here, in the ravings of this incoherent man upon the tumbled bed, was the solution to a mystery. Dr Zeitletz had no doubt concerning the identity of the "Sid" Barry mentioned. It was undoubtedly Sid Raupert. And the "lousy sheepman" was Carl Jacks. Carl Jacks, who had come to the Soltura district to buy lambs and who had been found dead in his rented buggy. That was the import of Tray Barry's raving. Zeitletz waited for Barry to go on but the man did not continue. He became obsessed with the fright of a "monstrous steer," a steer that, in his alcoholic fancy, occupied a corner of the room.

Out in the saloon Jack Brannigan stood behind the bar. There were only two men in the place, both natives, and they conversed low voiced beside the bar. The door opened and Sid Raupert came in.

"Hyuh, Jack?" Raupert greeted. "What's new?"

"Not much, Sid," Brannigan answered, sliding out

a little glass and a bottle. "Tray's finally got himself the d.t.s. He's back in my old room ravin'. I had to get Doc Zeitletz for him."

Raupert poured his drink with a steady hand. "Got the d.t.s, huh?" he observed, tossing down the liquor. "Talkin' some?"

"Talkin' a lot," Brannigan corrected. "There's a big steer penned in a corner, according to Tray, an' he's been talkin' about killin' somebody. Hell, Tray never killed nobody in his life. He ain't got guts enough."

Sid Raupert poured and downed another drink, no emotion showing on his narrow face. "An' you got Zeitletz for Tray, you say?" he asked.

"Doc's with him now," answered Brannigan. "Give him somethin' to quiet him down."

"Tray's a friend of mine," observed Raupert. "I'll go back an' set with him a spell. No need of runnin' up a big doctor bill. Tell you what, Jack. You send up to Welch's house an' tell old Allan that Tray's under the weather. I'll bet that Allan Welch will send down an' have Tray moved up there where he can be looked after."

"I'll do just that," Brannigan answered and spoke to one of the loiterers at the bar.

Sid Raupert, putting down his glass, strolled on back to the door that opened into Brannigan's room. Without knocking he pushed it open and went in. From his place beside the bed Dr Zeitletz looked up at the new arrival. Tray Barry was muttering still, his muscular twitching diminished.

Trigger Vengeance

"Jack told me that Tray was havin' the d.t.s, Doc," drawled Raupert casually. "I said I'd sit with him awhile. How is he?"

"He is quieting," Dr Zeitletz answered. "I've given him a sedative and it seems to be taking hold."

"No need for you to stay then," said Raupert. "I know how to handle the d.t.s. Feed 'em light an' keep 'em quiet. That's it, ain't it?"

Dr Zeitletz nodded. He felt the menace in Raupert's presence, the chilly aura that hung about the man. "That's it," he agreed.

"Tray been talkin'?" Raupert's question was entirely casual.

"He's afraid of a big steer he imagines is in the room," said Dr Zeitletz.

"That's what Jack said." Raupert pulled a chair out from the wall and sat down beside the bed. "You go ahead home, Doc. If we need you I'll send somebody up."

On the bed Tray Barry had stilled. Dr Zeitletz looked first at Barry and then at Raupert. He knew, did Dr Zeitletz, that if Tray Barry were to repeat the things he had said, he, Dr Fritz Zeitletz, would not walk out of the room. It was dangerous to stay but it was not the fact of danger that deterred Dr Zeitletz; rather it was Eliot Carey. He had to live awhile longer, had to live to see Eliot Carey firmly established in Soltura and because of that he obeyed Sid Raupert. "All right," agreed Dr Zeitletz. "I'll go then. Send for me if you need me."

The door had scarcely closed behind Fritz Zeit-

"Brannigan's Back Room"

letz' back before Tray Barry stirred. Sid Raupert bent close. "No need to kill him, Sid," whispered Tray Barry. "We can scare him out."

Raupert's lips were a thin, puckered, reddish line. "Uh-huh," murmured Sid Raupert.

He was sitting beside the bed, motionless apparently, when Allan Welch arrived, hurried and flushed. Brannigan came in with Welch and it was not until Brannigan had left that Raupert spoke.

"Tray's shootin' off his head," Raupert said thinly. "He's talkin' about that Jacks business."

"I told you there was no need——" Welch began.

"You wanted Jacks out of the country an' you paid for havin' him put out," Raupert interrupted harshly. "How it was done wasn't yours to say. The thing is that Tray is talkin'. I think he shot off his wind when Doc Zeitletz was here."

"My God!" Welch gasped. "If——"

"I don't know that he did," Raupert interposed. "I'm just guessin'. But Tray has got to be stopped, Welch."

"How do you mean? What do you mean?"

"I mean he's got the d.t.s an' he could have 'em again an' not so private," replied Raupert with asperity. "I'm not goin' to stick out my neck for a drunk like Tray an' neither are you. Men have died of the d.t.s before this."

Once more Allan Welch gasped, "My God!"

"You got a little bottle up at the store, Welch," Raupert said. "It's got knockout drops in it. I know. You go up an' get it."

Trigger Vengeance

"No!" Welch faced the thin-faced man. "Not that. Not——"

"You go get the bottle!" ordered Sid Raupert.

Eliot Carey scolded Dr Zeitletz when he got the small man into the house. He scolded him and put him to bed and swore that never again, no, not even to attend his appendicitis patient, would he leave Soltura unless Fritz Zeitletz promised not to go out on calls. Fritz Zeitletz was smilingly indulgent and offered no protest when Eliot Carey made him take a warm drink and a light sedative and go to bed. So preoccupied was the little doctor during the whole procedure that he undressed and swallowed the sedative without making objection.

It was some time before the sedative took effect and Eliot sat beside his mentor and told of the operation he had performed, describing it in detail. Fritz Zeitletz smiled faintly as he listened. Finally his eyes closed and he dozed off, then, blowing out the lamp, Eliot tiptoed from the room.

It was almost morning when Dr Carey heard the knocking at the door. Sleepily he found robe and slippers and lit the lamp. When he opened the door Sid Raupert stood on the steps.

"I come to tell you, Doc," said Raupert, his voice expressionless, "Tray checked out awhile ago. I guess Doc Zeitletz told you. Tray had the d.t.s. He was doin' all right an' all of a sudden he just up an' died. Heart wouldn't stand it, I guess. I thought I'd better come an' tell Zeitletz but you'll do."

"Brannigan's Back Room"

"Dr Zeitletz is sleeping," Dr Carey said wearily. "I don't want to disturb him. Do you want me to come?"

"Mornin' will be soon enough, I reckon," Raupert answered. "So long, Doc."

CHAPTER IX

Roybal Canyon

THERE WAS NO GREAT FUROR concerning the death of Tray Barry. Soltura did not mourn him. Dr Carey, going to Brannigan's place early in the morning, found Jack Brannigan and Sid Raupert there. Brannigan was anxious to have Barry's body removed and Dr Carey, after a brief inspection, gave consent. He had not spoken to Zeitletz concerning Barry's death before he left the house and the older doctor was not apprised of the occurrence until Eliot returned. Zeitletz had little to say when his associate reported, but Eliot had the impression that his friend was not satisfied. Jack Brannigan and Sid Raupert were chief among the mourners when Tray Barry's body was taken to Soltura's weed-grown cemetery that afternoon.

After the funeral Dr Carey, returning from a call, saw Sid Raupert coming down the steps of Zeitletz' house. Raupert nodded as he passed the young doctor, and when Eliot went into the house he found Zeitletz in the hall.

"What was Raupert doing here?" Eliot asked, appraising the grayness of Zeitletz' cheeks with knowing eyes. "Has he been bothering you?"

Dr Zeitletz shook his head. "He came to pay Barry's bill," the older man answered. "I don't feel well, Eliot. I think I'll lie down."

Fritz Zeitletz went into his room and Eliot, after glancing in on the older man, went on about his business.

With Thanksgiving past, winter really settled down on Soltura and the country about. The first storm in November had left snow on the ground that did not melt. Between the end of November and Christmas there were other storms. It was difficult for the mail buggy to come through from Feather Springs. The freight teams of Welch and Company, hauling supplies from the railroad, were hampered and hindered by the inclement weather, and Dr Eliot Carey, taking all of the out-of-town practice, was often gone from early morning until late at night, returning to the town only to find that there was another call awaiting him.

Dr Zeitletz definitely was slipping. He was an old, old man and a sick one. Still he rallied through the bad weather, staying at work as best he could and attending to the practice in the town itself.

Christmas Dr Zeitletz spent at the LS. Eliot Carey, invited to the ranch, was in Canyon Largo all through the day. A kerosene lamp had exploded in Narciso Duran's home in Canyon Largo and Narciso's three-year-old child was badly burned. Driving back to Soltura in the five-o'clock dusk, Dr Carey was heartsick and lonely. The baby had died of its burns despite all that Dr Carey could do, and he had left a sobbing mother and a stony-faced father behind him. Dr Carey had not the heart to take his troubles to the warmth and cheer of the LS. He went straight home after he had left his team in the livery barn and, eating a cold supper, went to bed. Nor did he get up when Dr Zeitletz came in with Laurence Irish.

New Year's Day passed; January wore along filled with work. Then came February and the snows ceased and the sky was bright and blue and the sun shone high. And in February there was fresh stirring in Soltura.

All through the winter months Eliot Carey had heard rumors—now here, now there—concerning Mark Neville. Strangers had been in and out of Soltura, stopping a day or two at Mrs Maybe's boardinghouse and then departing. The Wells Fargo Express Company had a long memory and the company had not forgotten the robbery of its express car. Mark Neville was rumored to be in the hills west of Soltura and gradually that rumor narrowed down until a definite place was named: Roybal Canyon.

Roybal Canyon was occupied, that was certain. There was a grizzled short-spoken man named Dunlop who had a cabin in Roybal Canyon. Dunlop had neither cattle nor sheep. He rode a rawboned black horse and had two pack mules, and these and the cabin comprised his worldly wealth so far as Soltura knew. Dunlop sold an occasional pack of furs: coyote, wolf and lion. He spent the proceeds of his sales at Brannigan's and at Welch's, becoming surlily drunk on his trips to town. Laban Benedict, Welch's bookkeeper, started the tale that Dunlop was buying far more food than he had ever purchased before. Jack Brannigan, taking his cue from Benedict, spoke of the fact that Dunlop was not drinking on his trips in but was buying whisky by the quart and taking it with him. Gradually the certainty came to Soltura's consciousness that Dunlop's cabin was harboring other than its owner.

Soltura paid little attention to rumor or even to certainty. Mark Neville had friends in Soltura. He had enemies also, chief among them being Sid Raupert, who had taken Tray Barry's place as deputy sheriff in the little town. Raupert and the Wells Fargo men who came and went perhaps had secret and more certain information than the others. At any event, in February, about the middle of the month, John Mason rode into Soltura, with five deputies following. Mason and his deputies, together with Sid Raupert and two hardy fellows from the express company's forces, forgathered in a room back of Welch's store. Certain of the townsmen were called in, notably Ben Fry from the livery barn and Laban Benedict from the store. Young Courtland Welch was present but it was noticeable that no one from the LS attended the gathering. Mark Neville had at one time punched cows for the LS and ranchmen and cowpunchers are loyal.

The meeting in Welch's back room broke up in the evening, the deputies staying in the store and making beds with blankets from Welch's stock. The townsmen, with stern faces, went to their homes and they did not talk, but all Soltura knew what had happened. John Mason and the Wells Fargo men were going after Mark Neville up in Roybal Canyon. That was the talk in Brannigan's saloon and in the adobe houses of Mexican town and all through Soltura.

John Mason confirmed that talk when he ate dinner with Fritz Zeitletz. Dr Carey was not present at the meal, being out on a call. Over the good food that María spread upon the table between the doctor and his guest John Mason told Zeitletz his mission.

"We're sure that Neville an' some more are up there at Dunlop's," the sheriff said. "We've got a kind of inside connection there, Fritz. There's one of the bunch with Neville that ain't suited exactly. He's got in touch with Raupert an' we know the whole layout. We're heading for the canyon early tomorrow morning."

Fritz Zeitletz toyed with the handle of his coffee cup and it hurt John Mason's heart to see how thin and clawlike was the hand of his friend. "Mark Neville," mused Zeitletz. "He is not a bad man, John. Mark Neville has done many a good thing."

Roybal Canyon

Mason nodded. "Sure," he agreed readily. "Mark ain't bad; he's just wild. That's the trouble. He's got some more with him. When he pulled that holdup on the Flyer there was just four of them: Neville, an' a fellow named Wiggins an' a couple more. Now he's got five men. One of the original bunch was killed when the train was robbed. Neville's got two new ones."

The sheriff was silent for a long interval while he drank coffee and thoughtfully buttered a biscuit, then he spoke again. "I know how it works," he said. "I know how Mark Neville got started. You see, it could have worked that way with me."

Zeitletz made no comment, waiting for the sheriff to continue. John Mason proceeded. "You take a young fellow and he's punchin' cows," Mason said thoughtfully. "He works all summer at a dangerous business. There's lots of action an' lots of life an' he spends his money when he comes to town. He gets shaved and gets a haircut and takes a drink or two and has a rip-snorting time. When the fall works close up the foreman lays him off. There's nothing to do till spring. He hangs around town and the money gets scarcer and scarcer and he lives on his credit. There's nothing for him to do, no excitement, no nothing. The first thing he knows he's broke and his credit's used up, and there he is with nothing but time on his hands and all that devilment that he could work off in the summer penned up inside him. Something happens and the first thing you know he's borrowed a little bunch of cattle or he's picked up a horse that doesn't belong to him or maybe he's robbed a train. There's nothing wrong with Mark Neville except that he was just too much man to stay still and wait. I know. It damned near happened to me."

For a long moment Mason was silent. Fritz Zeitletz stared at his plate. "Remember, Fritz?" Mason asked suddenly. "Remember when you first met me? I was going to bust into the Silver Dollar over in Feather Springs that night and take old Wink Patree's poker game for what was in it. Likely I'd have got killed. Old Wink was a salty old jigger. You came along and made me go with you out to where some woman on a work train was having a baby. Instead of holding up Wink's game, I rustled hot water for you and chopped wood until I was black in the face. Remember?"

Zeitletz nodded gravely. "I remember," he said. "Somebody will be hurt tomorrow, John."

Mason shrugged. "Mark and them ain't kids," he said. "We'll be playing for keeps and so will they. I'm going to start a bunch around to cut into the pass above Dunlop's so they won't go through to Packer Canyon and get away. The Wells Fargo men and me will go to the front door. It's too bad but it's got to be that way. Mark may be a pretty good fellow but we can't have him attracting all the wild kids in the country to him. First thing we'd know there 'd be another James gang."

Dr Zeitletz made no comment on Mason's statement but asked a question. "Won't it be bad going up there in the snow?"

"Slow us down," Mason agreed. "It will slow them down, too, though. Anyhow, the Wells Fargo boys are getting anxious." The sheriff paused a moment and then, looking keenly at his friend, spoke again. "You don't look so well, Fritz. How are you feeling?"

"I feel all right," Zeitletz answered. "My young man is taking all the work from me. He will not let me leave town, and when he is here he won't let me leave the house."

"That's a good boy, Fritz," Mason commented. "He——"

The front door opened and closed and Eliot's brisk steps were heard in the hall. John Mason watched Zeitletz' face light up and saw the affection in the old man's eyes as Eliot, tall and heavily coated, stood in the dining-room door. John Mason did not need to be told how Fritz Zeitletz felt about Eliot Carey.

The sheriff stayed the night with his friend but in the morning, before the doctors were up and dressed, John Mason left Zeitletz' home. Eliot commented on the officer's departure as he sat with his friend at the breakfast table but Eliot did not have time to listen to what Zeitletz had to tell him. An urchin arrived, breathless and panting and in need of a doctor, and Eliot, hastily gulping his coffee, accompanied the small boy.

When the young doctor was gone Fritz Zeitletz

sat for a while at the table and then, suddenly reaching a decision, got up, put on his overcoat and fur cap and, taking his medicine bag, went to the livery barn. Ben Fry was not at the barn but Zeitletz demanded his team and buggy from the hostler, and when it was brought climbed over the wheel, settled himself and drove out through the barn door. At the end of the street he turned west, heading toward the hills. He had decided that there was business in Roybal Canyon that needed the presence of a physician. Dr Carey, returning to the house an hour after he had left it, found Fritz Zeitletz gone. María could give him no information but Eliot did not believe that the older man had left town. It was not until dinnertime that he began to worry, and by dinnertime it was too late to worry about Fritz Zeitletz for Fritz Zeitletz was dead.

John Mason and his possemen left Soltura early. They rode out in the crisp morning, the breath steaming from their horses' nostrils and their saddle leather creaking with the cold. They were silent as they rode, for there was no need for talk. The ten miles to the hills were traversed and at the bottom of Primo Canyon the posse split. Roybal Canyon was a side canyon to Primo and before they could reach the mouth of Roybal they had to go up Primo Canyon for eight miles. Three of the possemen swung off toward the north, riding across the three miles that separated the mouth of Primo Canyon from the mouth of Packer Canyon. These three men were to ascend Packer Canyon until they came to the narrow pass that separated Packer from Roybal. The others of the posse waited, intending to allow the three time to take position before the main body of the posse proceeded on its mission. One of the Wells Fargo riders looked at his watch as the three rode off; the others, dismounting, tramped in the snow, moving about in order to keep warm. Some few hardy souls bared their hands to roll cigarettes, and John Mason talked low voiced with the men from the express company.

Time passed and the Wells Fargo man who had looked at his watch glanced at it again and then spoke to Mason. "Time to go," he announced. Mason nodded. The men who were on the ground mounted again and the little group of horsemen began the ascent of Primo Canyon.

They found the going easy enough. There was a settlement well up Primo Canyon and wood had been hauled down the twisting mountain road so that the trail was broken. John Mason and his men had no trouble in their ride up the canyon. Not so the three who had taken the Packer Canyon trail. They found their way beset with difficulties. Well up Packer Canyon the three came upon a snowslide which delayed them woefully. Of this Mason and the others knew nothing.

The eight miles of Primo Canyon took an hour. Where Roybal Canyon's wide mouth reached the main canyon Mason halted and the possemen clustered around him.

"You know how we planned it," Mason said

curtly. "Me and Mr Wade will ride in. The rest of you fan out down below and take some cover. Maybe we'll have no trouble and maybe we'll have some."

A rider grunted scornfully at Mason's optimism. The men in the posse suffered no hallucinations. They knew what they were going up against.

"Well then," Mason said heavily, "let's go."

The horsemen spread out and began to ride up Roybal Canyon. They did not know that behind them in Primo Canyon a team, hard driven, was coming along the road.

It was half a mile up Roybal Canyon before Dunlop's house was reached. Before the cabin came into view the posse had spread out clear across the gap. They halted and dismounted in the timber below the cabin, each man taking cover. Mason and the Wells Fargo man, Wade, waited until the possemen were in position and then slowly, their horses' hoofs creaking in the snow, rode up the beaten trail toward the cabin. At the pole fence that surrounded the cabin and the little shed barn the two riders halted and Mason, lifting his voice, hailed the house.

"Hello, the house!"

The canyon walls, white with snow, unblemished and unmarred, threw the words back to him.

"Hello, the house!" Mason called again. Somewhere in the timber a jay called raucously.

"We'll go on in," Wade declared. "They ain't there."

"I'm not too sure," Mason said. "Wait. . . ."

Wade had dismounted and opened the pole gate.

Roybal Canyon

He led his horse through and advanced boldly toward the lifeless cabin. Mason followed discreetly. He had smelled smoke as they rode up Roybal Canyon. John Mason was a cautious, canny man and smoke meant fire, and men about it.

Ten feet from the cabin Wade stopped short. He had heard something, movement in the cabin perhaps. A bold man, Wade, and a brave one, but foolhardy. He dropped the reins of his horse and whipped out the gun from its holster at his waist. He took two plunging steps, shouted, "Come out of there!" and fired a shot.

That shot was answered. A gun bellowed inside the cabin and Wade lurched and went down. For a fraction of a second there was no more fire, and then from the cabin and from the timber below the cabin all hell broke loose. John Mason, cool under fire, made a little rush and reached Wade. He bent over the man, straightened and, at a zigzag run, started for shelter. Once, in that run, he lurched and then, reaching a pile of fence posts, dived behind it. Silence descended upon the cabin and the timber.

For perhaps five minutes that silence held unbroken, and then in the timber a posseman thought that he saw movement and a rifle cracked. The shot was answered from the cabin and so a slow, steady firing began.

When that first shot was fired the possemen, following along behind their leaders, disposed themselves as they saw advantage. Ben Fry, on the left of the advancing line, had come up a gully that dropped below the level of the canyon floor. He could not see the others of the posse, save only Sid Raupert, who, like Ben, had picked the gully with the instinctive sense for cover that a good fighting man possesses.

Fifty yards below the cabin the gully was blocked by a fall of timber and into this Ben Fry worked his way, arriving eventually at the top of the tangle of logs and brush, sheltered from the cabin by the bole of a big pine that had fallen across the depression. It was a perfect fort and had the added advantage of blocking any attempt at escape from the cabin by way of the gully. From his vantage point Ben Fry could see the other possemen, and to his right Sid Raupert, also taking cover in the fallen timber, fired twice and then swore viciously.

"What's the matter?" Ben demanded, thinking that Sid might have been hit.

"Left my shells on my saddle," Raupert answered and began to work back through the fallen timber. Ben Fry grunted and took another shot at the cabin.

Dr Zeitletz halted his team at the mouth of Roybal Canyon. From above him, through the canyon mouth, came the sound of methodical rifle fire. Dr Zeitletz looked at the snow. He could not drive up Roybal Canyon. Alighting from the buggy, the little doctor tied his team and then, taking his medical bag, plodded steadily toward the sound of guns.

Dr Zeitletz found Ben Fry behind the big pine log. The livery man turned when he heard the crunch of Zeitletz' overshoes in the snow, saw who was coming and devoted his attention to the cabin once more. Dr Zeitletz, breathing heavily with his exertions, crawled up into the windfall and settled down behind Fry.

"Botched it," Ben Fry announced, not taking his eyes from the cabin. "John an' that Wells Fargo fello', Wade, went into the cabin. Wade got excited and threw a shot an' they cut him down from inside. He's dead, I reckon. John run over and looked at him, then made a run for that post pile. Made it, too, but he moved like he was hit before he got there."

Zeitletz was silent. Ben Fry went on talking. "Damn fool idea, if you ask me," he said. "Goin' up against a cabin like this. There's four-five men in there an' they ain't foolin' a bit. I mind one time in Texas——" Fry paused to fire twice swiftly. He slid down from behind the pine, stuffed shells into the magazine of his gun and turned to look at Dr Zeitletz. Zeitletz was gone. Indeed, he had departed when Ben Fry said that John Mason was hit. Fry grunted. A fighting man, Ben Fry, seasoned in the border warfare that flared incessantly in the Big Bend country. He crawled back up behind his rampart and peered over it.

Fritz Zeitletz, leaving Fry, went along the windfall and up the bank. He had, from where he crouched, a view of the cabin, the yard, the shed and the post pile. John Mason was huddled behind the post pile and Mason did not move. Beyond Mason Wade lay sprawled upon his back in the snow of the yard. Fritz Zeitletz settled his coat in place, tugged at his cap and stepped boldly out. Everybody in Soltura knew that little round, fur-capped figure. Everybody in Soltura and all the country around knew the dangling medicine bag. Sure of himself, sure of his immunity, Fritz Zeitletz trudged out into the open. He skirted the windfall and then dropped back into the gully. The post pile was just at the eastern edge of the depression and Zeitletz went along the bottom of the draw. He was screened from the possemen to the right; they could not see him because of the gully. He was in view only of Ben Fry and the men in the cabin.

When Dr Zeitletz was twenty yards from the post pile a posseman off to the right fired a shot, and with that for a start, a ripple of firing ran along the line. Dr Zeitletz, moving steadily toward John Mason and the pile of posts, halted, half turned and dropped in the snow.

Ben Fry had fired with the others. Now, as that fire died, he lifted his voice, yelling to his companions. "They got Doc. Damn 'em, they got him!"

He could see the others of the attacking force look toward him. Then a posseman, rising up, charged toward the cabin. The carefully planned attack had fallen flat, and now each man in turn caught the contagion of that first reckless charge and, leaving his hiding place, joined in. Only Ben Fry, a chew of tobacco bulging in his cheek, held his place and kept his head. It was Ben Fry and Ben alone left to stop the thing that next happened. When the possemen charged the door of the cabin swung open. Guns roared from door and window and the charge was stopped. As the men dropped down, seeking shelter from the slugs that smacked through the air toward them, men came running from the cabin door. Three of them made that mad short run from cabin to shed and were lost. Ben Fry lowered his hot rifle and swore. He had missed four shots.

A posseman cautiously raised his head, only to drop it again as a gun spoke from the shed. Another, unnoticed, crawled forward for ten feet before being checked. Then from the shed three horses pounded out, riders bent low, tight against the backs of their mounts.

Possemen, springing to their feet, answered that attempted flight with lead. The horses lunged through the snow, making their way up the canyon. A horse went down and scrambled up, and then the three, horses and riders, were in the timber and Ben Fry, standing atop the windfall, was bawling orders.

"Foller 'em! Git your horses an' foller 'em!"

The remaining representative of the express company and two others turned and ran back to where the posse had left their mounts. Fry was clambering down from the windfall and running toward John Mason. Others of the posse followed his lead. These were bending over Fritz Zeitletz and John Mason when the Wells Fargo man, Sid Raupert and another swept past. Fry, straightening up, saw them go and spat a brown stain into the snow before he bent over Mason once more.

"John's still goin'," he called. "He's shot pretty bad. How's Doc?"

Beside Dr Fritz Zeitletz a man stood up and answered, "Dead."

Once more Fry spat into the snow. "We got to get 'em in," he announced. "Look in the cabin an' see who's there an' one of you go get the horses."

CHAPTER X

. . . Of Which I Die Possessed . .

THEY BROUGHT Fritz Zeitletz back into town that afternoon riding in his buggy, a blanket-wrapped inert bundle under the buggy seat. The seat itself was needed for Ben Fry, who drove the buggy, and for John Mason, wan and white. There were three other blanket-wrapped bulks to transport. Wade, grizzled old Dunlop, who had died in the cabin, and a black-haired, black-eyed young fellow who also lay on the cabin floor. Some one of the possemen identified the black-haired boy as Harley Quinn, who, the summer before, had punched cows over east of Feather Springs. Ben Fry drove the buggy to Zeitletz' front door and the silent possemen carried John Mason and Fritz Zeitletz into the house. Eliot Carey was there to receive them.

He could do nothing for Dr Zeitletz. The men from the posse carried the little doctor into his room and placed him on the bed. Dr Carey reserved his attentions for John Mason. Mason could not move his legs, and when the sheriff was stripped and on the operating table in the surgery Dr Carey examined him. Mason had been shot low through the side, above the hip. From the course of the bullet Eliot decided that it had penetrated the great muscle of the back and lodged against the backbone. That and shock would account for Mason's partial paralysis. The doctor turned from the table and summoned Ben Fry and another of the posse.

"We'll go to work," he said crisply. "You'll help me."

Fry's protestations that he knew nothing of surgery made no difference to Eliot. While he scrubbed his hands and while the instruments boiled Ben Fry and the other man were given their instructions. Clean, and with his instruments in readiness, Eliot went back to the table and John Mason. Soon the sweetish, almost sickening odor of chloroform filled the surgery and John Mason lay unconscious.

Eliot carefully cleaned the lips of the wound, working swiftly and with wonderful dexterity. He found no foreign substance present where the bullet had entered and John Mason was turned upon his side. Now, boldly, Dr Carey went into the great muscle of the back, reaching in for the bullet. He found it lodged against the spine and lifted it out, an ugly, misshapen piece of lead held tightly in his bullet forceps. There was a small amount of bone from a shattered spinous process and this, too, the doctor removed. Then, still working at high speed, he closed the wound, bandaged it, and John Mason, operating table and all, was wheeled from the surgery into Eliot's own room where the sheriff was placed upon the bed. With his work finished for the moment, Dr Carey gave his patient a last inspection then walked into the room where Zeitletz' body lay.

All through the operation, all during the time he had worked over John Mason, Eliot Carey had been a detached, efficient machine. Now, standing beside Zeitletz' bed, he reached down his hand and turned back the blanket that covered the face of his friend. Fritz Zeitletz lay there, his eyes closed and his face peaceful. It seemed to Eliot that Zeitletz was smiling. For a long time he stood looking at that placid face and gradually his mind began to work once more. Fritz Zeitletz had been sentenced to die. He had not counted on many more days. There would have come a time when pain would have beaten him down, would have sent its fiery trace through his body, burning him. The time would have come when Fritz Zeitletz would have died and before that time what agony might he not have experienced? Perhaps this was best. Perhaps this was the way out, the way that Zeitletz—given a choice—would have gone. Had he, Eliot wondered, suffered after the bullet struck home? Dr Carey bent again and, moving swiftly as always, examined his dead friend. When he straightened he was satisfied. Zeitletz had been struck in the left side, far back, and the bullet had clipped directly through his heart. Fritz Zeitletz had suffered no pain.

Once more Eliot covered the quiet face and then

lowered himself to the edge of the bed and rested his hand upon Dr Zeitletz' lifeless arm.

How long he sat there staring at the wall where hung. pictures of round-faced foreign people, Dr Carey did not know. His mind was far from the room, traveling back over the time of his stay in Soltura. He was awakened from his reverie by Ben Fry's appearance at the door.

"John's beginnin' to wake up, Doc," Fry announced. "You want to come in?"

Eliot got up from the bed and followed Fry into his room. As he came out into the hall he saw that it was filled. Men and women stood there, silent, quiet, almost breathless. María was among them, red eyed, but mute as the rest.

Eliot Carey spoke to María. "It's all right, María," he said gently. "He didn't suffer. It's all right." Behind María Father Revelet spoke, his voice low as he echoed Dr Carey's words in Spanish.

"You better come, Doc," Ben Fry urged impatiently. "John's got his eyes open." Dr Carey went on to do what he could for the living.

He was with John Mason for the remainder of the day. Ben Fry and others were in and out of the room. There seemed always to be someone there to do as the doctor ordered, to bring the things he desired. It was late that night when Eliot, getting up from the chair beside Mason's bed, first took real cognizance of the people in the room. There was a quiet-faced woman, a stranger, at his side and Eliot looked at her in wonder.

"I'm John's wife," said the woman, her voice as calm as her face. "Doctor——?"

"We've done what we can." Dr Carey answered the unspoken question. "He's resting and his heart is strong. All the broken bone is gone from the wound and the bullet has been removed. He will live, Mrs Mason. He will be all right in time."

The quiet-faced woman collapsed at Eliot Carey's feet.

They took John Mason's wife into the living room and placed her on the couch. Spirits of ammonia and cold water revived her and she lay there, her big eyes fixed upon Eliot Carey's face. The doctor spoke reassuringly, and Mrs Maybe, wheezing with her asthma, planted herself beside the couch as though she meant to stay. Dr Carey went back down the hall for another look at the sheriff and then, reassured, returned to the surgery. There, because he must have something to do, because his hands needed occupation, he cleaned the instruments he had used, washing them and putting them in the little sterilizer. He took the bloody sheet from the table and, wadding it, threw it in a corner, only to retrieve it and carry it out to the clothes hamper. He did all that he could do, and when he could no longer find occupation for his hands he sat down at the desk and stared at the cubbyholes. It was there that Clem Maybe found him.

"How are you, Doc?" Clem Maybe asked awkwardly.

With a start Eliot looked up at his questioner.

"Why . . . why, I'm all right," he answered, wonder in his voice.

"I thought maybe you'd need a little drink," said Clem. "I brought you some. I . . . Well, Doc, this has been pretty hard on you."

In a detached, curious way Eliot realized that Clem Maybe was sorry for him, that Clem Maybe was trying to help, to be sympathetic. "Thank you, Clem," he said.

"You want that drink, Doc?"

"No . . . no, thanks, Clem. I don't need a drink."

Maybe stood beside the desk, shifting from one big foot to the other, nervous and not understanding the calm of the young man who sat so motionless. "Why . . . all right then," Clem said. "All right, Doc. The missus is goin' to stay with Mrs Mason. Ben's back with John. I thought—— You know, Doc, when I hauled you over here I thought maybe you wasn't goin' to do. I was all wrong, Doc. I take it all back."

Dr Carey made no answer and after a moment Clem Maybe tiptoed out into the hall. There he met his wheezing wife. "He's just sittin' there," Clem reported. "Just sittin' starin' at the wall."

On the day following the fiasco in Roybal Canyon the town of Soltura buried Fritz Zeitletz: the town of Soltura and all the country about it. Feather Springs was represented and there were people that Eliot had never seen before. To that funeral he rode with Laurence Irish and Janice, the girl, her face set and expressionless, sandwiched between the two men.

Fritz Zeitletz had believed in no particular religious creed, but Father Revelet was beside the grave, as was Duncan Loeder, the Protestant circuit rider from Feather Springs.

When the frozen earth had rattled down upon the coffin and when the last of the mourners had turned away to walk or to ride slowly back to the town Laurence Irish spoke, his voice more harsh than Dr Carey had ever heard it. Even Janice, surprised at the unnatural timbre, turned to look at her father's face.

"That is all," Laurence Irish grated. "This country will see the biggest man hunt it has ever seen. There's nowhere now that Mark Neville can find a man to hide him."

The words were the first that Eliot had heard concerning Neville and he questioned Irish. The ranchman was abrupt and short spoken.

"Neville and two others," he said, answering Eliot's question. "They got away. The men who were to have gone up Packer Canyon were held up by a slide. Neville and the two others crossed the gap and went on across Packer and into the hills. Raupert and one of the express-company men followed them until dark. In the morning they lost the trail and they came back to town. I thought you knew, Doctor."

Eliot shook his head and Irish went on, his voice rasping. "They've gotten away," he said. "For a while they've gotten clear but not for long. There is not a man in the country that did not owe Fritz Zeitlitz something. The whole country will be up in arms. I intend to take every man I can spare from the winter work and to hire others to track down those killers. And we'll find them! When we do——" Seeing the horror in his daughter's wide eyes, the ranchman stopped abruptly.

For a long interval Eliot remained quiet, immersed in his thoughts. Perhaps if he had not been so clever with his scalpel, perhaps if he had not been so deft and so sure that night in Julio Chavez' rock house in Manueles Canyon, this would not have happened. Perhaps . . .

"We'll miss him!" said Laurence Irish. "God, how we'll miss him!"

No one in the buggy spoke further during the short drive to town. When they reached the doctor's house Irish stopped the team and, without invitation, alighted from the buggy and tied the horses. Janice, her father and Eliot on either side, went up the walk and the doctor opened the door for their entrance.

María met them in the hall. She had come straight to the house from the cemetery and now she spoke swiftly to the captain. She had not finished her speech when the round face and pince-nez glasses of Sam Thomas appeared in the living-room door.

"I've been waiting for you," announced Thomas soberly. "Will you come in here?"

He did not pause for an answer but stepped back

into the living room and Janice, her father and Eliot beside her, followed the attorney. Thomas, as though he were the host, gestured to chairs and the three sat down. María also slipped into the room and stood beside the door.

Sam Thomas cleared his throat, drew a folded paper from the inner pocket of his coat, cleared his throat again and made an announcement.

"Fritz Zeitletz left a will," he said impressively. "Some months ago he had me draw the document and he executed it in my presence. His heirs are assembled here and with your permission I shall read."

Once more the attorney cleared his throat and then began to read the will.

Stripped of its legal verbiage, Fritz Zeitletz' will contained a few definite statements. To María the little doctor left a thousand dollars on deposit in a Kansas City bank. He bewailed the fact that he had no more to give his faithful servant. To Janice Irish he bequeathed certain of his personal possessions: his watch, a few pieces of jewelry and, mentioned specifically in the will, his diary. "Not," the will read, "because it is of value, but because I would not have it fall into unfriendly hands and because it is a little part of me that I want Janice to have."

There were tears in Janice's eyes as Sam Thomas read the passage and Thomas, visibly affected, stopped and cleared his throat once more.

The remainder of his property, the house, the

medicines, the instruments in the surgery, the team and buggy—everything of which he died possessed Dr Zeitletz left to Eliot Carey. There were no strings attached. The little doctor made but one request: that as long as she wished it Eliot employ María.

Sam Thomas finished reading and silence descended upon the room. Into that silence the attorney injected speech again. "Dr Zeitletz told me, when this document was drawn, that he possessed a small income as long as he lived. This income derives from an estate in Austria and ceases with his death. He asked me to tell you that, Dr Carey. I will take his will with me and probate it if that is your wish, Doctor."

Eliot nodded silently. He could not speak. There was nothing to say, nothing that he *could* say. The others seemed to recognize that fact. Laurence Irish came up impulsively out of his chair, crossed to where Eliot was seated and placed his hand upon the young doctor's shoulder.

"Fritz Zeitletz was my friend," Captain Irish said. "I hope that I may stand in the same relationship to you."

"And I," Sam Thomas echoed.

"I——" Eliot's voice choked. "I—— Thank you, gentlemen." Instinctively his eyes sought Janice Irish's face. The girl was looking at him, her eyes wide, her face quiet and reposed. Eliot could not read the look. There was something in the eyes, some question that he could not answer. After a moment the girl's glance lowered and Eliot stood up, Sam Thomas and the captain on either side.

"If you will excuse me," he said, "I—— Will you excuse me?" He did not wait for an answer but strode from the room. Irish and Thomas looked at each other understandingly.

"It's hit him hard," Irish said suddenly. "Hard, Sam!"

Thomas nodded. "I won't talk to him any more at present," he said. "I'll wait. Now, Miss Janice——"

The girl sprang up from her chair. Two swift steps took her to her father and she threw her arms around his neck. The captain held her close, her bright head on his chest and her body shaken by the sobs she could no longer suppress.

"You'll have to wait awhile on her, too, Sam," Laurence Irish cautioned. "You'll have to wait."

Sam Thomas looked at the girl and her father and then, turning abruptly, strode to the window and stared out across the dusk-darkened snow.

It was late when at length Sam Thomas left Fritz Zeitletz' home. He accepted Captain Irish's invitation to spend the night at the LS and, accompanied by Janice and the captain, bade Eliot good night. There was not room for anyone other than those already present to stay at the white house.

John Mason occupied Dr Carey's room, his wife sitting beside him keeping constant vigil. Mason's pulse was fairly strong but, save for a brief interval after he had come from the anesthetic, he had been in a sort of semicoma.

Trigger Vengeance

With Thomas and the Irishes gone Eliot stayed with Mason awhile, ordering Mrs Mason to eat something and get some rest. When the woman returned, quietly taking her place beside her husband, Eliot went out into the hall. Restlessness possessed him. He could not go into Zeitletz' room and lie down. He remembered too well the last occupant of that bed. From the hall he wandered through the house, to the kitchen, the dining room, into the living room and on to the surgery. The surgery held him. He stook there before the desk with its littered top and stuffed pigeonholes and presently sank down into a chair. The lamp burned on the table and Eliot Carey, nerves tight as a drumhead, sat in the chair and stared at the desk. He heard movement in the hall as Mrs Mason went to the kitchen, heard her return and then his name was called. Instantly Eliot was on his feet and in motion toward the call. When he went into the sickroom he saw that John Mason's eyes were open and Mrs Mason, face white with fright, was looking at him.

"He tried to talk," the woman whispered.

Eliot bent down over the man on the bed. Mason's eyes were clear. His head, under the doctor's hand, was hot and Eliot knew that fever was rising. "Get me some water," he directed, "and my black bag from the surgery."

Mrs Mason hurried away. On the bed the sheriff stirred and his lips moved as he tried to speak.

"Fritz?" questioned John Mason.

... Of Which I Die Possessed ...

"It's all right," Eliot said. "Take it easy, you're going to be all right."

There was a vitality in Mason that would not down. His eyes were bright with fever and his face, waxy from loss of blood, showed a flushed spot on either cheek. Again his lips moved and Eliot caught the words.

"They killed him," said John Mason distinctly, and then his voice failed. Eliot could see from Mason's eyes that there was more that he would say but could not.

Mrs Mason returned with the black bag and a glass of water and Eliot hastily mixed a draught and, lifting the sheriff's head, administered it, the sheriff fighting weakly against the potion. For a while after drinking the sedative he lay on the bed, nervous twitching showing his restlessness. Then he was quiet, his eyes closed and his breathing became more regular.

"He will rest now," Eliot assured Mrs Mason. "He has some fever but I'll be close by."

The doctor got up, relinquishing his chair to the woman, and went to the door. He stood beside the door watching Mason's peaceful face. Eliot nodded. John Mason had every chance. He had not lost too much blood. The bullet was out and the wound, as far as Eliot could tell, was clean. Barring complications, barring some internal injury, John Mason would live. The course of the bullet had been through the thick loin muscle of Mason's back, not through the abdominal cavity.

Trigger Vengeance

Once more Eliot spoke to the silent woman beside the bed. "He has every chance," the doctor assured. "Every chance in the world of getting well. This condition now is principally shock and loss of blood. He'll be all right, Mrs Mason."

The woman looked her gratitude and, turning, Eliot went out again into the hall.

Back in the surgery he resumed his seat before the desk. After a time he put his arms on the papers and books on the desk top and lowered his head to his arms. The lamp flamed low and the house was silent.

Dr Carey did not sleep. He thought, thought so deeply that he lost all sense of time or place. He was brought from his reverie by a tapping at the window and, lifting his head swiftly, saw the face of Littlebit Mann beyond the glass. Littlebit beckoned and Dr Carey, rising from the desk, went out into the hall and to the door.

When he opened the door Littlebit was on the porch. Eliot stepped out and joined the rider, closing the door behind him. Littlebit's voice was hoarse as he spoke.

"How's the sheriff?"

"I can't tell you yet," Eliot answered. "I think he will be all right but it's too early to say."

"Can you leave him?" Littlebit demanded.

"Why?" Eliot asked.

"You're needed bad." There was urgency in Littlebit's voice. "Bad, Doc."

"I might leave him for a little while," Eliot

granted. "Who needs me and what for, Littlebit?"

"There's a man hurt," Littlebit replied.

Instinct told Eliot Carey why he was wanted. "Neville wants me?" he demanded.

"Not Mark. July Wiggins was hit. Mark's managed to bring him close."

"Do you think I would go out to attend one of the men who killed——" Eliot began.

Littlebit stopped him. "Yo're a doctor, ain't you?" asked Littlebit simply.

For a long minute Eliot Carey stood silent on the porch. Then he answered, his voice thick. "Yes," he said. "God forgive me, I'm a doctor. I'll go with you, Littlebit."

By a devious route Littlebit Mann took Dr Carey through the town. At its edge they reached an adobe and, leaving Eliot, Littlebit went to the door. When he returned for the doctor Eliot noted that Littlebit held a weapon in his hand and smiled thinly. They were not going to trust him and they were right.

Inside the adobe there was candlelight. Mark Neville stood across the room from the door, facing Eliot as he entered. Wing Lackey, face sullen, was against the further wall, and the man, July, lay upon a pallet. Eliot did not know to whom the adobe belonged. The owner was not present. He did not look once at either Neville or Wing but went to the man on the pallet. Swift examination told him that there was nothing he could do for July Wiggins. How July had managed to last so long was a miracle. Dr Carey straightened up and faced Mark Neville.

Trigger Vengeance

"He can't live," the doctor pronounced. "He's dying now."

Neville, face drawn and haggard with strain and weariness, spoke quietly. "I had to give him his chance, Doc."

"You had to drag our necks into a noose," Wing flared, "bringin' July here. You think we won't be caught. This doctor will have 'em down on us like wolves. He'll leave here—— No, he won't!"

Wing Lackey moved as he spoke, jerking at his gun under his unbuttoned sheepskin coat. Littlebit Mann raised the weapon he held, pointing it at Wing, but Mark Neville, with a long step, was between Wing Lackey and the doctor.

"Put it down, Wing!" he commanded. "Drop it!"

Eliot, fascinated, watched the play of emotions on Lackey's face. Fear was there and hatred. Slowly Wing relaxed and Neville, not turning his head, spoke to the doctor. "I'm sorry, Doc," he said. "You can pull out now if you want to."

Dr Carey did not move to obey. On the pallet July Wiggins drew a harsh breath and, slowly, let it go. Looking at the man, Eliot saw his chest move a little and then collapse. He bent down, was quiet for a long moment and then lifted his head. "Your friend is dead," said Dr Carey.

"He was a good man." It seemed as though Neville was offering an argument. "He had to have his chance."

No one spoke in the adobe following that declaration. Littlebit Mann stirred restlessly and Wing Lackey moved against the wall.

"I'll take you back, Doc," Littlebit offered in the silence.

Eliot picked up his medicine bag.

"Doc," Neville spoke suddenly.

Dr Carey faced the speaker. Neville's blue eyes were very earnest as they met the doctor's. "It wasn't us in the cabin, Doc," Neville said. "It wasn't us that killed Zeitletz. We saw him come out from the timber an' we didn't shoot. Dunlop had already stopped one. Wing was at the door. Harley an' July an' me held down the windows. Doc Zeitletz dropped before we ever let go. It wasn't us."

Into Eliot Carey's mind flashed the words that John Mason had spoken "They killed him!" Mason had whispered.

"I don't believe you," Eliot declared flatly.

Neville shook his head impatiently. Wing Lackey growled, "It don't make a damn if you believe it or not. You——"

"Shut up, Wing," warned Neville. "Look, Doc. Why would I lie to you?"

"To keep me from killing you," Eliot answered simply. "I would, you know."

Neville grunted. "You done something for me, Doc," he said. "Maybe I am an outlaw but I wouldn't lie to you. I'll prove we didn't hit Doc Zeitletz."

"How?" Eliot was frankly incredulous.

"Where was Zeitletz hit?" asked Mark Neville. Eliot thought before he answered. He had seen the bullet hole in Zeitletz' side. He spoke slowly. "Far back on the left-hand side."

"An' that proves it!" exclaimed Mark Neville triumphantly. "Doc was to our left an' in front. If we'd downed him we'd of hit him in front, wouldn't we?"

Neville waited for Eliot to answer. Dr Carey was trying to think. He could not say exactly, could not give a definite answer. "It looks that way," he admitted grudgingly. "Maybe *you* didn't shoot him, Neville, but how about the others that were with you?"

"Damn you!" Wing Lackey snarled.

"Shut up, Wing!" again Mark Neville commanded. "I'll tell you, Doc. Wing here was at the door. It was closed. Dunlop had stopped one an' was on the floor. Quinn was up in the loft an' he was dead. July an' me was at the window an' I know we didn't hit Zeitletz. It was one of his own bunch."

Eliot shook his head. He could not believe Neville, and yet there was a sincerity, an honesty in the man's words that made Dr Carey hesitate to disbelieve.

"How about that other man you killed?" Eliot demanded, taking a fresh tack. "And how about John Mason?"

Neville shrugged. "They had a job," he responded. "They was paid an' they took their chances the same as us."

Eliot could not answer that and Neville spoke again. "We'll take July along a ways. It wouldn't do to leave him here. You can pull out, Doc. Tell

Raupert an' them we're here. We won't be here when they come."

"I'll tell nothing!" Dr Carey's voice rasped. "I don't know, Neville. You said you didn't kill Zeitletz. Maybe you didn't. I'm going to find out. . . . And if you did all hell won't hide you!"

He turned abruptly, grip swinging in his hand, and without a backward look walked to the door, jerked it open and stalked out into the night. Behind him the door closed and, somewhere back of the adobe, a horse stamped.

CHAPTER XI

Welch . . . and Company

IN DEFERENCE to Fritz Zeitletz the store of Welch and Company was closed. Allan Welch, going to the store after the funeral, sought the comfortable chair in his office and, with the fire in the stove warming the room to comfort, seated himself and relaxed. There was no one else in the store, no clerks, no one from the warehouse, none to distract him. For the first time in a considerable period Welch was at leisure to think.

The reflections were pleasant. It seemed to Allan Welch that he was by way of becoming a rich man. He had come a long way, he thought, a very long way. There was a wide step between Allan Welch, a peddler working from door to door, and Allan Welch, merchant. Welch had made that step and, reflecting upon it, found it good. The manner of advancement did not matter; it was the advancement that counted. He could forget the poverty, the denial, the almost starvation now, just as he could forget the scheming, the fawning upon others, the cheating and the fraud. That was a part of life that was past. This was another portion.

A year or two, Welch believed, would see him finished with this particular phase of his life and embarked upon another. Selling merchandise, buying wool and lambs, speculating a little in grain futures— these things were all well enough, but there were larger and broader fields of opportunity. Complacently Welch stroked his black spade beard. He would presently explore those fields.

With an effort, because his legs were short and his stomach had become somewhat protuberant, he placed his feet on the top of his desk and leaned back in his chair. He had come a long way; he would go much farther. He was not an old man and he was ambitious. Thoughtfully he considered the things he owned: his property, his family, his investments, checking up on them mentally to see if they would do to take with him upon his future journey. Satisfied, he nodded.

His wife was weak but she obeyed his every wish and command and she satisfied his present needs. Of course there was the woman, Sofia, whom he maintained so discreetly in an adobe at the edge of town. For the present she was a necessity. Still his wife had brought him money and in a way she had brought him Welch and Company. He would cleave to his wife. There would be, as he advanced, other Sofias.

He remembered distinctly how, twenty-two years

ago, he had wooed and won the present Mrs Welch. She had been Cathrine Snyder then and her father, old Ed Snyder, had run a little store in Soltura, a store that on Saturday was filled with natives trading, and where now and again a cowpuncher might be found sitting on a counter eating canned fruit with a long-handled spoon. Ed Snyder had taken in his new son-in-law as a clerk and almost immediately business had become better.

Complacently Allan Welch patted his stomach with the tips of his short white fingers. He had always been good at finding and stopping leaks.

The children had come along, Courtland and then Emma, and with their advent he had needed more money and earned it. Then, after what was years of slavery to Allan Welch, after years when he had taken orders from Ed Snyder, his father-in-law had died. There had been other heirs beside Cathrine, growing stout now and satisfied with her life in Soltura. Allan Welch had fought those heirs to have his way. He had won them over and, little by little, he had bought them out. At one time he had thought of putting the store into bankruptcy but had decided against it. He was glad of that decision now. He could not have obtained the credit he needed if he had gone through bankruptcy. Still in those days the store had shown very little profit and Ed Snyder's heirs, in Boston and in Brooklyn, had been glad to get out of so unprofitable and distant an adventure.

Unlocking his hands, Welch leaned forward and, grunting with the exertion, took a cigar from a box on the desk top. When he had lighted the cigar he leaned back again. The lean years, the years of scheming against Snyder's heirs, were over, were passed.

He had seen, during those years, that the money that came to Soltura was made with sheep. The natives with their little flocks were independent. They paid their bills. They lived simply but well. Sheep had given them that living. Allan Welch was ever one to cut the distances. There was too much distance between himself and the money from the wool and the lambs. He had built the warehouse and gradually, extending credit from one season to the next, he had found that the natives could be cajoled and lured into overextending themselves. That had been the beginning. The drought had been the end. The drought had been a blessing to Welch. During the drought the small sheepmen about Soltura had gone deeply into debt. They owed Welch and Company. And they still owed Welch and Company. Welch had seen to that. Tray Barry and Sid Raupert, under his orders, had discouraged wool buyers and lamb buyers from coming into the country. He had a working agreement with the stores in Feather Springs. He did not enter their territory and they avoided his. He was able to control the price of wool and the price of lambs. He controlled the price of merchandise. He had working for him a number of native families. They took their pay in groceries and clothing, and their labor was assured by the debts they owed and by mortgages on their sheep, their household furnishings, their little plots of land. When one became obstreperous, as had Abrán Fernandez, Allan Welch closed down. He could not have his people getting ideas. The insurgent was removed and another more complacent man put in his place. It was business, Welch thought; good business. As truly as though he owned the town and the country about it, he controlled Soltura. Men voted as he dictated, they obeyed his wishes, they did as they were told, and all because of a debt at the store and a few signed pieces of paper. Once more Welch tapped complacently upon his belly with his pudgy fingers. Business!

Welch had left the front door of the store unlocked, not because he wanted anyone to come in but because it was his habit always to be available to a possible customer. Now he heard that door open and close and, bringing his feet down from the desk top, he leaned forward so that he might see around the office partition. Courtland Welch and Emma had come into the store and were standing near the door talking. Welch leaned back again. They would be talking about him, he knew, arguing as to which should see him first. Apparently Courtland won the argument for it was Welch's son who first made his appearance at the office door.

"Come in, Courtland," Welch ordered brusquely.

The young fellow came into the office and stood before his father. Courtland was a larger man than his father, his size and features inherited from his mother. He waited a moment as though he wished

Welch . . . and Company

Welch to speak and then, when Welch did not, shifted his weight nervously.

"John Rhyn and Wayne Hubbard were in town today," Courtland said as though offering an apology. "They came over to the funeral. They want me to go back to Feather Springs with them for a day or two."

Welch weighed the announcement. John Rhyn was the son of J. T. Rhyn, one of Feather Springs' merchants. Wayne Hubbard's father had a sheep ranch east of Feather Springs.

"May I go, Father?" Courtland asked.

Deliberately Welch nodded his head. It would not hurt Courtland to be friendly with either boy, and it would not hurt Welch's business to have his son a friend to the sons of Rhyn and Hubbard. "You can go for four days," Welch decided. "Be back Tuesday."

"Thank you, Father." Courtland was grateful. "I'll come back Tuesday then. John said that he would bring me home."

Welch felt expansive. "Invite the boys to stay a day or two with you," he ordered.

"Thank you, Father," Courtland said again and turned from the door. Welch could hear the young man's feet in a rapid tattoo as he almost ran toward the front of the store. A good boy, Courtland, properly humble and properly afraid. Welch waited. The store door closed.

Presently, as he surveyed the door of the office, he saw Emma coming briskly toward him, a letter

in her hand. Welch smiled. If Courtland was like his
mother in appearance, Emma resembed her father.
There was something of Welch's decisiveness in her
manner as she came in and without bidding took her
seat in a chair opposite the desk.

"I've heard from Aunt Agusta, Papa," Emma
announced.

"So?" Welch asked.

Emma nodded. "She wrote me." The girl colored
faintly. "You remember I wrote to her and asked
about Doctor Carey?"

Welch bobbed his head in affirmation. "What does
your aunt say?" he asked.

The color brightened on the girl's cheeks and,
watching her, Welch was pleased. Emma had the
same toughness of fiber, the same regard for money,
the same tenacity to obtain an objective, that he had
himself. Welch recognized these things in the girl
and was glad. Emma could be counted upon and,
withal, she was handsome, pleasing in appearance
and knew how to dress. Emma had never lacked for
money. Where he was almost niggardly with Courtland, Welch gave money to Emma without question.

"Aunt Agusta writes that the Careys have no
money." The girl answered her father's question.
"Doctor Carey's father is dead and his mother lives
on a small income."

Welch pursed his lips as though he had bitten
into something that was distasteful. "That is bad!"
he said.

Emma's eyes studied her father's face. "Perhaps

not so bad," she commented. "A young man without much money can be gotten into debt."

Welch's eyes twinkled. Emma, he knew, had decided that she wanted this tall personable young physician as her own. Her father had not been consulted in the matter. Emma rarely consulted him; she made up her mind and then went ahead. It amused Welch to have his daughter use him. He watched her maneuverings with delight. Emma would carry on the Welch line. Courtland was weak, but not the girl!

"So," he said, "you want me to place the young man in debt?"

Emma shrugged. "You can be nice to him," she said. "You can help him."

"So that he will like my daughter?"

Again the girl flushed. "I like him, Papa," she said directly. "I think——"

"Well . . . well . . . we will see." Welch granted the girl's request. "I have told Courtland that he can invite John Rhyn and Wayne Hubbard to visit him for a few days. Perhaps you will have a party?"

Emma considered, then she shook her head. "Don't let Courtland have Wayne Hubbard come," she said. "That would be too many men. Courtland can ask John to bring his sister. That will make a girl for Courtland, and then if I invite the doctor——"

Welch laughed, interrupting his daughter, "—and

two young men for you to play against each other," he completed. "I will tell Courtland."

"When are you coming home, Papa?" Emma, her eyes alight with gratification, got up from her chair.

"Presently. Presently, Daughter," Welch answered. "You run along and tell your mama that I will come by and by."

"Thank you, Papa," Emma said demurely and left the office.

When she had gone Welch sank back into his chair once more. A smart girl, Emma, a very smart girl. If she wanted this young man, if she desired Dr Carey, why, then, Welch would get him for her. He smiled to himself as he mused.

Once more Allan Welch's meditations were interrupted by the front door's opening. He heard bootheels thumping as a man came deliberately toward the office. Once more Welch lowered his feet. Sid Raupert came into the office, walked to the desk and, taking a cigar from the box, bit off the end, his small eyes fixed unwinkingly on Allan Welch. Welch was uneasy as he gestured toward the chair Emma had occupied.

"Sit down, Sid," he invited. "Sit down."

Raupert seated himself, deliberately scratched a match on the white paint of the partition and lit the cigar.

"It was too bad about Doctor Zeitletz," Welch offered, looking at the brown blemish the match had made on the white paint. "Too bad. I expect that the whole country will hunt Mark Neville now."

Welch . . . and Company

Raupert blew out a smoke cloud, removed the cigar from his mouth and eyed it speculatively. "Likely," he agreed.

Welch was at a loss. He had nothing to say. Raupert returned the cigar to his mouth, again blew out smoke and laughed, a short harsh bark of sound. "Funny that they'll hunt Neville when I done it," he stated. His eyes were narrow and speculative, watching Welch through the smoke.

"You?" Welch was startled.

Raupert nodded. "I'd been figurin' on it for a long time," he said nonchalantly. "Zeitletz was down at Jack Brannigan's place the night Tray kicked off. Tray had been talkin' an' I think he talked in front of the doctor. I couldn't take any chances."

Welch shuddered. This small man sitting so complacently and smoking with so much relish frightened Allan Welch. Raupert was so cold blooded and, Welch admitted, so useful.

"It looked like a good chance," Raupert commented. "I took it. They'll blame the killin' on Neville."

"But," Welch began, "you don't know that Doctor Zeitletz had heard anything. He had said nothing. He——"

"I can't take chances in my business," Raupert said raspingly. "He might have been gettin' ready to pop off."

There was silence in the little office. Allan Welch stirred restlessly. "I don't think you needed to——" he began.

"You don't do the work I do," Raupert interrupted. "You just hire it done." He laughed the short harsh bark once more. "Mason was stirred up about the Carl Jacks business," he concluded. "He was right touchy. Anyhow, I owed Neville one."

Welch said nothing and Raupert smoked for a moment. "John Mason's goin' to live." Raupert broke the silence. "They didn't do a good job on him up in Roybal. You throw a lot of weight around here, Welch. Next year you'd better run me for sheriff."

Welch considered the possibilities of the idea. He had already recovered from his shock at Raupert's revelation. With Sid Raupert as sheriff he could expand further. There would be no need of keeping his agreement as to territory with Rhyn in Feather Springs. But Raupert was expensive. His price came high and as sheriff would go higher. Welch made a decision in his mind. It was about time to get rid of Sid Raupert. The little man was dangerous. Like a weasel, he killed for the sheer love of killing. Still Welch nodded his head. "You could beat Mason," he commented.

Raupert seemed to read Allan Welch's thoughts. "I could with your help," he said. "You'll give it to me, Welch. I've got a friend or two in the country and I've done a little writin'. Anything happens to me an' some of my friends will have somethin' interesting to read."

"Why, Sid." Welch forced surprise into his voice. "You don't think I'd——"

"I don't trust you as far as I can spit," Raupert

interrupted coarsely. "You're all right while you need me, but if you ever figured you didn't you'd try to get rid of me. I ain't to be got rid of, Welch."

Welch did not answer. Sid Raupert knocked the ashes from his cigar. "The Mexicans are right peeved about Zeitletz," he said. "They're boilin' like a hornet's nest down in Stringtown."

Welch shook his head. "Bad business," he commented.

"Worse if he knew somethin' an' talked," Raupert retorted. "He won't do any talkin' now. Say, Welch, if I was you I'd tie this young doctor up to me. A lot of folks are beginnin' to like him. The LS boys think he's just right. Better tie him up."

Again Welch retired into the tortuous twistings of his mind. There was a possibility in what Raupert had said. He could . . . Emma wanted the young doctor. It might be . . . "Maybe you're right," he agreed.

"You bet I'm right." Sid Raupert got to his feet. "An' say, Abrán Fernandez is doin' a lot of talkin' an' he's clear out of line. Maybe I'd better put him where he belongs, huh?"

Welch was still thinking. "Abrán should leave town," he said absently.

"All right then"—Raupert was brisk—"I'll look after it. An' I want a hundred. I'm short."

Methodically Welch arose from his chair. He crossed the room to the safe and twisted the combination knob. The bolts clicked as he slid them back and the hinges were silent as he opened the safe's door.

Trigger Vengeance

Taking out a sheaf of bills, he counted greenbacks from the top and held out a little bundle of currency. Raupert took it.

"You will be nice to the new doctor, Sid," said Allan Welch. "I think perhaps you are right. I think maybe I can use him."

CHAPTER XII

Financial Arrangements

JOHN MASON got well. Three weeks' interval stretched between the time of the fight in Roybal Canyon and the day that the sheriff left Dr Zeitletz' house for Feather Springs. Three long weeks. But Mason got well. During the three weeks that the sheriff lay in bed the manhunt for Mark Neville and Wing Lackey raged through the Soltura country. The State Mounted Police took a hand. Lieutenant Gar Arning, a quiet-faced, smooth-moving man who commanded the force, dropped unobtrusively into Soltura one night, spent the next few days in the country; and Laurence Irish, good as his promise, put on extra hands, men that had been laid off during the winter. The manhunt went forward, but to all intents and purposes the earth had opened and swallowed Mark Neville and Wing Lackey.

When he was able to sit up and to have visitors a stream of people came to see John Mason. On the day he was to go back to Feather Springs he and Eliot Carey had a conversation.

Eliot had come into the sheriff's room to make a final examination and assure himself that Mason was ready to travel. Mrs Mason, who during all the time her husband was ill had stayed close beside him, had gone out to make some arrangement for their leaving, and Eliot and John Mason were alone. It was the sheriff who broached the subject of Mark Neville, speaking abruptly after Eliot had said that he was satisfied with his patient's condition.

"I'm going to get Mark Neville," the sheriff stated. "If it's the last thing I do and takes my last breath I'm going to get him. Fritz would be alive today if it wasn't for Mark Neville."

Eliot shook his head. "I don't know," he said. "Doctor Zeitletz had cancer, you know. He hadn't long to live. I'm not sure but that this might have been an easier way for him to go."

John Mason grunted. "You talk like you were a friend of Neville's," he said and then, shrewdly, "You saw Neville, didn't you?"

Eliot's brown face flushed and he made no answer.

Again Mason grunted. "You're the same kind Fritz was," he observed. "Always trying to find some good in everybody. I know you saw Neville. The night after they brought me in it was. My wife heard you go out. She hadn't heard anybody come to the door. I know you went on a call and I think you went to see July Wiggins. You knew that we found July?"

Eliot said, "No," surprise in his voice.

Financial Arrangements

"Found him two weeks ago," Mason announced. "We been keepin' it quiet. He'd been buried over by Manueles Canyon and they didn't have time to put him very deep. Something dug him up and one of the LS boys saw the buzzards and went over and found him."

The sheriff paused for Eliot to comment, and when the doctor did not speak went on.

"The way I figure it, Neville called you to look after July. You went and found July dead or about dead. Then Neville told you that they didn't kill Fritz. Am I right?"

Eliot remained silent, regarding the question, but in turn made a statement. "Doctor Zeitletz was shot in the left side, far back," Eliot said. "The wound looked as though the bullet had come from behind him."

"And who in that posse would shoot Fritz?" Mason scoffed. "Everybody in this country owed Fritz Zeitletz for something. They stuffed you, Son."

Again Eliot flushed and his voice was very earnest when he spoke. "Might not someone have shot Doctor Zeitletz accidently? He might have been shot by accident and the man who hit him afraid to own up to it. Couldn't that be possible?"

John Mason considered the possibility. Finally he shook his head. "I didn't take any pilgrims with me on that trip," he said. "There wasn't a man there but had been in a fight. No, that bunch lined their sights and knew where they were shooting."

"But it is possible," Eliot insisted. "Why would

Neville want to kill Doctor Zeitletz any more than one of the possemen? Surely Neville knew the doctor. Surely——"

Mason held up his hand and Eliot stopped abruptly. "You talk pretty good, Son," Mason said. "Sure Mark Neville knew Doc. Doc had done some things for Neville, I reckon. Maybe Mark didn't do the shootin' himself. Maybe it was Wiggins or that other one that got loose. I'll give Neville the benefit of the doubt but that ain't going to prevent his being hung when I catch him."

"No," agreed Eliot, "it isn't."

"Maybe Neville didn't kill Doc," Mason observed, "but it was one of his bunch." He looked swiftly at Eliot. "He tell you who did do it?" the sheriff demanded.

Eliot shook his head. "I don't know who did it," he said, "but I intend to find out."

"What would you do if you did know?" Mason's eyes were shrewd.

Flame lanced in the doctor's brown eyes, instantly to be extinguished.

John Mason nodded. "That's just what I thought," he said. "Now listen, youngster. You were Fritz's boy and that makes you a friend of mine. I'd feel the same way about you even if Fritz hadn't thought you were just the proper thing. Don't you go taking things into your own hands. You might find out something and those fool ethics you doctors have keep you from telling me about it. You come to me if you learn anything. I'll hang the man that killed

Financial Arrangements

Fritz Zeitletz, so high the buzzards won't have to come down to feed on him. You tell me now, you understand?"

Eliot did not reply and John Mason shook his head. "You're as stubborn as Fritz was," he said. "Well . . . anyhow, I like you, Carey. I think you'll do."

At that moment Mrs Mason returned with blankets in which to wrap her husband. The conversation was broken, and shortly Eliot helped the sheriff out of the house and into his buggy.

There followed a slack time for the young doctor. The sheriff was gone. There was not much sickness in Soltura and not many calls. Winter had tightened its grip again in a last effort. Eliot moved back into his own room (he had been sleeping on a cot in the kitchen, leaving Dr Zeitletz' room untouched), worked in the surgery, studied and attended the few patients that called him. He found, during this slack season, that Fritz Zeitletz had not kept any real set of books. There was a record of calls but it was incomplete. During the time he had spent with Zeitletz Eliot had reported such calls as he made, leaving it for Fritz Zeitletz to make the charges and collect the bills. Zeitletz had paid Eliot promptly every month and Dr Carey had some money saved from those payments. He lived on that money and the little that was paid him by patients who came into the office. He was puzzled, for he knew that Dr Zeitletz must have kept some sort of books but he could not find them.

Trigger Vengeance

A few weeks after the departure of John Mason found Eliot facing the end of the month. Bills came in, a bill from Welch and Company among them. Examining his store of coin, Eliot Carey found that he could not pay all the bills. He had been brought up in dread of debt for, with his father dead, Eliot's mother had been forced to live economically within her small income. Eliot had the Yankee desire to pay cash and be unincumbered, and it seemed that under the present circumstances it was impossible. Accordingly he put on his outer clothing and, dreading the mission, went to Welch's store to make some arrangement concerning his bill.

Allan Welch was in the office in the back of the storeroom when Eliot came in and he greeted the young doctor cordially. Eliot was ill at ease but Welch talked about the weather and the cold and the nearness of spring and seemed in no hurry to come to business. Finally, however, he broached the subject.

"You had some business with me, Doctor?" he suggested.

"I came in to see you about my bill here," Eliot answered brusquely. "Collections have been slow and while I'm certain that Doctor Zeitletz had a good many outstanding accounts, I can't find his books. I'm sorry, Mr Welch, but I'll have to ask you for a little time."

Welch laughed pleasantly. "No need to worry, Doctor," he said. "You can have all the time you

Financial Arrangements

want. Your credit is good with Welch and Company."

Eliot was relieved. "Thank you," he said. "I'm very grateful, Mr Welch."

Welch seemed to consider some idea for a moment and then offered a suggestion. "We do a credit business here," he said. "It is necessary in this country. Money comes in only twice a year, when the wool is sold and when the lambs are shipped. We carry our customers from one season to the next. There is very little ready cash." Welch hesitated and Eliot eyed him, wondering what was coming next.

"It's really sort of a banking business that we do," Welch continued. "I'll tell you, Doctor, why don't you do this: when you need money come to us. You can turn your accounts over to us and we'll credit you and give you what money you need. Then when the wool is sold or the lambs are bought we'll collect. We'd be glad to do that for you."

It seemed very fair to Eliot Carey. He nodded his head and Welch spoke quickly. "Of course we can only do that with people who are our regular customers," he said and then, laughing, "But that includes about everyone around Soltura."

"That's very kind of you." Eliot was considering the proposition in his mind. "I'll think it over, Mr Welch, and tell you what I decide in a day or two. It seems very fair to me and it would certainly be an accommodation."

"Let me know." Welch waved an airy hand. "What are you doing tonight, Doctor? You've been keeping much to yourself since my friend Doctor Zeitletz passed away. That is not good for young people."

"I've been studying," Eliot answered. "There has not been a great deal of practice and I've had a lot of time to myself." He smiled ruefully. "I suppose I'll be at home tonight," he concluded. "I've been there every night this week."

"Come and visit us," Allan Welch urged. "There are some young people at the house now and we would be glad to have you. Come to dinner and stay and visit us. Come about six."

Eliot Carey was feeling very kindly toward Allan Welch at the moment. He had misjudged the man, he believed, and, impulsively, he wished to make amends for his unfairness. "Thank you," he said. "I'll be glad to come, Mr Welch."

The doctor left then, and when he was gone Allan Welch walked over to the stove in the corner and warmed his hands. A little smile played over his face. He had, he believed, done a good stroke of business. There ought to be a profit in carrying the accounts of Dr Carey on the store's books. About a hundred and six per cent, say. People were slow to pay doctor bills to doctors but they would not be slow in paying doctor bills to Welch and Company. And, unless he was mistaken, he had made a friend of that stand-offish young man. Welch, his hands warm, went back to the desk. Perhaps Emma was right. Perhaps this broad-shouldered, long-faced young man was the proper person for her. Welch studied the matter.

Financial Arrangements

He would wait awhile and see. It might be that he needed Dr Eliot Carey for a son-in-law.

That night, well fed and enjoying the evening, Dr Carey excused himself from Emma and her friends long enough to seek Allan Welch in his study. "I've thought over your offer, Mr Welch," he said. "You are being very kind and I would like to take advantage of it."

Welch put his hand on the doctor's shoulder. "Fine," he said. "You bring down your accounts and we'll go over them. Now run along back to the youngsters, Doctor. They're calling for you."

Eliot went back to the parlor where a game of five hundred was in progress and Welch reseated himself in his easy chair. Both men were well content.

As an upshot of the conversations in the store and at Welch's house Eliot took the books he had kept since Dr Zeitletz' death and called upon Allan Welch. They spent half an hour going over the books together, and at the end of that time Welch and Company had added a hundred dollars and more to their accounts, and Eliot Carey was in possession of some cash and his own bill with the store was clear. Eliot went back to his office well satisfied with himself and Allan Welch took a list of names and figures to where Laban Benedict worked in his glassed-in enclosure.

"You can add these to the accounts named here, Laban," directed Welch. "See here." He presented the bookkeeper with the paper. "Here are the names and here are the figures. I've penciled in the amounts you are to add." Welch smiled broadly and Benedict, a gaunt, narrow man, echoed the smile." After all," Welch commented, "twenty-five dollars is not much for having a baby. Fifty is better, and then we are entitled to a little profit, aren't we, Laban?"

With the first of March Dr Carey found himself comfortable and without worries. María looked after his home and his food, Ben Fry took care of his team and buggy and Welch and Company were his financial agents. His grief at the loss of his friend was not gone but, what with work and time, the bitter edge of it had dulled. Eliot missed Dr Zeitletz, missed him woefully. There were times when, returning from a call late in the evening, he saw the cheery light coming from the windows of the little white house and a pang of grief shot through him. He had not relinquished the idea of finding the man that had killed the doctor. Doggedly he clung to that promise he had made himself; but he was busy again, the furor in Soltura had died down and, for the first time in his existence, there was no one to whom Eliot Carey had to render account.

The visit to Welch's had been followed by others. Emma often asked the doctor to call; Laurence Irish invited him to the LS where he spent several evenings talking with the captain and watching Janice's bright hair as she bent over a book or above some mending that she was doing for her father. Dr Carey was troubled by the two girls.

Thrown a great deal into the company of Emma

Financial Arrangements

Welch, he found that he liked the girl. She flattered him, she asked him questions and listened intently to his answers, and from time to time she gave him money—following that first twenty-five dollars—always asking that he use it for charity and listening with interest to his reports of what he had done with the sums. And still there was something about Emma that did not ring quite true; something that the doctor could not quite place. Once or twice, talking to the girl, he had looked up and found her watching him intently with an oddly possessive look. Dr Carey was not quite at ease in the presence of Emma Welch.

Nor was he at ease in Janice Irish's presence. Save on two occasions Janice had kept a barrier between herself and Dr Eliot Carey. The day he had set Calico's leg Eliot had had a glimpse of the real Janice Irish, and on the day before Thanksgiving the girl had let down the barrier when she was in the surgery. He knew that Janice was a very real person. He knew that there were many people in Soltura to whom she was almost a deity. The girl brought happiness with her into otherwise drab homes and her charity was of a closely personal kind. Where Emma Welch gave Eliot money to bestow for her, Janice Irish might go into an adobe house and take the care of the children from the toilworn mother's hands for half a day, giving the weary woman time to rest. Eliot wished desperately that he might lower the barrier between himself and Janice Irish. He would have liked to become a hero in the eyes of the redheaded girl, but when at the LS he recounted to

Trigger Vengeance

Laurence Irish some experience, something that he had done, and then glanced at Janice for approbation he was apt to find the girl staring quizzically at him, and on one occasion, when he had perhaps boasted a little, Janice had been frankly and indulgently smiling when Eliot looked at her. The smile had hurt. He had seen a similar smile on his mother's face when, as a small boy, he had boasted of his exploits.

When Eliot tried to talk to Janice on a personal basis he found himself led deftly into impersonal discussions. When he tried to get Janice Irish to himself he found that her father or Littlebit Mann or some other was always at hand, and on the rare occasions that he found her alone she always managed to have work to do. It seemed to Eliot Carey that Janice Irish just simply did not care for his company.

And so the new year plodded into March and a warm wind came, melting the snow that was dirty with its blowing. The roads were impassable. Allan Welch sat in his office or passed among the patrons of the store, a smile on his face and his mind busy. John Mason, from Feather Springs, quietly directed the work of the sheriff's office, listening to this man and that, sorting conjecture and surmise from fact. Interviewing, one at a time, the men who had accompanied him that fateful day to Roybal Canyon and questioning them slowly and cunningly. Somewhere in the hills and canyons Mark Neville and Wing Lackey hid and ran to hide again, the net that Mason spread tightening about them. Neville met the force with force, the cunning with cunning, but

Financial Arrangements

Wing Lackey, resentful of Neville's leadership, hard pressed and frightened, stood on an edge of indecision. Wing Lackey was ready to make his own peace and let Mark Neville take the brunt of it.

Courtland Welch, under his father's restrictions, doled out money in niggardly quantities, sought surcease from restraint. Not directly as a stronger man might have done, but furtively, slipping out at night when Welch's house was dark, finding consolation as best he might, sheltered from his father's wrath by his mother.

Emma Welch, her campaign progressing, was satisfied. She could afford to wait. All her life her father had got her the things she wanted and those things he had been unable to obtain she had secured for herself. Eliot Carey liked her, she knew. Give her a little time and she would change that liking into a stronger sentiment.

Janice Irish, tending her father's house, smiled in her work and was happy. Sometimes the happiness was less apparent and the girl was sober, sitting at the table without speaking, or asking her father searching questions that troubled blunt Laurence Irish. Janice was growing up. Already a woman in body, she was becoming mature in mind, and Laurence Irish, recognizing the change, still did not understand it and disliked it.

Dr Carey went about the routine of his profession. He lanced boils brought on by a diet of pork and flour and beans. He doctored colds, dispensing cough syrup and liniment and physic. He compounded a prescription for Mrs Maybe's asthma and listened while that good woman recounted her woes. He went here and there as the calls came, doing what he could, standing by sometimes to see an old man die, triumphant again when death passed by, dealing in life and happiness, death and grief, missing his friend Fritz Zeitletz, missing his counsel, his comfort and his cheer and vaguely dissatisfied with himself and what he was doing.

Down in the livery barn Ben Fry sat upon a bench and chewed a straw, blissfully unaware that he held hidden in his mind the key to a mystery. Sid Raupert strode along the streets or rode across the country, a narrow, cold-faced man. A man with no inhibitions and no conscience. Jack Brannigan dispensed drinks and was falsely jovial. Laurence Irish watched his daughter and wondered at her unhappiness. Soltura went on, day after uneventful day. And March ended.

March ended and with its end Abrán Fernandez, once driven out of Soltura, crowded out to seek a living for himself and for his family, came home, and with Abrán Fernandez came another, unseen, unknown, dreaded: diphtheria!

CHAPTER XIII

Diphtheria!

DR CAREY was taking his daily Spanish lesson. He had persuaded María to talk to him solely in Spanish, this despite María's pride in her slight knowledge of English. And every day, when he was not on a call or otherwise engaged, the young doctor followed María about the house as she set it to rights, asking questions in awkward Spanish and laughing with the woman at the mistakes he made. He was in the kitchen talking to María when the summons came. A small tattered urchin was at the door when Dr Carey opened it and the fright on the boy's face was apparent.

"¡Mi padre!" he gasped. "Pronto, Señor Doctor. Mi padre está muriendose."

This was not the customary summons of some frightened youngster. Eliot recognized the urgency and, stepping back into the surgery, pulled on his coat and hat and picked up his bag. With the boy preceding him he hurried down the walk and followed the youngster toward the town. At that same adobe house where Eliot had tried to hand Abrán Fernandez the money Emma Welch had given him the boy stopped. *"Aquí,"* he said. *"Mi padre——"* Eliot did not wait for the end of the sentence. He pushed open the door and went in.

There was already a sense of death within the adobe, a something—aura, sensation, feeling—call it what you will, that Death brings with him. Eliot crossed the room to where two women, a man and two children stood beside a bed. The room was not well lighted but on the bed the doctor could see a man, face dark with his choking, mouth open as he fought for breath. The man on the bed was Abrán Fernandez and as Dr Carey bent down he caught the typical odor of diphtheria.

"Traeme la luz," he snapped. "Bring the light."

A match scratched and a lamp shed its feeble yellow glow over the contorted face. Dr Carey looked into the throat. Abrán's throat was swollen, almost closed. Eliot Carey reached for his bag. He must open the throat, let breath get to the lungs and he must do it immediately.

With a hastily twisted swab Dr Carey attacked the spreading membrane. Part of it he lifted free, clearing the passage to some extent, and the man on the bed breathed easier. There was blood following the removal of the membrane but no severe hemorrhage. Eliot Carey disposed of the swab by throwing it in the fire burning in the fireplace and

Diphtheria!

faced the two awed women and the man. He was thinking swiftly. He had seen and used diphtheria antitoxin, but that had been in Vienna and in the East and there was none in this country, he knew. He must fight the disease with the materials at hand until better weapons could be supplied.

"I will make some medicine," he announced, speaking in Spanish slowly as he thought of the words. "I will bring it and show you how to use it. Have any of you a sore throat?"

As he asked the question he looked at the children. Children are particularly susceptible to diphtheria's ravages and the doctor's voice was sharp and anxious. The younger of the two women echoed his question and Dr Carey saw the boy who had come to call him gulp. He singled out that boy with a pointing finger. "Let me see," he ordered.

Taking the boy to the window, Eliot had him open his mouth. There was a suspicious redness in the child's throat and Dr Carey shook his head. "I must see the others," he stated.

One by one he examined Abrán Fernandez' family, the examination accompanied by the hoarse rasping of Abrán's breathing. Only the older boy showed any symptoms and, somewhat relieved, Dr Carey spoke again.

"Not one of you must go out of the house," he ordered. "You must let no one come in. I will make the medicine and come back and show you how to use it. This boy must go to bed."

The young woman, mother of the children, nodded

her understanding and, with a final look at Abrán, Eliot Carey hurried out.

Back in his surgery Eliot made up a weak solution of bichloride of mercury. He made a large bottle, took a package of absorbent cotton and a bundle of swab sticks and, so equipped, hurried back to Abrán's adobe house. There, using first Abrán and then the boy as subjects, he demonstrated the application of the bichloride, swabbing out the throats and destroying the swabs as before. He ordered the two children younger than the boy to be isolated in the second room of the house, gave directions as to food and the sterilization of utensils and dishes and generally outlined the routine to be followed. His Spanish was insufficient for the occasion and he was forced to piece out his directions in English, not sure that they were perfectly understood.

"Every half-hour you will clean the throats," he said, illustrating his point by taking out his watch and following the course of the minute hand from twelve to six. "Every half-hour. And I will come every day to see if you have done it properly. And if he"—gesturing toward Abrán on the bed—"becomes more sick you must call me."

Abrán's wife Consuelo nodded agreement and Dr Carey left again, more relieved than he had been. Only the boy with the sore throat had shown the slightest trace of fever when he had taken the temperatures and that boy was now in bed. There was nothing else that Dr Carey could do except watch his patients constantly. Nothing else . . . Yes! There

Diphtheria!

was another thing. He wheeled and retraced his steps toward the town, going to Welch's store.

Welch himself welcomed the doctor to his office, drew out a chair and bade the young man be seated. "What can I do for you, Doctor?" he asked expansively.

"There is diphtheria in town, Mr Welch," Eliot answered. "Abrán Fernandez has it and one of his children. I have just come from there."

It seemed to Dr Carey as though Welch drew back a little. The two dread plagues of this Western country were smallpox and diphtheria.

"I have done what I could for them," Eliot continued, "but I'm afraid that it isn't enough. There are three children there and two women beside Abrán and his wife's father. I'd like to send to Kansas City and have some antitoxin shipped out immediately. I wonder if you would send for me."

"Antitoxin?" Welch questioned.

"A material that counteracts the poison of the disease," Eliot explained. "Mulford manufactures it in this country and I am sure that it can be obtained in Kansas City at any wholesale drugstore. I know you have connections there and I wonder if you won't telegraph for a supply.

Welch pondered the problem. "Certainly we will send for it," he agreed. "We do business with a drug wholesaler in Kansas City. I'll be glad to do it for you, Doctor."

"Thank you." Eliot smiled at the merchant. "Can

you send someone to Feather Springs today to put a message on the wires? It seems to me that speed is essential here. One of the Fernandez children already has the disease and I'm afraid the others will get it. I've isolated them as best I can but there are only two rooms in the house and the other children might get the contagion. You'll send at once, Mr Welch?"

"Surely." Welch nodded. "You write down what you want, Doctor, and we'll get it as soon as we can."

Eliot said, "Thank you" and, taking a pad from Welch's desk, wrote in detail the name of the antitoxin, the amount he desired and the manufacturer. "I'm surely grateful to you, Mr Welch," he said, giving Welch the sheet of paper. "I appreciate this a great deal."

Welch said, "Not at all," and as Eliot turned toward the door, "Is there any danger of its spreading, Doctor?"

"I hope not—if they observe the quarantine," Eliot answered cheerfully. "I'm going down to the school now and see if there are any sore throats, then I'll go back to Fernandez'. Good-by."

He went on out of the office, leaving Allan Welch staring at the paper in his hand.

For some time Welch studied the sheet whereon Eliot Carey had written, then, carrying it, he walked out to where Laban Benedict worked over the books. "How much does Abrán Fernandez owe us, Laban?" he asked.

Benedict shrugged. "Some," he answered. "We've

Diphtheria!

been charging him the usual twelve per cent a month and it's mounted up. He wasn't quite clear when we foreclosed on him."

Welch said, "Hmmmm" and, still carrying the paper, returned to his office. Dr Carey had said for him to telegraph for this medicine. To send a telegram he would of necessity have to send a messenger to Feather Springs—a long, cold ride. An unnecessary ride, he thought. A letter would do just as well. He would write a letter now and Clem Maybe would pick it up and take it to Feather Springs in the morning. The next morning the train East would carry the letter on, and so in three days—no, four days—it would be in Kansas City. That was fast time, Welch thought. Fast enough. Eight days and the medicine would be back in Feather Springs or in Soltura. Dr Carey had been urgent but there really was no use in so much haste. Allan Welch dipped his pen into the inkwell and, drawing a letterhead toward him, began to write.

Back in Abrán Fernandez' adobe house Eliot Carey bent over the man on the bed and listened to his breathing. It was hoarse and rasping as Abrán fought for breath. Shaking his head, Eliot straightened up.

"You have used the medicine?" he asked.

"*Sí.*" Abrán's wife nodded her head. "*Sí, Señor Doctor.*"

It was midnight before Dr Carey went to bed. Early the next morning he was up and at Abrán's bedside. There was but little change in the man. His throat was still open to the passage of air but his general condition was not good. Dr Carey did what he could and, returning to his surgery, stopped at Welch's store. Welch assured the doctor that the antitoxin had been ordered and Eliot went on home. There he pondered his problem, reading what material he could find and wishing mightily that Fritz Zeitletz were alive to consult with him. Fritz Zeitletz had seen and done a great many things and Eliot missed the little doctor's resourcefulness. In the surgery, too, Eliot sought for and found an intubation set, a rarity among the instruments, and, having cleaned the tubes, he wrapped them in gauze and put them in the sterilizer. The case with the handles he placed in his bag.

Eliot knew that Abrán's case was one that required careful watching and intelligent nursing. Abrán's wife had been up all through the night swabbing the throats of her husband and son with the bichloride solution. The woman had done well but it was apparent to Eliot that she could not for long maintain the pace. She must have assistance and Eliot debated upon the matter. It would be hard to get anyone. The fear of diphtheria would militate his getting help.

He was still considering the problem of someone to stay with the Fernandez family when Captain Irish arrived. Laurence Irish's ruddy face was troubled and, when Eliot answered the captain's knock, the ranchman blurted out a question before the doctor could greet him. "Have you seen Janice?"

Diphtheria!

Irish demanded. "She came to town this morning and I can't find her."

Eliot shook his head. "Why, no," he answered, wondering that the captain should be so concerned about a short absence. "I haven't seen her."

Irish explained why he had come to Eliot. "I've heard about this diphtheria," he said, "and I'm worried. Janice, just as likely as not, is nursing somebody that's sick. If she got diphtheria——" The ranchman's troubled face showed his feeling.

"There are just two cases in town," Eliot said quickly. "Both at Fernandez'. We'll go down there."

"Come on," Irish ordered.

Eliot joined the captain in his buggy and they drove down the street. At Abrán Fernandez' adobe the captain stopped his team and Eliot jumped out and without waiting for the slower Irish went to the door. Janice opened it to his knock. Red hair shining about her oval face, lips smiling a welcome, she greeted the doctor. "Won't you come in?"

So surprised that he had no answer, Eliot went into the house, the captain crowding in after him.

It was evident that Janice had been busy. The room was clean and Abrán's bed was freshly made. It seemed to Eliot that there was fresh peace in the room, but the harsh breathing from the bed still spoke of a battle's being fought. Eliot went to Abrán's side and Laurence Irish, drawing his daughter away from the bed and to a corner of the room, spoke to her low voiced. As Eliot examined Abrán he could hear the murmur of their voices as the captain and his daughter talked.

Despite the freshly made bed and the clean room, Abrán was no better. Indeed, he was worse. His throat was still open and he could breathe, but the poisons of the disease were gaining on him, sapping his strength and stealing it away. Dr Carey straightened up from his examination to find Janice beside him and the captain, anxious faced, standing beside the door, his hand on the knob.

"Consuelo is asleep," Janice said. "The poor woman is worn out, Doctor. I'll stay through the day and relieve her. I've been swabbing Abrán's throat and the little boy's every half-hour. Is that right?"

Automatically Eliot nodded.

"And I've boiled the dishes and hung out Abrán's bedding in the sun," Janice continued. "Is there anything else that I should do?"

"They need food," Eliot said thoughtfully. "If Mrs Fernandez and the children that are well could have something better than beans and salt pork, it would help. They need strength to fight off contagion."

Janice turned to her father. "Will you bring some beef, Captain?" she asked.

Irish nodded glumly and Eliot spoke again. "I don't like to have you here, Miss Irish," he said. "Diphtheria is very contagious and———"

"It's no worse for me than for you, Doctor," Janice Irish reminded.

Eliot flushed. "It is a doctor's duty———" he began.

Diphtheria!

"I think it is my duty too," Janice said quickly. "Are you going with the captain, Doctor, or is there something else for you to do here?"

"Nothing right now," Eliot answered. "I'll come back this afternoon. But I don't think you should expose yourself like this."

"Someone has to," Janice said cheerfully. "I'll look for you this afternoon. Don't forget the beef, Captain."

Just how, he hardly knew, Dr Carey found himself outside the door with Laurence Irish beside him. Eliot scowled at the door and then transferred that scowl to Captain Irish. "You should have made her go home with you," he announced. "She has no business in there."

"I didn't see you getting her to go," Irish answered with asperity. "You're a doctor; why didn't you tell her to get out?"

"She's your daughter," Eliot pointed out. "I'm not——" He grinned suddenly. "It looks like neither one of us had much to say," he concluded.

Laurence Irish laughed ruefully. "I've never been able to run Janice much," he confessed. "On a thing like this she does what she wants to. Is there much danger, Doctor?"

"There is always a chance of contagion," Eliot answered. "Still she seems to know what she's doing. I think that she is reasonably safe."

"She'd stay anyhow," Irish said with finality. "I'll take you downtown, Doctor, if you're going that way. If you aren't I'll take you back to the house."

Trigger Vengeance

"I'm going to the school," Eliot answered. "I'll ride to town with you."

He climbed into the buggy and sat beside the captain while Irish turned the team and started back toward Soltura's business street. Neither of the men spoke while they traveled the distance, but when the captain stopped the team and Eliot got out of the buggy Laurence Irish voiced his thoughts.

"She needs somebody to boss her," Irish announced, nodding his head back in the direction from which they had come. "If you ever get married, Doc, don't let your wife run it over you. You be the boss!"

Eliot offered no comment and Laurence Irish drove on down the street.

When the buggy had gone Dr Carey started toward the school. Miss Annabelle McKenzie, fifty years old and with an acid tongue, instructed some twenty of Soltura's younger generation in a one-room building, teaching all the grades up to and including the sixth. Eliot had a profound respect for Miss Annabelle, her common sense, her sharp tongue and her big heart. He wanted to make sure that there were no sore throats at the school and he wanted to talk the situation over with the teacher. In time of trouble such as this he believed that Annabelle McKenzie would be a tower of strength.

He had not reached the school when Emma Welch called to him from across the street and Eliot paused in his progress. Emma beckoned to him and reluctantly Eliot crossed to her. He did not want to see Emma Welch, he did not want to stand talking of

Diphtheria!

frivolities or discussing the possibility of more diphtheria in Soltura. However, there was no courteous way of avoiding the encounter and perforce Eliot crossed the street. When he reached the girl Emma impulsively put her hand on the doctor's arm.

"Isn't it awful?" she exclaimed. "I've just heard that Abrán Fernandez is very sick with diphtheria and that one of his children has it too."

Eliot nodded. "Abrán is sick," he agreed, "and the oldest boy has the disease."

"Do you think there is any danger of its spreading?" Emma asked and shuddered.

"I can't tell," Eliot answered calmly. "No one can tell about diphtheria."

"Is there anything I can do, Doctor?" Emma asked, smiling up into his face. "I can make bandages if you need them and if——"

"I'm afraid that bandages aren't very useful in treating diphtheria, Miss Welch," Eliot interposed. "I was just going to the school. I wanted to talk with Miss McKenzie. Children are particularly susceptible to diphtheria."

He was trying to rid himself of Emma Welch and go on about his business but the girl would not let him go so easily. "I do hope there is no more sickness," she said. "I'm so worried. If—— Do the Fernandez need any money, Doctor? If they do I'll give them some."

Money! Eliot could not but think of bright-haired Jane Irish calmly walking into Abrán's home and taking charge. There was the difference between

Trigger Vengeance

Janice Irish and Emma Welch! Janice saw the thing that was needed and did it; Emma asked if money was needed.

"They don't need money," Eliot blurted, "they need help. Intelligent nursing. Miss Irish is down there now helping Mrs Fernandez. The poor woman is worn out. I don't think that they need money, Miss Welch. They need nursing and good food and warmth. If you'll excuse me now I must go on to the school and then back to the office. I can't tell what calls may have come in while I've been gone."

His voice was brusque and he turned abruptly on his heel, striding away. Emma opened her mouth to call him back and then closed it with an almost audible snap. She was not used to such cavalier treatment and she resented it. Just who did this young man think he was that he could treat Allan Welch's daughter so? An angry flush spread over Emma's face. She watched the broad back of the doctor as he strode along toward the school.

And so Janice Irish was down there nursing Abrán Fernandez and his brat? And the doctor thought it was a wonderful thing, did he? And the Fernandez needed nursing and care, and money was not the prime need! Emma turned, almost flounced about. Janice Irish! She had always thought that Janice Irish was a little show-off and now she knew it. And there wasn't anything that Janice Irish could do that she couldn't do! She would show Janice Irish, and Eliot Carey too!

Dr Carey was not particularly concerned about

Diphtheria!

being shown anything. Annabelle McKenzie's long, plain face looked very good to the doctor. The rough Scotch burr of Annabelle's voice when she informed him with asperity that there were no sore throats in her school and that she would see that no one with a sore throat eluded his attention sounded fine. Miss Annabelle's impatience with him made him feel elated, and when he left the school he heartily wished that Miss Annabelle were twins. Given a couple of Miss McKenzies to turn loose on Soltura, and there would not be much for a doctor to worry about. Eliot went back to his house feeling much encouraged but still uneasy about Janice. He wished, he most devoutly wished, that Laurence Irish had more control over his willful daughter!

He went back to Fernandez' late that evening, hoping to find Abrán improved. It was a vain hope, he felt, but still he had not been called during the day and there was a possibility that Abrán had rallied. When he entered the adobe he was surprised. Emma Welch, clothed completely in white and with a big white kerchief fashioned into a cap adorning her dark hair, came from Abrán's bedside and hurried to him.

"I was just going to send for you, Doctor," she said. "It seems to me that Mr Fernandez is better. He is breathing more easily."

"What are you doing here?" Eliot snapped.

"Why, you said that they needed help." Emma's tone showed her injury. "Of course I came to help them."

Trigger Vengeance

"Where is Miss Irish?" Eliot demanded.

"She left when I came," Emma answered innocently. She did not tell Eliot Carey that Janice Irish had gone only because of the captain's insistent demands, and then only because Laurence Irish promised that she could return in the morning.

Eliot made no comment on Janice's departure but went at once to Abrán's bedside. "Have you been swabbing his throat?" he asked.

"Yes, Doctor," Emma answered. "Every half-hour. The little boy's throat too."

Eliot, examining Abrán, grunted. True, Abrán breathed more easily, at least so it seemed, but the breathing was shallow, quick, only part of the lungs in use. The man's pallor was intense and his pulse was a tiny rapid thread in his wrist. Abrán was definitely worse.

It was an hour before Eliot left Fernandez. When he did leave there was a sheet pulled over Abrán's face and Consuelo Fernandez, red eyed but hardly comprehending what had happened, was sitting beside the bed, holding the baby and rocking back and forth in her dumb misery.

Dr Carey did not talk as he conducted Emma Welch through the quiet streets back to her home. There was nothing that he wanted to say. Emma, after one or two fruitless attempts, respected his silence. She had hoped that there would be a closer bond between herself and the doctor but it was not there. Rather, it seemed to the girl that a definite

Diphtheria!

barrier separated them. At her door she said, "Good night," low voiced and restrained.

Eliot Carey wakened from his thoughts long enough to give directions. "Take a hot bath," he ordered brusquely. "Put some disinfectant in the water if you have any. Gargle your throat and boil those clothes before you wear them again. Good night, Miss Welch."

He turned away and the girl, standing beside the door, watched him swing off down the walk. She had failed. She knew that she had failed.

And Eliot, striding off through the night, did not think of Emma Welch. It might have afforded Emma some consolation had she known that he was not thinking of Janice Irish either. He was thinking of the dirt and the squalor in Abrán Fernandez' house and in the other adobe houses of the little town. He was thinking of the meager food and the wasted bodies of the children, bodies that had not the strength to throw off disease, to resist attack. The West, Dr Carey thought, the glamorous, glorious, wide-flung West! In it he had found conditions that would rival the worst slum on Manhattan Island. Eliot Carey stopped in his stride and with his clenched right fist struck the palm of his left hand. He would change that thing. He would, God help him, give these people a chance if he could. He would fight ignorance and poverty and dirt and superstition!

In the morning, returning to the adobe house, the scene of death, Eliot found the place packed. Despite his warnings, despite his orders, Abrán Fernandez' friends and neighbors had come to see him as he lay and they had brought their wives and their children. They were sullen when Eliot ordered them to leave; they moved sluggishly, loath to go. It was not until Father Revelet, just returning from a missionary visit to Rinconcito, arrived at the adobe house and seconded Eliot's commands that the room was cleared. Even the natives lingered outside the door, crowding about it.

Eliot talked plainly to Father Revelet. "I told them to allow no one in here," he said. "I told them the place was quarantined. And now this morning I find the whole place full of people, women and children too. I don't know what will come of this, Father. So far we've had these two cases and if we could have kept them confined, there might have been no more; but there is no telling what has gone out of here this morning."

The priest nodded. "It is hard," he said. "They are children. They do not understand."

"I wish the antitoxin I ordered would come," Eliot said. "I've nothing to fight with, Father."

"You must do the best you can, my son," the priest comforted. "We here are used to doing with very little. I will help you all I can."

"Then make them understand that they must not come in contact with the disease," Eliot directed. "Make them keep away from any person who is sick and tell them that if anyone, particularly a child, has a sore throat, they must come to me immediately."

Diphtheria!

Father Revelet nodded his understanding. "I will do that," he promised. "Is there anything else, Doctor?"

"I'm worried about Mrs Fernandez," Eliot answered. "Losing her husband was a blow to her. I wish I could get someone to help her."

"I will arrange that too," the priest agreed.

"Thank you, Father." Eliot placed his hand on the priest's arm. "I must go in now and see the boy. He was reacting very well last night."

He left Father Revelet in the center of the little room and went to the bed whereon lay Abrán's son. The boy looked up at him with bright feverish eyes.

When Eliot had attended his patient and was making ready to leave the old grandmother came to him. She clutched his arm and, almost inarticulate because of her lack of teeth, told him that the baby had a sore throat and cough. Eliot immediately went into the other room where the children had been kept. The baby, as the old woman had said, was restless, feverish, showing a degree of temperature, and her throat was reddened. Here was another victim, and Eliot counseled that the child's throat be swabbed and that the baby be put to bed immediately.

When he left the house he went directly to Welch's store. Allan Welch was not in but Laban Benedict assured the doctor that the antitoxin had been ordered and that it should be heard from soon. Going back to the white house, Eliot was worried and distraught.

CHAPTER XIV

Message from the Dead

ABRÁN FERNANDEZ' funeral was held the next morning. Despite Eliot's warning, there was a crowd at the church. Dr Carey, going to Welch's store to see if anything had as yet been heard from the antitoxin, saw that crowd and hurried across the street, forcing his way through the people and at last finding Father Revelet. The natives gave way sluggishly as he worked a passage through them, and they were openly resentful. Eliot, sensing that hostility, could not understand the attitude exhibited toward him. In his stay in Soltura he had been treated kindly by the native population, meeting with smiles and a *"Buenos días, Doctor"* when he passed along the streets. Now there were scowls and sullen, resentful undertones.

Father Revelet, in his robe and surplice, was in the small preparation room of the church and to him Eliot spoke harshly. "I told you, Father," he chided, "that these people should not congregate. I told you that they should avoid anyone who has been in contact with a case of diphtheria. Mrs Fernandez is out there and her father and mother and one of the children. Do you *want* to start an epidemic in Soltura?"

The priest looked his surprise. "But surely in the church, Doctor," he said. "There is no danger in the church."

"I've never heard of a disease respecting a religion," snapped Eliot. "In the church or anywhere else. These people *must* avoid crowds and they *must* not come in contact with the disease."

Upon Father Revelet's face appeared the same stubborn, resentful expression that Eliot had encountered in the crowd. "I cannot forbid a wife from mourning her husband," Father Revelet said coldly, "nor can I forbid friends from showing their respect for the dead."

"Very well." Eliot Carey's tone was rasping. "I only hope that you will be able to forbid diphtheria from attacking the wife and the mourners. I'm trying to help here, Father Revelet, but I can do nothing if the intelligent men of this community will not help me."

The priest took affront at that. His face was stony as he looked at the doctor. "Then perhaps you should appeal to your friends," he said. "Perhaps Mr Welch can help you. He is an intelligent man. Almost as intelligent as you are, Doctor, and as prone to take advantage. You must excuse me now."

Father Revelet left the doctor then, going through

the little door into the church, and Eliot stood in the small room, angry and not a little puzzled by the words of the priest. After a moment's pause he shrugged and went on. There was nothing he could do about the assemblage in the church. The people were there; he could not order them to leave it. He could only hope that nothing bad would come of meeting.

Allan Welch had nothing to report to Dr Carey when the doctor reached the store. He was bland and smiling and unworried and Eliot took some consolation from Welch's ease. Still he was not pleased with himself, with conditions in Soltura or with Welch when he went back to the white house. Reassurances were all very well but Dr Eliot Carey wanted action.

For three days it seemed that the doctor's worries were needless. Daily he called at Welch's, inquiring about the antitoxin. Daily he received assurances that it was coming, that it should be in Soltura immediately. The Fernandez children seemed to improve under the application of the bichloride solution. They were getting better. No fresh cases appeared, at least none were called to the doctor's attention and, lulled into false security, Eliot felt relief and relaxed. Then on the fourth day he was wakened at dawn by Father Revelet. The priest was agitated when Dr Carey conducted him into the surgery.

"I have come from Con Abeyta's," Father Revelet announced. "I am afraid that there is diphtheria there. Can you come, Doctor?"

Message from the Dead

"As soon as I dress," Eliot answered. "Will you wait for me?"

The priest nodded and Eliot hurried to his room.

At Abeyta's he found not one case but three cases of diphtheria: two children and a woman. The symptoms were advanced, the membrane already present in the throats, and when he had made his examination Dr Carey faced the priest. "Why was I not called, Father?" he demanded. "I should have seen these patients yesterday or the day before."

Father Revelet shook his head. "I am not sure," he said. "Con Abeyta came for me early this morning when the baby began to breathe badly. I have heard . . . I am not certain, Doctor Carey——"

"We will have to begin applications immediately," Eliot announced. "If only that antitoxin would come. It should have been here. I can't understand why it hasn't arrived."

"You can help these people?" Father Revelet asked anxiously.

"I can treat them," Eliot agreed. "I can't understand why I was not called. I'll go back and make up some bichloride solution and bring it here and show them how to use it. That's all I can do right now. This is bad, Father."

Father Revelet nodded his agreement and seemed about to speak. Eliot, not noticing that the priest wished to tell him something, hurried out, and Father Revelet, turning to Con Abeyta who stood by frowning, asked a question.

Trigger Vengeance

"Why did you not call the doctor?" the priest demanded.

Con Abeyta shook his head. "He charges too much," Con answered. "He says one price and means another."

"Tell me!" commanded Father Revelet.

"The doctor tells Ramón Archuleta twenty-five dollars for a baby," Con stated. "Welch comes with the bill and it is fifty dollars. Too much. Two, three times that happens."

Father Revelet shook his head. "Where is Ramón?" he asked. "I must find out about this."

Con shrugged. "*A casa,*" he said.

The priest was torn by indecision. "I must see Ramón," he announced. "I will—— No, I will wait until the doctor comes back."

Within fifteen minutes Eliot returned. He had a bottle of bichloride solution and cotton but no swab sticks, his supply of sticks having run short. With Father Revelet standing by to interpret when necessary, the doctor showed Con Abeyta how to make a swab, splitting off a splinter of wood from a box and smoothing it with his knife. He showed Con how to twist a swab and use the bichloride on the throats of the patients and warned him to destroy the used swabs. He gave directions as to food and warmth and the sterilization of utensils and gradually the dour expression left Con's face. Con could see, as could Father Revelet, that Dr Carey was genuinely interested and concerned. When Eliot finished Con asked a question.

Message from the Dead

"¿Cuanto, Doctor?"

"Never mind about that," Eliot snapped. "You take care of these people."

Father Revelet echoed the doctor's words in Spanish and the last question departed from Con's eyes as he nodded his approval.

Eliot turned to the priest. "I'm going down to Welch's," he said. "Surely that antitoxin must have come in by now."

Father Revelet nodded. "I hope so," he agreed. "I will stay here a little while, Doctor."

Eliot nodded and, putting on his hat and coat, went out. Father Revelet turned again to Con.

At the store Eliot Carey found Welch in the office. He hurried in, not waiting for an invitation, and Welch, seated at the desk holding a letter, looked up and smiled at the young doctor.

"We've heard from that order," Welch announced. "Doolittle's, the wholesalers I wrote, didn't have the serum on hand. They write that they are ordering a supply from Mulford's and it should be here inside a week."

"They wrote you?" Eliot asked, not comprehending.

"Answering my letter," Welch said blandly.

"Your *letter?*"

"I wrote to them the day you asked me to order this serum," Welch explained. "I do a good deal of business with Doolittle and———"

"You *wrote* to them?"

Trigger Vengeance

"Certainly. You asked me to order this antitoxin and I wrote immediately."

Eliot Carey was young. Normally he was a pleasant, personable young man. But he was a doctor and inside him—restrained most of the time but there—was a temper. He was like a violin, smoothly harmonious when properly handled and in tune, but with a tension upon him that could break suddenly. Now he exploded.

"I told you to telegraph for that antitoxin," the doctor snapped. "I tried to impress it upon you, Mr Welch, that speed was essential, that we must have it immediately. And you *wrote* a letter! You chose the slowest possible means of making our needs known. Naturally the concern you wrote to thought that there was no particular hurry. Mr Welch, you are a fool! There are three new cases of diphtheria in town now. At the best you're a fool, and if one of these people die you'll be no better than a murderer!"

Eliot wheeled and stamped out of the office, leaving the astonished Allan Welch still seated at his desk.

Outside the office Eliot's anger gave place to concern. There were three cases of the disease and they were advanced. He could not tell how many more cases of diphtheria there might be hidden in the town. He must make sure of the number and he must make arrangements to have a supply of antitoxin shipped in immediately. He walked down the street, moving slowly because he was deep in thought, and as he walked, Laurence Irish, with Janice beside him, drove into Soltura's main street.

Captain Irish and his daughter had been in and out of Soltura all through the week. Eliot had seen Janice and her father at Abrán Fernandez' the morning after Abrán's death. He had had no opportunity to speak to them. Father Revelet had found a woman to supplant Janice as nurse and since Abrán's death Eliot had not seen the girl. Now, as the buggy came abreast of the walking man, Laurence Irish stopped his team and hailed the doctor.

"Doctor Carey!"

Turning, Eliot saw who had called him and, leaving the sidewalk, went out onto the rutted street.

"How are you, Doctor?" Irish greeted. "We've been aiming to come in and see you. Janice was pretty much upset about Abrán. She's spent some time down there and I've been busy. I hear you have some new cases."

Eliot nodded. Janice's blue eyes were searching his face anxiously. Eliot did not look at the girl.

"I was just going down to your house," Irish continued. "Get in. We'll take you home. We—— Why, what's the matter, Doctor?" There was concern in the ranchman's voice.

With a rush of words Eliot blurted out his troubles. "I sent for a supply of diphtheria antitoxin over a week ago," he snapped. "This morning I find that Welch wrote for it in place of telegraphing, as I asked, and the supply house has just answered his letter. They are out of the serum and are ordering it—by mail. I've got to get a supply here immediately. There are three new cases in town and no telling how many more. I've got to get telegrams off to Denver and to Kansas City and get that serum here. I've got to——"

Laurence Irish crowded over on the buggy seat. "Get in, Doctor," he ordered. "We'll take you home and I can drive to Feather Springs and send your telegrams. Get in."

Eliot climbed into the buggy and Laurence Irish sent the bay team trotting down the street.

At Eliot's home the captain and his daughter followed the doctor into the house. There in the surgery, while he stripped off his overcoat, Dr Carey outlined the situation in Soltura as he saw it.

"There is every chance that the disease will spread," he said. "A crowd of people came to the Fernandez funeral and most of them had been at the house the morning he died. It may be that there will be no more cases but I can't take a chance on that. I've got to stop this thing right here if I can and I've got to have something here to fight it with. If I can get a supply of antitoxin I can stop it. If I can't we'll lose three out of every ten people that come down with it. That's the record of diphtheria. And anyone may be a carrier. He might be perfectly well and still be carrying the disease germs in his throat."

"Write your telegrams," ordered Captain Irish. "Janice and I will take them to Feather Springs. We'll make arrangements to have the stuff brought over as soon as it comes."

Message from the Dead

Eliot sat down at the desk, pulled a pad of paper to him and thought a moment. "I'll send to Denver and Kansas City both," he decided, and began to write.

When he had finished the messages he gave them to the captain. "If you'll get these off," he said, "we ought to have an answer at once. And, Captain, you had better speak to John Mason about this. We're going to need help in maintaining a quarantine here."

Laurence Irish nodded. "I'll do that," he agreed. "Come, Janice."

Janice Irish had removed her coat and her hat. She smiled disarmingly at her father. "I'll stay here, Captain," she announced. "Perhaps Doctor Carey can find something for me to do."

Laurence Irish knew his daughter. He recognized the finality in her voice. The captain shook his head. "You can't——" He began his fruitless argument.

"I can't go with you," agreed Janice. "That's right, Captain. You hurry to Feather Springs. Doctor Carey needs this medicine."

Laurence Irish stood, undecided. Janice sat down in the surgery. She was there and it was evident that she meant to stay. "Go on, Captain," she urged.

"Well, I——" Irish began.

"I'll keep her here," Eliot said. "But if you want me to send someone else, Captain——"

"I'll go," Irish decided. "Janice, you stay right here."

The captain scowled at his daughter and went on

Trigger Vengeance

out. From the study Janice Irish and Eliot Carey heard the team trot away. The girl smiled brightly at the doctor.

"Now what is there for me to do?" she asked. "The captain will be in Feather Springs in four hours."

Eliot shook his head. "You should have gone with your father," he answered. "There's nothing for you to do here."

Janice got up and walked to the window. "I'm in the way then," she said. "I suppose that you think you will have to look after me but I'm perfectly capable of looking after myself. I—— Why, here comes Miss McKenzie! I wonder——"

Eliot was already on his way to the door.

Annabelle McKenzie's strong homely face showed her worry. Without waiting for Eliot's question when he opened the door the woman stood on the porch and gave the reason for her visit. "There are two sore throats at school, Doctor," she announced. "Tomaso Quintana and Eloy Vigil. Eloy says that his little brother has a sore throat too. Can you come?"

"I'll be right with you," Eliot snapped. "Wait till I get my coat."

In a moment, with no further word to Janice, he rejoined the teacher and the two went hurrying off down the walk. Janice watched them go, looking out through the surgery window at the brown muddy street. Eliot had his hand under Miss Annabelle's arm and was hurrying her along. When they were out of sight the girl turned from the window and walked slowly back across the surgery to the roll-top desk. She should have gone with the captain, she thought. Here she was only in the way.

Dr Carey did not return and Janice examined the surgery. She had not as yet taken those articles left her by Fritz Zeitletz in his will and, leaving the surgery, she went along the hall, stopping at the door of the room Dr Zeitletz had occupied during his life. For a time she hesitated before that door and then, opening it, went into the room.

Janice had been in this little room many times during Zeitletz' lifetime. Now she found it just as it had always been. The big chair, the table, the bed, the pictures on the wall—each occupied its customary place. The room was clean, swept and dusted, and there was a fresh spread upon the bed. Janice Irish, pausing beside the table, looked about her and nodded. Eliot Carey had kept the room just as Dr Zeitletz had kept it. Standing there, the girl could imagine that there were times when the young doctor came into this place to stand and commune with its departed occupant.

She finished her inspection and looked at the table. Fritz Zeitletz' watch lay there ticking off the hours, wound, the girl knew, by Eliot Carey. The watch was hers. Dr Zeitletz had willed it to her, together with his diary and other personal possessions. And the watch was running! There must be, Janice thought, a good deal of hidden sentiment in Eliot Carey. She touched the watch and from it her fingers strayed to the square leather back of Fritz Zeitletz' diary. The girl picked up the book, half opened it and then hesitated. Here was the story of Dr Zeitletz' life. She wondered. . . . Fritz Zeitletz had given it to her; he must have meant that she should read it. The girl opened the book and glanced at a page or two. She turned further into the volume. What had Fritz Zeitletz to say concerning Eliot Carey? Janice leafed through the pages, looking for a date.

As she turned the pages she noted that portions of the diary were written in German. The girl turned back, making a more thorough examination. Fritz Zeitletz had alternated, one day writing the events in his precise English, the next day using his native language. Janice smiled. How like Dr Zeitletz this was. With no one in Soltura speaking German, he had kept up in his diary his practice in his native tongue. Regularly the sequence ran, first the Germanic script, then the English. The girl paused. Fritz Zeitletz had known that she had no knowledge of his native tongue. But Eliot Carey spoke and read and wrote German. Had Dr Zeitletz shrewdly suspected that to have his diary interpreted she must take it to Dr Carey? Had he willed her the book with the idea that it would throw her into the young doctor's company? She believed that he had. She could almost see Dr Zeitletz chuckling. She knew that Zeitletz had loved her and she knew that he had loved Eliot. Would it not be likely that the rotund little man had planned to put his two most dear ones into intimate contact with each other?

Message from the Dead

The girl flushed and continued to turn through the pages. Presently she found the thing she sought.

"This day my young man has come," Fritz Zeitletz had written in his heavy, careful script. "He is all that I could wish. I must keep him."

The girl read on, sinking down into the big leather-covered chair beside the window, puzzled occasionally by some ill-written word or phrase but continuing steadily on, skipping over the entries written in German.

So engrossed was she in the thing she read that she failed to hear Eliot come in and go out again. And Dr Carey was so busy, so preoccupied, that he failed to note Janice's absence from the surgery. He had found three fresh cases at the school and the probability of another at Vigil's. Miss Annabelle had sent the children home, closing the school, and was now at Vigil's investigating the sore throat of the baby. Dr Carey, in the small room where he kept his drugs, measured out bichloride of mercury and added water. He must have more cotton but fortunately there was plenty of bichloride. If only the antitoxin would come! Dr Carey poured solution into bottles and corked them and thrust them into his grip. He would go to Vigil's and join Miss Annabelle.

In Fritz Zeitletz' room Janice Irish continued to read. She was nearing the end now, nearing the place where blank pages supplanted the written. The pages she read were filled with the life of Soltura, the hidden things that Dr Zeitletz had entrusted to his diary. They were filled, too, with Eliot Carey, his kindness, his courage, his never-failing courtesy toward an older man. Janice Irish was having a picture drawn for her, a picture of Eliot Carey, drawn by Fritz Zeitletz.

And now she reached a page and read it through and stopped to read again.

"This day," Fritz Zeitletz had written, "I was called to attend Tray Barry, who had been drinking too heavily. Barry is suffering from delirium tremens. I administered a bromide and was compelled to give another. Barry is possessed with a fear of Sid Raupert with whom he has been associated. From his ravings I gathered that Barry—who is our deputy sheriff and whose appointment was urged by Allan Welch—and Sid Raupert were concerned in the murder of Carl Jacks. Indeed, Barry's delirium was concerned chiefly with that murder and his fright of Raupert. He said as nearly as I can remember: 'He was nothing but a sheepman. I told him to get out, that no one but Welch bought sheep here. He deserved to be killed.' And then he said: 'I won't tell, Sid. I won't tell on you.' From this I gathered that he and Sid Raupert had killed Jacks."

There was a blank below the words and then Fritz Zeitletz had written, "I must remember that my duty is to the sick." There followed quotation marks and then Fritz Zeitletz had written: " '. . . whatsoever things I see or hear concerning the life of men, in my attendance upon the sick or even apart therefrom, which ought not to be noised abroad, I will keep silent thereon, counting such things to be as sacred trusts.'" And following that, "What is a doctor's duty?"

The writing on the next page was in German and Janice Irish closed the book upon her finger, marking the place of the page, and stared out of the window. What was a doctor's duty? What was her duty? Fritz Zeitletz had written in the diary the things he knew. *He* had held them as secrets but what of Janice Irish? Should she continue the silence? She wondered. Had that been Fritz Zeitletz' intention when he had willed her the diary?

No, this had been written after the will was made. Dr Zeitletz had willed her this book so that she might know Eliot Carey, so that she might know how a man looked at the young doctor. That was the purpose; Janice knew it. And this other? What should she do with it? There was only one person whom she could ask: Eliot. He was a doctor, just as Fritz Zeitletz had been a doctor, and he would tell her what she must do.

For a time the girl sat there musing, thinking of what she had read, stirred by it to wonder at the depths that run beneath the surface of men. She was in the big leather chair when Eliot Carey returned and, hearing him, she arose and went out into the hall.

"Doctor Carey," Janice began, "I have been——"

Eliot saw the book in the girl's hand and recognized it. "That is yours, Miss Irish," he said. "And the doctor's watch is there on the table and some of the other things he left to you. I have kept the watch wound and running. I had intended getting all those things together and bringing them to you. I'm sorry I've been so negligent."

"But that isn't what I wanted to talk to you about," Janice expostulated. "I have been reading in the diary——"

"Will you excuse me, please?" Eliot interrupted. "I have just come from town and I must go back at once. I'm afraid that we have a diphtheria outbreak on our hands here, Miss Irish, and we have very little to fight it with. There are four new cases and Father Revelet is going from house to house asking if there are any sore throats among the children. I must make up some bichloride solution and take it back to Miss McKenzie. She is staying with the Vigil children."

"Of course," Janice answered. "Can I help, Doctor?"

"You can learn to make up bichloride," answered Eliot.

The girl followed the doctor into the surgery. Eliot removed his coat and hurried into the little drug room. Janice stopped at the desk. "You are busy now," she said, "but there is a part of Doctor Zeitletz' diary that I want you to read. I want your advice."

"Put it on the desk," Eliot called from the drug room. "I'll read it as soon as I can find time."

Janice marked the place in the leather-bound book, put it on the roll-top desk and went to the drug-room door. "I've put the diary on the desk with the place marked in it," she said. "Now what is it you want me to do, Doctor?"

"I want you to learn how to make this solution," Eliot answered. "See? You put this weight on the scales and weigh out enough dry bichloride of mercury to tip the balances. So. Then you shake the powder into a bottle and use the graduate to measure out four ounces of water. Use the water in this jug, please. Then mix the water and the bichloride in the bottle, cork it and paste one of these poison labels on it and write 'Bichloride of Mercury' on the label. I'll send for the solution as I need it. Probably I'll want some cotton to make swabs too. Can you do that for me, Miss Irish? Can you spare the time?"

"Of course," Janice answered. "How do you use this, Doctor?"

"Swab the throats with it every half-hour," Eliot answered, "then burn the swabs. It is the same thing that you used at Fernandez'. I wish there were some way to make these people understand that they must not come in contact with cases of diphtheria, and I wish that I could make them isolate the cases and boil the dishes that the patients use. It seems almost impossible to make them do that."

He was putting on his coat as he spoke, and now, thrusting the freshly prepared bottle of bichloride solution into a pocket of the coat, he picked up his bag and his hat.

"Good-by, Miss Irish," he said. "I've got to find Father Revelet and leave this with Miss McKenzie."

"Good-by, Doctor," Janice Irish answered.

CHAPTER XV

At Fuente Duro

FIVE HUNDRED DOLLARS is not a big reward but it is enough to make a man worry when it is placed upon his head. Wing Lackey had worried about the reward and he had worried about the constant movement that was forced upon him by that reward. Wing Lackey looked askance at every man; they might want five hundred dollars. He looked askance at every man and he hated Mark Neville. Mark Neville was his only companion: Mark Neville, who did not worry and who had padding in his boot where his toes should have been. Wing hated Mark because he did not worry; and because he was cheerful, and because he ordered Wing about, casually, as though it was his right to give orders. He hated Mark Neville because, he reasoned tortuously, it had been Neville's fault that there was only fifteen hundred dollars in the express box; and because that money was gone, and because Neville had taken July Wiggins to a doctor. He hated Neville because when they rode together Neville always rode in the lead; and because Neville would not leave the country, and because Neville was not afraid. There were numerous reasons for Wing Lackey to hate Mark Neville.

Hatred can craze a man, make him more or less insane, but insanity does not mean that a man loses his cleverness. Wing Lackey had a sort of animal cunning, the kind of cunning that makes a coyote avoid a trap that is cleverly placed and concealed and then walk into a trap put openly upon the bare ground. It seemed to Wing Lackey that he could not tolerate Mark Neville any longer. Constantly the temptation to rid himself of Neville confronted him.

But to rid himself of Neville he must take a chance and Wing feared to take a chance. And, too, killing Neville, while it would rid Wing of the man, would do him no other good. Wing Lackey brooded over the situation as they moved from place to place, hunted, always moving, trusting no man. As he brooded he became more cunning, and the day came when Wing Lackey laid a plan. It stood to reason, in Wing's cunning mind, that if the leader, if Mark Neville, were taken or killed the hunt would stop. And it stood to reason that the man that turned Mark Neville over to the authorities, even though he himself was an outlaw, would get a break. That was just common sense, wasn't it? It seemed so to Wing Lackey. That was his plan and that was his reasoning, and while diphtheria raged in Soltura, Wing Lackey set his plan in motion.

Trigger Vengeance

They were in Manueles Canyon when Wing Lackey carried out his design. For three days the two had been hidden away in a rock shack that Julio Chavez maintained for a sheep camp. Julio, bound to Mark Neville by ties that he would not have broken had he been able, had brought them food and spent some time with the fugitives. Julio had a cousin who had come down from Colorado and was staying with him. Julio's cousin, Bevan Chavez, had no ties and knew no one in the country. It was possible for Wing Lackey to see Bevan alone and give Bevan a message and some money. It was possible for Bevan to make a trip to Soltura. So it was that Sid Raupert received a message inviting him to meet Wing Lackey by Fuente Duro, a big spring that, because of the hardness of the water, no one used. The Fuente Duro was well up the canyon, almost at the top.

Sid Raupert got the message in Soltura. The fact that Soltura was threatened with a diphtheria epidemic, that there were ten cases of diphtheria in the little town, did not worry Sid Raupert at all. "What the hell!" Sid said to Jack Brannigan. "It's the Mexicans that's got it, ain't it?" Sid was not worried by the diphtheria. He kept away from it. But when he got Wing Lackey's message he did some thinking. As an upshot of that reasoning he rode out of Soltura on the morning that Laurence Irish drove to Feather Springs to order antitoxin. Sid straddled his big roan horse and he had a rifle under the right fender of his saddle. Sid Raupert had a hen on.

When he reached the rimrock above Fuente Duro

he hid his horse and then, choosing a vantage point, watched the canyon below him. He saw Wing Lackey appear in the canyon, dismount and, after a furtive investigation, sit down to wait. Still Sid remained hidden. He stayed up on the rim for an hour, stayed until he was positive Wing was by himself. Then Sid mounted the big roan and went down to the spring.

Neither he nor Wing had much to say until Sid had left his horse and seated himself opposite the outlaw. Then Wing broke into his idea. "You want Mark Neville, don't you?" Wing began, asking a needless question.

Raupert nodded his head and chewed the small cud of tobacco in his mouth.

"I'll tell you how to get him," Wing continued. "But I got to be protected, Sid."

"Well?" said Sid.

"Well . . . Mark is in the country. I know where he is."

Raupert appeared uninterested. "Uh-huh," he said.

"An' I can tell you where to get him," Wing continued.

"Uh-huh," Raupert grunted again.

"Don't you want him?" Wing blurted.

"Sure," Sid Raupert drawled.

"Then listen. What 'll I get out of it?" Wing bent forward. "They want Mark for that express job an' they want him for killin' Doc Zeitletz, don't they? It ought to be worth somethin' for me to turn him in."

Raupert rolled the cud across his mouth from one

cheek to the other. "What do you want?" he asked.

"I want a cut of the reward on Mark an' I want to get out of the country."

"That all?"

"That's it." Wing was eager. "It ought to be worth that to you fellows, what with Mark killin' Zeitletz an' all."

There was a streak in Sid Raupert, a boastful, bold characteristic, a sadistic desire that would not let even Wing Lackey credit a deed done by Sid Raupert to someone else. If he had not meant to kill Wing Raupert might have restrained that desire, but there was a double-barreled derringer in his hand that Raupert held beside his leg and in his mind the firm intention to kill Wing Lackey. Raupert spoke out.

"Mark didn't kill Zeitletz. I done it."

"You?" Wing's eyes were wide with astonishment. Then, recovering himself, "Anyhow, there's a reward on Mark an' I know where he is!"

"I know where he is too." Raupert's eyes did not leave Wing as he spat out his chew. "He's down at Chavez! An' there's a reward on you, Wing!"

Too late Wing saw the trap set on the bare ground. He read his fate in Raupert's blank eyes and clawed for the gun he wore at his hip. Deliberately, because there was plenty of time, Sid Raupert shot Wing Lackey, shot him twice through the chest with the .41-caliber derringer and, with the little pistol smoking in his hand, stood up and watched Wing writhe on the ground and then become still.

At Fuente Duro

"I'd take you in," Sid Raupert said, addressing the motionless Wing, "but I reckon I'd better go down an' watch Julio's place awhile. Maybe Mark will be lookin' for you."

Reloading the derringer, Raupert mounted his big roan horse and, looking back at the body on the ground for a brief instant, rode up the rough trail to the rimrock and then north along it. There was a place above Julio Chavez' where a man could lie down and, over his rifle sights, survey all that went on about Julio's rock house. Sid Raupert knew that place well.

Wing lay where he had fallen. He was unconscious when a horse and rider came through the timber on the south slope of the canyon and he did not see or hear Mark Neville dismount and come limping over to bend down above him. Neville shook his head. He put his hand on Wing's chest and felt the heart beat. Limping over to the spring, Mark Neville returned with his hat full of water. He spilled a little water on Wing's upturned face and then a little more. Then, pulling a dirty handkerchief from his pocket, he dipped it into the hat and bathed the upturned face. After a long time Wing opened his eyes. The eyes were blank and Mark Neville, voice strong, asked a question.

"Was it Sid? Was it Sid Raupert, Wing?"

Some comprehension came into Lackey's eyes and again Neville asked his question. "Was it Sid Raupert?"

Trigger Vengeance

Wing Lackey said, "Yes" very weakly and a little bloody froth formed on his lips.

Neville wiped the froth away. "Don't talk," he said. "I knew you were gettin' nervous, kid. I knew that you were goin' to break. You sent for Sid to meet you. Bevan told me this mornin'."

"Yes," Wing whispered.

"An' Sid downed you," Mark continued. "I could have told you, Wing. It's my fault. I reckon I've been hard to get along with."

Wing made no movement, uttered no sound and Neville repeated, "It's my fault. It's been a bust all along, kid. First there wasn't enough in the express box to make it worth while. Then Dunlop an' July an' Harley got killed. An' now you——"

"Don't go back," Wing managed.

"No. I won't go back to Chavez' place," Neville assured the dying man. "Sid will be watchin' there. I'll have to even with Sid, I reckon."

"Sid . . . killed . . . Zeitletz. . . ." Wing spoke each word with an effort. "He . . . told . . . me. . . ."

"I been thinkin' it was Sid," answered Mark Neville. "An' that's another score."

"You—— I'm . . . sorry, Mark. . . ." Wing whispered and closed his eyes. The breath no longer came bubbling through the froth at his lips. Once more Mark Neville wiped away that bloody froth. No more formed. Mark Neville sat there holding the wet handkerchief.

For a long time he sat unmoving, then, getting

up, he emptied the water from his hat and walked to where his horse cropped the brown grass.

Sid Raupert lay on the rimrock above Julio Chavez' cabin all that day. He chewed tobacco and waited, his rifle laid out before him. He saw Julio and Julio's wife and Bevan, Julio's cousin, come and go about their business. He saw nothing of Mark Neville. When evening came and it was too dark to see his front sight Sid Raupert got up stiffly and went to the roan horse and untied him. There would be another day and another time, and in the morning he would bring Wing Lackey into town and be five hundred dollars ahead.

In Soltura Dr Carey was busy all through the day. It seemed to the young doctor that he would not be able to finish the work that there was for him to do. Father Revelet, reporting to Eliot, had found several homes in which there was illness. Eliot visited these homes. Of the four he visited, three contained diphtheria. The fourth, he found with relief, was simply a stomach rash on a baby. In each home he entered Eliot met with a sullen resentfulness. It seemed to the hurrying doctor that he would not have been tolerated in those homes except for the presence of the priest. He commented on the fact and Father Revelet looked at him questioningly but forbore to comment. It was not until late in the afternoon, when each of the patients had been given a second inspection, that the priest told Eliot the reason for Soltura's sullenness and suspicion.

"These are a clannish people, Doctor," Father

Trigger Vengeance

Revelet said as the two walked back together toward the doctor's house. "If a man wrongs one native he is suspected by them all."

Eliot nodded. "Doctor Zeitletz told me that," he said. "I've tried to be fair with all of them, Father."

"Have you?" Father Revelet asked.

Eliot nodded. "I don't understand their attitude," the young doctor continued.

"Don't you?"

"No." Eliot shook his head.

They walked along in silence for a time and then the priest asked a question. "What do you charge for a call, Doctor?"

"That depends," Eliot answered. "When they come to the office I charge fifty cents. If the call is in town I generally charge a dollar and if I have to take out the buggy I charge from two to five dollars."

"And for a maternity case?" Father Revelet persisted.

"From fifteen to twenty-five dollars," Eliot answered. "It doesn't seem to me that I'm unreasonable. Of course when I have to prescribe medicine I charge for that but I ask as little as I can. After all, Father, you know that a good half of the work I do will be charity work. I'll never get a cent for it. I've got to live and I must have a supply of medicines and drugs. I can't work for nothing, although I'll admit that I'd like to. I wish that I could do all the work that is needed here, clean up this dirt, educate these people, give them something to live for."

Father Revelet cleared his throat. "What sort of

arrangement do you have with Welch and Company?" he asked and then added quickly, "Not that it is my business——"

"Why," Eliot interposed, "I don't mind telling you. I was in debt to the store and Mr Welch suggested that I turn some of my bills over to them and they would credit me. He discounts the bills I hand him, six per cent for the service." He went on then, hastily describing his financial arrangement with Welch.

The priest nodded. "One more question, Doctor. How much did you charge Ramón Archuleta when you delivered his wife's baby?"

"Twenty-five dollars," Eliot answered. "I was there all night and I had to make five calls after the baby came. Why, Father?"

"Because"—Father Revelet spoke slowly— "Welch gave Ramón your bill and it was for fifty dollars. Because every bill you have given to Welch and Company has been doubled at least, sometimes more than doubled. That is why these people mistrust you, my son. You have told them your charge and then the bill has come in for greater amounts, and Welch is a merciless collector. If his accounts are not paid he charges twelve per cent a month interest. He—— Where are you going, Doctor?"

Eliot Carey's brown eyes were almost hidden by his slitted eyelids. His mouth was a hard straight line in his brown face. "I'm going to Welch's store," he said thinly and, turning from the priest, strode rapidly back along the street. Father Revelet took

Trigger Vengeance

two steps after the doctor and then stopped, his troubled eyes continuing the pursuit.

Dr Carey, reaching Welch's store, strode straight through until he came to the office. There were men in the office talking with Allan Welch, but Eliot took no heed of them. Eyes blazing, he confronted Welch.

"What do you mean, Welch?" demanded Dr Carey. "What do you mean by taking my bills and doubling them when you put them on your accounts? I'll have an explanation of this!"

Allan Welch's face paled. Here were Sheriff John Mason and Prosecutor Sam Thomas come over from Feather Springs, brought to Soltura by Captain Irish's news concerning the epidemic. Unable to locate Dr Carey, they had come to Allan Welch, the big man of Soltura, to talk things over and decide what was best. And here this madman came raging into the office!

"Now, Doctor," said Welch placatingly. "You know that I was just trying to help you out."

"That's a lie!" Eliot snapped bluntly. "You've been using me to swindle these natives. I turn in a bill for twenty-five dollars and you double it. You've been charging twelve per cent a month interest on the bills you did not collect immediately. I thought you were offering me an accommodation. I thought you were honest and I find you about as low a cheat as ever lived!"

Welch was frightened. He did not know what this angry man across the desk from him might do. "It's business," he purred. "I bought those bills from you.

224

At Fuente Duro

You assigned them to me. You haven't a leg to stand on legally."

"I'll find out," promised Dr Carey grimly. "I'll find out, and in the meantime, if you try, if you even mention collecting one of my bills, I'll have personal satisfaction from you. Understand?"

He did not wait for Welch's reply but, turning, stalked out of the office. John Mason followed him out, but Sam Thomas, little eyes twinkling behind his glasses, walked over to the desk and, placing one plump leg across the edge of the desk, perched there like a small pudgy bird.

"What's all this, Allan?" questioned Sam Thomas.

Welch thought rapidly. "An agreement I had with Doctor Carey," he said, assuming an injured tone. "He was in financial difficulties and I suggested that as we did more or less of a banking business here he could assign some of his accounts to us and we would advance him money and collect the account. It's legal, Mr Thomas, entirely legal. I assure you——"

Sam Thomas' smile was gentle and benign. "Of course it's legal, Allan." The prosecutor's voice was comforting. "Entirely legal. The doctor hasn't a leg to stand on, just as you say."

Welch took confidence from the man's tone. "We have made it a practice to add a small interest charge for handling the accounts," he said smoothly. "We can't carry these people for nothing. Money costs us money, you know."

Thomas nodded. "But hardly twelve per cent a month," he said softly. "Hardly that much. That's usury, you know, and the law forbids usury. I know that Doctor Carey has no grounds to proceed against you but there might be some others, eh, Allan? Some of these people that have had to pay usury. I believe I'll just look into the matter. You won't mind, will you?"

Thomas took his plump leg from the edge of the desk and stood on his feet. More than ever he looked like a plump bird. He smiled at Allan Welch and, humming a little tune, adjusted his hat and walked on out of the office.

Welch watched him go. For a long time after the lawyer had departed Allan Welch sat there, then heavily he got up from his big chair and, picking up his hat, started toward the door. At the door Laban Benedict, hurrying forward, intercepted him. "Mr Welch," he said, "there's a matter here—— Why, what's wrong?"

"I'm going home," Allan Welch said, his voice low. "I don't feel well, Laban. I'm going home. And, Laban——"

"Yes, Mr Welch?"

"Never mind," said Allan Welch. "I'm going home, Laban," and he walked on, leaving Laban Benedict to stare curiously after him.

Allan Welch plodded up the hill, his mind filled with mixed emotions: chagrin, fear, hatred, hatred particularly toward Eliot Carey. As he opened the door of his own big house his wife came down the stairs.

"I was going to send for you, Papa," Mrs Welch

announced, seeing her husband. "I've put Emma to bed. She has a sore throat and the back of her neck hurts and she doesn't feel well. Do you think I'd better send for Doctor Carey?"

"No!" Welch almost shouted the word. "I don't want that ingrate in my house. I won't have him, do you understand?"

Mrs Welch recoiled before the outburst. When Welch calmed she spoke again, her voice mild but stubborn. "But Emma's sick, Papa. With all this diphtheria around I'm afraid——"

"Send for Doctor Weede at Feather Springs then," snapped Welch. "And don't bother me with these things. I've got business to think of."

Business! That had been the taboo of Allan Welch's home. When Welch had business to consider, the family walked softly and did not interrupt his thoughts.

Mrs Welch said, "Yes, Papa," and went back up the stairs, and her husband, placing his hat on the hall tree, went into his study and closed the door behind him.

CHAPTER XVI

The Doctor Finds His Fight

CAPTAIN IRISH came back to Soltura late that night. He had left his team in Feather Springs, changing horses there, and he was weary from the long trip but he brought news. Denver had replied to Eliot's telegram saying that there was no supply of antitoxin there, but Kansas City had answered with the assurance that they were shipping immediately. Irish had made arrangements to have the serum brought to Soltura as soon as it arrived. He had also spoken to Dr Weede at Feather Springs, but his report on Weede was not encouraging.

"Weede's drunk, as usual," Irish said, sitting in the surgery, with Janice, John Mason, Sam Thomas and Eliot Carey gathered about him. "He wouldn't be any help here and I didn't ask him to come. I got what absorbent cotton he had and brought it over. It's there in that bundle, Doctor."

"Thank you," Eliot said. "Then we can expect

the antitoxin day after tomorrow, can't we? It will be a relief when that gets here. I tell you, gentlemen, we can save some cases with the treatment I'm using. It's good and it has been used for years; but this new therapy, this serum treatment for disease, saves lives that otherwise we would lose."

John Mason nodded. Through the evening he had been helping Dr Carey, organizing and installing a system in the town. There were five deputy sheriffs in Soltura now, men whose duty it was to see that no one broke quarantine. Sam Thomas had been busy, too, but in another field. Thomas at the moment looked like a plump canary that had frightened away a cat. Despite the seriousness of the situation, Thomas was cheerful.

"I think we can hold our ground," Dr Carey said thoughtfully. "If we can keep these sick people from getting any worse, and if we can find any new cases that develop at once we can hold on until the antitoxin gets here. We may lose some even with the antitoxin—it isn't perfect—but it gives a two-to-one chance to live, where without it there are three chances in ten of dying."

Mason stretched and yawned. "I'm going to turn in," he said. "Ben Fry is looking after things tonight. I reckon he won't let anybody break their quarantine. María's made me down a bed in the kitchen and I'm going to use it. Good night, all."

The sheriff's boot heels thumped on the worn carpet of the hall as he went toward the kitchen and Eliot turned to Laurence Irish. "I wish you would stay here tonight, Captain Irish," he said. "You could use Doctor Zeitletz' room."

"Why don't you, Captain?" Janice seconded Eliot's words. "I can go to Welch's. You'll take me up there, won't you, Mr Thomas?"

"I'll be delighted, Miss Janice," Thomas answered gallantly. "But I don't think I'll go in." He chuckled as though he remembered some good joke. "No, I don't think I'll go in," he repeated.

"I am tired," Captain Irish admitted. "If you'll go right to Welch's, Janice, and not try to nurse one of these sick people I think I'll accept Doctor Carey's offer. You look as though you could use some sleep yourself, Doctor."

"I'll go with Miss Irish to Welch's," Eliot answered. "Then I can come back. I want to drop in at Vigil's and at Con Abeyta's. Miss McKenzie is at Vigil's and Father Revelet at Abeyta's and I should see them."

"They can perfectly well look after things," Janice interposed. "And I don't intend having you take me to the Welches'. Mr Thomas will do that. You're tired, Doctor. You should get some rest. After all, we'd be lost if you weren't able to look after things."

"I'm stopping at Mrs Maybe's," Thomas seconded. "I can take Miss Janice to Welch's and then go on to my bed. There's no need of your coming, Doctor."

And so it was arranged. Eliot showed Captain Irish to Dr Zeitletz' room, lit the lamp and left the captain there. Janice Irish, face bright and eyes

The Doctor Finds His Fight

eager, was with Sam Thomas in the hall when Eliot returned from seeing that the captain was comfortable. They were ready to leave and Eliot took them to the door, standing in the opening and watching them as they went down the walk. When they had passed through the gate he closed the door and went back into the surgery.

He could not relax. There were too many things to consider, too much for him to think about for his nerves to release their tension. Eliot sat down at the desk and stared blankly before him. He realized— how well he realized—his youth and inexperience, his gullibility and his lack of knowledge. Here he was with sickness all about him and the people of Soltura trusting him, their lives in his hands. The thought awed the young doctor. He was frightened, frightened at the enormity of the task. So far one man had died in Soltura. There had been no chance to save Abrán Fernandez. How many others would die? How many of these people could an older, more experienced man save? The young doctor placed his arms upon the desk and lowered his head. What a task this was! Was he big enough to meet it? It seemed to Eliot Carey that he was not. For the first time in his experience he realized the fact that a doctor stands alone, that his is the decision that may make the difference between life and death, that living lies in his hands. And he knew so little, so pitifully little! He was so woefully inadequate.

"Doctor!" Janice Irish was in the doorway of the surgery. "Doctor!"

Trigger Vengeance

Eliot lifted his head.

"Emma Welch." Janice's voice showed her concern. "She's ill. She has diphtheria, Doctor!"

It took but a moment for Dr Carey to don overcoat and hat and pick up his bag. Then, with Janice hurrying along beside him, he left the house. As they walked swiftly toward Welch's Janice told Eliot her experience.

"Mr Thomas took me to Welch's," she said. "Mrs Welch met me at the door. She said that Emma wasn't feeling well and that she would put me in the room next to Emma's. Mr Welch wasn't there. Mrs Welch said that he had gone out. We went upstairs and I opened Emma's door to speak to her. Her voice sounded as though she were ill and I went in with a lamp. I asked her to let me see her throat, and it was red, Doctor, and there were little white splotches on the sides. Mrs Welch told me that they had sent to Feather Springs for Doctor Weede and that he would be here tomorrow but she was frightened. I asked her to let me get you and she told me to go."

Eliot listened silently to the recital, hurrying the girl along, his hand under her arm. He could appreciate why Dr Weede had been called. It was natural, in view of what had happened, that Allan Welch would not send for Eliot Carey. But the thought of refusing the call did not enter Eliot's mind. He was a doctor and personal likes and dislikes had no place in the business of attending the sick.

The Doctor Finds His Fight

Mrs Welch was waiting for them in the hall when they arrived and gestured for silence. "Mr Welch has come home and is sleeping," she whispered. "This way, Doctor."

Eliot followed the stout woman up the stairs, Janice walking beside him. In Emma Welch's room the doctor put down his grip and removed his coat. Emma, her cheeks flushed, looked up at him from the bed.

"I'm not sick, Doctor," she said. "Janice insisted that I call you."

Mrs Welch had placed a chair beside the bed and, seating himself, Eliot took out his watch and possessed himself of Emma's wrist. "May I have a glass of water and a spoon?" he asked.

Mrs Welch hurried away and Eliot counted the girl's pulse. Already it was becoming thready and rapid. He took Emma's temperature when Mrs Welch returned and then, using the spoon handle for a tongue depressor, examined Emma's throat. It was red and, as Janice had said, there were small white patches appearing on the pillars. Eliot's eyes showed his concern as he reached for his grip.

"How do you feel, Miss Welch?" he asked.

"The back of my neck hurts," Emma answered petulantly. "It's just a headache, Doctor. What are you doing? What——" The sentence broke off with a cough.

Dr Carey was twisting cotton about the end of a swab stick. He took up a bottle of the bichloride solution, dipped in the swab and held it poised.

"Now, Miss Welch," he said, "if you will open your mouth——"

"It's diphtheria!" Emma's voice rose almost to a shriek. "I've got diphtheria. I'll die. I know I'll die!" She struggled against Eliot's hand, knocking the swab away.

Eliot tried to calm the frightened girl. "This won't do," he said brusquely. "I'm trying to help you, Miss Welch. I'm trying to keep you from being sick."

Janice Irish's strong hands rested upon Emma's shoulders and pushed the struggling girl back upon the pillows. "Emma"—Janice's voice was calm and cheerful—"you're acting like a baby. The doctor wants to help you, dear. Lie back and be quiet now."

Gradually, under Janice's chiding, Emma Welch relaxed. She allowed Eliot Carey to apply the solution to her throat, whimpering a little when the swab was removed and lying back on the pillow, her eyes closed. Beside the door Mrs Welch, face pale, was sobbing audibly. Eliot looked at Janice Irish. There was no need to expect help from Mrs Welch.

"I'll stay here and look after her." Janice answered the doctor's look.

Eliot got up from the chair and went to the door. Janice followed him. Outside the sick room, in the hall, the two stopped and talked low voiced.

"You must swab her throat every half-hour," Dr Carey directed. "Keep her warm. There should be some air in that room; it's stuffy.

"You're going to have trouble here, Miss Irish.

The Doctor Finds His Fight

They don't want me for a doctor or I would stay, but we can't wait until Weede gets here. That's a bad throat now. No telling what it might be by morning."

Janice nodded. "I think you——" she began.

"You know what to do about the dishes and any utensils she uses," Eliot interrupted. "I've left a bottle of solution and some swabs and cotton. She's frightened. That makes it bad. And I'm afraid that Mrs Welch will not be much help," he added ruefully.

"I can look after her," Janice said confidently.

"You must be careful," Eliot emphasized. "When you swab her throat you had better tie a handkerchief across your mouth and nose. Don't let her struggle or become hysterical and so waste her strength. She's going to need it all." The doctor proceeded then, outlining diet and giving further directions. When he had finished Janice Irish nodded her understanding.

"I don't like to leave you here," Eliot said. "I don't—— You will be careful, won't you?"

"Surely, Doctor." Janice smiled. "You must not worry about me."

"I'll have someone here to relieve you in the morning," Eliot promised. "If she gets worse during the night, or before Doctor Weede comes, you will call me, won't you?"

Janice promised and, bidding the girl good night, Eliot collected his belongings and went on down the stairs and out of the house. Janice went back into Emma's room.

Trigger Vengeance

The two girls had been friends for years. Not intimate friends but casual, speaking, playing together as youngsters, later meeting at Soltura's few social gatherings. Mrs Welch was beside the bed talking to Emma, her voice high and excited. With difficulty Janice got the large woman from the room, telling her that she must rest for Emma's sake and that she would be called if she was needed. Mrs Welch left, still protesting against her expulsion, and Janice, glancing at the watch pinned to her shirtwaist, proceeded to swab her patient's throat again.

When she had finished that task she placed the bottle of solution on Emma's dresser and sat down beside the bed. The girl on the bed lay quiet, her eyes closed. Presently Emma opened her eyes. "I'm going to die," she said calmly.

"Nonsense," Janice snapped. "You're going to get well. Doctor Carey says you have every chance."

Emma closed her eyes again and was still for so long a time that Janice thought she slept. But Emma was not asleep. "No," she said after a time. "I won't get well. Do you love Doctor Carey, Janice?"

Janice Irish flushed. "No," she answered, not knowing whether or not she told the truth.

"I do." Emma's weak voice was musing. "I love him. I took him some money so that I would attract his attention and I've thrown myself in his way every chance I had. He doesn't care a thing about me."

"Of course the doctor likes you." Janice refuted the words.

"Maybe he likes me," Emma admitted. "I want

him to love me. That's why I'm sick, Janice. On his account and because of you. Doctor Carey loves you."

"No, he doesn't," Janice said cheerfully. "He wouldn't look twice at me if it weren't for the captain. He likes the captain. What makes you think he loves me, Emma?"

"Because"—Emma's voice was dreamy—"I tried to give him some money for Abrán Fernandez. He told me that they didn't need money, that they needed someone to nurse them. He said that you were down there nursing. That was why I went. I was jealous of you."

The dreamy voice lapsed and Janice Irish sat staring at Emma's face, pallid and with spots of color on either cheek. Emma's breath came more evenly and the girl seemed to be asleep. Janice Irish, relaxing in her chair, let her mind wander from the present; wander back to a day that seemed long ago when she had driven with her father in a buggy from the depot to Feather Springs, a young, brown-bearded man riding behind them; to the time she had held a threshing black-and-white head while Eliot Carey and Littlebit Mann grunted and tugged and set a horse's leg; back through the months, each touched with some high spot, some marked day or hour when she had been with Eliot Carey. Emma said that Eliot was in love with her. Janice remembered the solicitude in his voice as he cautioned her, remembered the strength of his hand as it gripped her arm. The color on her cheeks suddenly matched that of Emma Welch resting on her bed.

Dr Carey, leaving Welch's house, paused at the end of the walk and, turning, looked up at a dimly lighted window. He had not wanted to leave Janice Irish in the house, had not wanted to leave her with Emma Welch, to nurse Emma and run her chance of contagion. If Janice were to take diphtheria—— Eliot realized that all his world would come tumbling down without Janice. He wanted her, wanted her desperately, wanted her soft warmth in his arms, wanted her shining hair to touch his cheek, her lips against his lips. He took a step back toward the house and from the darkness at the corner of the lot came a cheerful voice.

"Still at it, Doc?" Ben Fry lounged up the walk toward him, his hand ruffling against the pickets of the fence.

"Still at it, Ben," answered Dr Carey, turning.

"Somebody sick here?" asked Fry.

"Miss Welch," Eliot answered.

"That's tough." Ben Fry spoke meditatively. "Diphtheria don't go around respectin' folks, does it, Doc? Seems to kind of take 'em as they come, diphtheria does; the little ones and the big ones too."

"It seems that way, Ben," Eliot agreed quietly.

"Well," said Ben Fry, "you better go on home an' get some sleep, Doc. You're likely to have a hard day tomorrow."

Eliot nodded. Tomorrow would be another day and a hard one. "Good night, Ben," he said.

The Doctor Finds His Fight

"Good night, Doc," answered Ben Fry.

Eliot went on down the walk, Ben Fry watching him go. When the doctor had disappeared into the night Ben Fry stared up at the lighted window. "I ain't sayin' it's right," Ben Fry commented half aloud. "I ain't sayin' it's right, you understand, but it sure seems like a judgment someway."

Dr Carey was up at six the next morning, called to Con Abeyta's where the youngest child was very ill. He watched that baby die and could not remain because of another urgent call. From house to house he hurried, doing what he could and lending strength to weary women and frightened men. It was the women, Eliot found, who had the strength. The men gave up; they saw their young ones ill, almost at the point of death, and they stopped fighting. The mothers, frightened, worried, worked until it seemed they could work no more, forced a smile for the doctor and for the patient and went to work again. The women: they were the ones that kept fighting, that refused to count the battle lost.

At ten o'clock Dr Carey managed to snatch a hasty meal and by noon, having made the rounds and learning from John Mason and from Father Revelet that there were no new cases, he relaxed a trifle. But at two o'clock he was called to Welch's. Dr Weede had not come from Feather Springs.

He found Welch there when he came, a bitter-faced, scornful man who would not speak and who turned his head away when the doctor came through the door. Not so Mrs Welch. She was weeping and she hurried Eliot up the stairs, intermingling her panting with sobs.

"Papa wouldn't let me send for you this morning," she said when they reached the top of the stairs. "He thought that Doctor Weede would be here, but he didn't come and I just said we had to have you. Emma's worse, Doctor. She's a lot worse. She——"

"We'll see, Mrs Welch." Eliot forced cheerfulness into his voice. "You stay out here and I'll go in and look after your daughter. Perhaps you just think that she is worse. She may be much improved."

He left Mrs Welch at the door and went across Emma's room to the bed. Janice Irish came to meet him, her face drawn from lack of sleep, and when Eliot looked questioningly at her the girl shook her head. Eliot did not ask questions but sat down beside the bed and took Emma's pulse. It was weaker, more threadlike and very rapid. The girl did not open her eyes until Eliot asked to see her throat, and then when she did open them they held no recognition for Dr Carey. Eliot shook his head when he examined the girl's throat. The membrane was spreading down toward the larynx and the passage was closing. Still he forced cheerfulness into his voice when he reported to Mrs Welch.

"She isn't getting along very well," he said honestly, "but we can make a fight for it, Mrs Welch. We must pull her through." Mrs Welch brightened at the doctor's words and Eliot went on.

"Can you stay with her today?" he asked. "Miss

The Doctor Finds His Fight

Irish must get some rest. She can show you what to do."

"Yes." Welch's wife was eager. "I've wanted to nurse Emma. I want to be with her. I'll stay with her, Doctor."

"That's fine then," Eliot said.

Janice followed him out into the hall. "She's much worse, isn't she?" the girl asked, low voiced so that the mother could not hear.

Eliot nodded.

"You'll have to send someone else to help," Janice went on. "Mrs Welch means to do things exactly right but she fusses at Emma and hangs over her and won't let her rest. Emma slept awhile early this morning."

"I'll get someone else up here," Eliot promised. "You must get some rest, Janice. You ought not to stay here."

"Father came this morning and tried to get me to leave." Janice Irish smiled faintly. "I wouldn't go. I'll stay, Doctor. I'll lie down when you have sent someone to stay with Emma but I won't leave."

Eliot nodded.

"Is there anything else that we can do?" Janice asked.

"We can give her a stimulant if her heart begins to fail," Eliot answered. "That and swabbing her throat and keeping her warm. That's all we can do now."

"If only——" Janice began.

"If only the antitoxin were here," Eliot completed. "That would give her more chance. It will be here tomorrow. Perhaps——"

He did not finish the sentence. He did not believe that Emma Welch would be alive tomorrow.

"If her throat begins to close, call me," he directed after an instant's pause. "The membrane is spreading to the larynx and we may have to open her throat. I'll go now, Janice." Unconsciously he used the girl's first name. "There are some others that are waiting for me. You'll call me if her breathing gets worse?"

Janice nodded and Eliot went on down the stairs.

He was busy throughout the day. Father Revelet promised to see that someone was sent to take Janice's place at Welch's during the day. Eliot called upon the patients he had not seen in the morning and repeated his calls upon those who needed him most. There were twenty-two cases of diphtheria in Soltura, all needing constant attention. In addition to the other work a man in Canyon Largo had been inconsiderate enough to break a leg. His brother brought him to town and, between calls on the diphtheria cases, Eliot set the leg, the little surgery filled with the odor of chloroform and the brother standing by, sweat upon his forehead.

At nine that night Eliot was called to the Welches' again. Courtland let him in the door and silently followed him up the stairs. Janice Irish, Welch and Mrs Welch were in Emma's room and Eliot could hear the girl gasping for breath as he mounted the stairs. When he reached Emma's bedside he saw that she was far gone. Her face was suffused and she was choking. Eliot had to act instantly, had to decide and act upon his decision. There was no time for surgical cleanliness, no time to do anything but what he did.

From his bag Eliot removed the intubation set, carried against just this need since the outbreak of the epidemic. Selecting a tube from one of the six in the gauze packet, he tied a string, also from the packet, about the top of the tube and fitted a handle. Now he was ready. The mouth gag from the set was put in place and carefully Dr Carey inserted the tube into Emma's throat, working deftly, gently and rapidly. As the throat was opened by the silver tube the girl's breathing became less strained, easier and not so audible. Eliot removed the gag, straightened and stood up, holding his hands away from his sides.

"I'd like hot water and a wash basin," he requested.

Mrs Welch padded away, to return bringing the basin of water, and Dr Carey scrubbed his hands, using blue surgical soap. He dried them on a towel, sat down again and reached for Emma Welch's wrist.

"Now we'll see," said Dr Carey.

Emma's pulse was a bare thread under his fingers. He called for water, dissolved a pill in a spoonful that he boiled over the lamp and, filling his hypodermic syringe, administered a stimulant. Then he waited for the pulse to become stronger. Through all this Janice had worked beside him, her hands supplementing his, her shoulder touching against the doctor's own. Eliot had not noticed before but now he was keenly aware of the girl's presence. Her eyes questioned him and he shook his head. "I can't tell," he said briefly, forgetting that they were not alone in the room. "It may work; it may not. If only we had the antitoxin!"

He was silent for a long minute. Beside the door Mrs Welch sobbed quietly, her head on her husband's shoulder. Welch himself, his arm awkwardly placed half around his wife, stared at the bed, not seeing it or the doctor or Janice Irish. In Eliot's fingers Emma's wrist was lax. He felt the feeble touch of her pulse grow more faint. The breathing through the tube was more shallow. Releasing the wrist, Eliot reached again for the hypodermic syringe. The stimulant was not holding the girl. Once more he prepared a charge for the hypodermic, bent down, lifted the girl's arm and then slowly replaced it on the covers. There was no need for a stimulant, no need for anything.

"Is she——" Janice began.

Eliot nodded. Beside the door Mrs Welch screamed once—sharp, high, agonized. Welch, his arm tightening, led his wife out into the hall. They could hear her sobbing as her husband took her to another room.

For some time neither the doctor nor Janice spoke. Then Eliot, his voice harsh and filled with fatigue, broke the silence. "I couldn't save her," he said. "I tried——"

The Doctor Finds His Fight

"Of course you tried." Janice tried to reassure the weary man. "Of course you did, Doctor."

Eliot did not hear her. He went on, not talking to the girl but voicing the thing that filled his mind. "I thought that I could stay here," he said. "I thought that I could help these people. I was going to beat ignorance and filth and superstition and I can't save a girl's life. I've failed."

Janice Irish put her hand on the doctor's shoulder. "You're tired," she said, compassion in her voice. "You haven't failed. You're just tired."

The doctor became aware of the girl, of the hand resting so lightly and yet so strongly upon his shoulder. He reached up and covered that hand with his own. "You are kind, Janice," he said. "I'd dreamed of what I could do here. Remember when you told me that if you were a doctor you would find something that needed to be changed and that you would fight to change it? Remember?"

"Yes." The girl's voice was soft.

"I thought I'd found it here," Eliot continued. "I thought that I could help these people. I've failed. I can't beat death. I can't."

Under the doctor's hand that other hand, soft and warm and supple, turned until it was palm uppermost. The fingers closed around Dr Carey's fingers, a strong, reassuring pressure. "You can try," Janice Irish said softly. "You can try, Eliot. I . . . I'll help you if I may."

Eliot Carey made no movement. The hand under his own stirred, shifting as though to ask release.

Trigger Vengeance

Dr Carey turned his head and looked up into blue eyes, tear filled now. "I love you, Janice," he said simply. "You know . . . ?"

Janice Irish bent her shining head and swiftly, light as the touch of a butterfly upon a flower, her lips touched the doctor's cheek. "I know," she whispered.

The girl straightened, withdrew her hand from beneath the doctor's. Mrs Welch's sobs came from the hallway, muffled by intervening space and walls. Welch's voice sounded as he tried to comfort his wife. Eliot got up and turned toward Janice. The girl had retreated until she was at the door, her face flushed, her eyes wide at the miracle that had been done in that room of death.

"I must go to Mrs Welch," she said hurriedly. "She needs me. I must go. You——"

"You must go," Eliot agreed quietly. "And I must go." There was strength in the man's voice again. "But you won't forget this, Janice? You weren't just sorry for me?"

"No." The girl was breathless. "No, I wasn't just sorry. I—— Oh, I must go." She turned and fled through the door.

Eliot Carey turning from the door looked down at the other girl upon the bed. He bent down and with the string removed the tube from her throat. It might be needed again in this fight that had just begun. He wrapped the tubes and the set in a towel and placed them in his bag, closed it, and then, standing beside the bed, reached down and gently covered Emma Welch's quiet face. There was nothing more that he could do for Emma Welch, nothing that he could ever have done for her; but there were others waiting, others that needed him and that he could help. Eliot Carey picked up his grip, took his hat and coat from a chair and, on tiptoe, as though he might disturb the dead, left the room. There was a fight in Soltura that needed him. He had lost ground—but he would not lose the fight.

CHAPTER XVII

Kill to Cure

LITTLEBIT MANN, riding hard, pressing Calico along over the rutted road from Feather Springs, brought the diphtheria antitoxin. Littlebit came in at ten o'clock in the morning, having made the distance from the railroad in less than three hours. Calico was wringing wet and stood swaying on widespread legs while Littlebit, at a stumbling, pigeon-toed run, carried his precious package up the walk to Eliot Carey. Littlebit thrust the parcel into Eliot Carey's waiting hands and, like the horse, stood swaying, legs spread to hold him up, while Dr Carey ripped away the wrappings. It was there, the small boxes that contained bottles of an innocuous-appearing lifesaving liquid. Armed with that fluid and his hypodermic syringe, Dr Carey sallied forth to do battle.

He had trouble. He was forced to call upon Father Revelet to help him, to stand by and give reassurance while the doctor cleaned a small brown back or

Kill to Cure

belly with alcohol and picked up a fold of skin, slipping the beneficent needle under the skin and pressing home the plunger. Father Revelet scolded and commanded and quieted crying children who choked and coughed even while they cried. Father Revelet was stern with frightened men and women who would have resisted the dose.

By one o'clock Dr Carey had made the rounds, administering the antitoxin, and almost at once the magic of that colorless fluid began to be felt. Eliot had hardly returned to his white house, had barely called cheerfully to María telling her that he was at home again, before Con Abeyta was on the porch, bowing, scraping, grinning and with the word that his boy was feeling better. Five times during his hasty luncheon Dr Carey got up from the table to go to the door and assure some smiling father that there was no need to give another dose of *la medicina* as yet; that there was plenty of *la medicina* and he would come and give more if it were needed.

The diphtheria antitoxin took hold of Soltura and, as the inoculations began to take effect, Soltura took hold of herself. The danger was not over, the epidemic was not finished. There might yet be new cases, there might yet be deaths, but Soltura gained confidence. Soltura had fresh ammunition in the battle, ammunition that would shoot home and deal a death blow to those little club-shaped rods that stole so stealthily from throat to throat and choked and burned and brought death. The tenseness lifted from Soltura and men began to move about once more, and women, thrusting their heads from quarantined houses, called cheerfully to their neighbors.

"Juanito está bueno, gracias a Dios," they called. Or, *"Como está Rosa?"* and the answer: *"Bien. Bien, gracias."* Only in Welch's house up on the hill, and in Welch's store, and in Jack Brannigan's saloon did the tension remain.

In Welch's house Mrs Welch sat and sobbed, her son Courtland beside her, trying to comfort her, while in a casket from the storeroom of the warehouse Emma Welch lay white and quiet and waiting. In the store Allan Welch, hat pulled down over his eyes, sat in his office and stared wearily at his desk, the thoughts running around and around in his mind like a toy train on a circular track. Emma, his pride and his joy, was dead. Emma was dead, was dead, was dead. And he had killed her. He had written a letter. He had written a letter when he should have sent a telegram, and that quick decision had cost him his daughter. There was no doubt in Welch's mind, his wife had left him no doubt. Somehow Mrs Welch had learned of the letter and the time consumed. She had risen up, her voice high and hysterical, and before her accusation her husband had fled.

In Brannigan's saloon John Mason talked quietly to Sid Raupert. "You'll get the reward all right," Mason said and could not hide his contempt. "You'll get the money, Sid, but you're through working for me. I made you a deputy because Welch asked me to. You can turn in your star now and your commission." And John Mason held out his hand.

Kill to Cure

Sid Raupert, his eyes burning behind their narrowed lids, looked to right and left and saw that there was no one with him. Even Jack Brannigan, behind his bar, polished a whisky glass and refused to meet Raupert's look. Slowly Sid Raupert unpinned his deputy's star and placed it in Mason's waiting hand.

"You killed Lackey," said Mason, pocketing the star, "and you brought him in. The reward was dead or alive and you'll get your money. Where would you want it sent, Sid?"

Once more Sid Raupert looked about him. In the eyes of the men that gathered around, in Littlebit's eyes and in Ben Fry's and Lem Calder's and Laramie Jones's, he read the thing that he had heard from John Mason's lips. He was done in Soltura, through, finished, dismissed and ordered to leave.

"I'll let you know, Mason," Sid Raupert said hoarsely. "I'll write and tell you where to send it. Set me out a drink, Jack."

Silently Jack Brannigan shoved out a glass and a bar bottle, and Raupert poured his drink while Mason and the others drew away, giving him space to drink alone.

"I wouldn't wait, Sid, if I was you," John Mason said, moving toward the door. "No, I wouldn't wait to go."

Raupert drank his whisky and made no answer, and John Mason and the rest filed out of Brannigan's.

"Damn them!" Raupert swore when they were

gone. "Damn them! I brought in Lackey, didn't I? Hell, they didn't have the guts to go an' get him. They weren't smart enough. They——"

Jack Brannigan came around the end of the bar carrying a broom. "I'm going to sweep out, Sid," Brannigan said. "I'll make a lot of dust. Maybe you'd find it better outside."

In Welch's store, where the owner sat so still, Laban Benedict moved behind the high desk which held the books. Laban had cleaned the desk drawers of his personal possessions and now, with his sleeve protectors and his thin alpaca office coat bundled under his arm, he came to Welch.

"I'm leaving, Mr Welch," said Laban firmly. "I'm going to move. Sam Thomas has been talking to Ramón Archuleta and Con Abeyta and some of the families in Canyon Largo and at Rinconcito. He was out yesterday and this morning. I hear he's going to start suit against you for charging usury. I think I'll leave. I took what money was coming to me from the till. Good-by."

Laban Benedict tramped off, a just man, an elder in the church. Allan Welch did not lift his head. The ship of Welch and Company was sinking. It was natural that the rats should leave it. Sam Thomas was starting suit for usury, and when the word spread out the wholesalers would come, demanding their money, and the whole vast structure that he had built so laboriously would go down in a sea of lawsuits and assignments and scorn and hatred. And Emma

Kill to Cure

was dead, and Courtland and Cathrine were leaving for the East, going to Cathrine's sister Agusta. Courtland had told him so, standing straight and scornful and brave. Courtland, who had always been afraid of his father! They were leaving after the funeral, hiring a buggy from Ben Fry's livery to drive them to Feather Springs and the railroad.

Welch lifted his head. It was all because of that young doctor. All because of Eliot Carey! Rage against Eliot Carey burned in Allan Welch's brain. He would settle with that upstart. He would——— But he dared not. He could not. The men who obeyed his commands were gone and he was alone. Slowly Allan Welch got up from his chair and crossed to the safe. Opening it, he searched within and brought out a bottle, the small bottle that, so long ago, he had carried to Brannigan's saloon. The black letters on the label spelled, "Chloral Hydrate," and some of the fluid had run down across the letters, making a stain.

There was perhaps an ounce or two of liquid left in the bottle. It didn't take much. Not a great deal. A man went to sleep, just as Tray Barry had gone to sleep, and he slept and slept the while his heart beat more and more slowly, and finally stopped. After the funeral, after Emma was laid in the ground and the dirt thrown over her coffin, after Courtland and Cathrine had driven away in their hired buggy, there would be solace in the bottle. Solace and consolation. It was a temptation not to wait, a temptation to lift the bottle and drink and sink away into sleep. Allan Welch put the bottle back into the safe. He would wait until they were gone, wait until Emma was hidden under the brown earth. And then . . . and then the little bottle would be waiting to soothe and shield him. But now it was time to go to the funeral.

Eliot Carey rode back from the cemetery with Laurence Irish and Janice. They were quiet as they rode. Janice's eyes were bright with unshed tears but under the lap robe her hand was tight in Eliot Carey's grasp. Captain Irish was aware of those clasped hands but said nothing, only looking at his daughter and the doctor with questioning blue eyes and then watching the road and paying attention to his driving. At the doctor's house he stopped the team to let Eliot alight. Laurence Irish and his daughter were going to the LS, but first they were to stop in town, for John Mason and Sam Thomas had asked the captain to meet them for a consultation. When Janice and her father had driven away, Eliot went into the house, removed his hat and coat and, hanging them on the hall tree, walked into the surgery.

Dr Carey was happy. He could still feel Janice's hand, warm in his own, and the touch of her shoulder against his as they rode in the buggy. And there was another reason for the doctor's well being: the effect that the antitoxin was having on the diphtheria cases.

At the desk in the surgery for the first time in

Kill to Cure

two weeks Dr Carey relaxed. His eyes were happy and his lips pursed to make a little tuneless whistle. María, hearing that whistle as she worked in the kitchen, smiled to herself.

The brown leather of a book cover caught the doctor's eye and he reached out a hand and lifted the book. Janice had asked him to read in Fritz Zeitletz' diary something that she had found there. Janice! How lovely she was. How strange she was. How she could strengthen a man and how she would cleave to him!

The place was marked and Eliot opened the book. He glanced at the entry and the date and saw, just as Janice had seen, that Dr Zeitletz had alternated his entries, using first German and then English as a medium for his thoughts. But where Janice Irish had been unable to read the Germanic script, Eliot Carey could read it as easily as the English. A young doctor doing postgraduate work in Vienna would be lost unless he could read and write and speak German. Reading the first entry, Eliot wondered what it was that the girl had wished him to see. There was nothing unusual in the things that Dr Zeitletz had recorded. But the opposing page was different. The opposing page was in English and Eliot Carey read it through, read the story of Fritz Zeitletz' visit to Tray Barry at Brannigan's saloon, the words that Barry had said and the implication Zeitletz had drawn from them. Hastily Eliot turned to the next entry.

Here, hidden from Janice Irish but plain to Eliot,

was the answer to a question. Dr Zeitletz, in meticulous German script, had recorded facts. Sid Raupert, he wrote, had called upon him. Raupert had threatened, telling the doctor that if he spoke of what Tray Barry uttered in his ravings he would be killed. Eliot, translating freely, might have written as an interpretation:

"Raupert believes that I know he killed Carl Jacks. He threatens me with death if I speak of what I know. I ordered him out of my home, telling him that a doctor does not violate the confidences of a patient, even when those confidences are uttered by a delirious man. Raupert means to kill me if he dares. He does not know that Nature will save him the trouble."

Dr Carey read no further. Was this the answer to Fritz Zeitletz' murder? He must learn one more thing and then he would know. Decisively he closed the leather book, got up and, putting on his outer wraps, left the house. María heard the door close and sighed resignedly. She must keep the supper warm in the oven and it would not be good. Her doctor had gone out again.

At Fry's livery barn Dr Carey found Ben Fry cleaning the alleyway between the stalls. Ben greeted the doctor cheerfully when he came in. "Hello, Doc. Want your team?"

"No, Ben," Eliot answered, his voice strained. "Not the team this time. I want some information."

Ben Fry liked the young doctor. "It's yours if I've got it," he said.

Kill to Cure

"Who was in the posse that day up at Roybal Canyon?" Eliot asked. "I'd like to know, Ben."

Fry scratched his head. It was an odd question for Dr Carey to ask. Still there was no telling about the young doc. He was full of queer ideas. Some of them worked, though. "Why . . ." said Ben, "let's see, Doc." One by one he named the possemen, finishing with a question. "What's on your mind?"

"Not much," Eliot answered shortly. "Where were those men, Ben? Can you tell me?"

"I reckon I can," Fry answered. "I was on the left end of the line. Raupert was with me—— No, he went back to get his cartridges off his saddle. He'd left 'em. I didn't see him after that. You see, Doc Zeitletz come up an' learned about John an' went out to get him. They shot Doc from the cabin an' the whole thing blew up. The boys lost their heads an' charged the cabin after I'd yelled that Doc was hit. They all went haywire. It's a wonder some of 'em didn't get it."

"But where were the men, Ben?" Eliot persisted quietly. "Do you remember?"

"Sure," Ben Fry answered. "I won't never forget that fight. I've been in some before that but I won't forget that one. I was in this brush pile, see?" Ben Fry bent down and, using the stiff butt of a straw, began to trace a map in the chaff that lay on the floor. Eliot squatted beside him. "Doc went up this gully," said Ben Fry. "John was layin' behind a pile of posts right at the edge of the gully. Doc got pretty near to him an' they let go from the cabin an' Doc went down. No, somebody over at the east end of the line let go first, an' they answered from the cabin, then we all took a shot. That was when Doc got it."

"Could they see into the gully from the east?" Eliot asked.

Ben Fry glanced up into the doctor's set face. "Why . . ." he said slowly, "no . . . no, I guess they couldn't. I could see Doc, an' they could see him from the cabin—anyhow, well enough to hit him—but I don't reckon the other boys could see him. They didn't know he'd been hit until I yelled."

"And you could see all the others?" Eliot insisted.

"Yeah," Fry agreed. "I could see 'em. They began to run in after I yelled that Doc was hit. Then Mark Neville an' them broke from the cabin an' made a run for their horses. I was all alone. I couldn't stop 'em. Sid Raupert come up behind me a minute later but he wasn't any help. They'd made the shed by then. Say, Doc, what are you gettin' at? What's stickin' in your craw? You don't think any of the boys hit Doc by mistake, do you? I was the only one that could have hit him an' I know damned well that I didn't!" There was a challenge in Fry's voice.

"No," Eliot said quietly. "You didn't hit him, Ben. I know that. Thanks." Dr Carey straightened, nodded to Ben Fry and without another word walked out of the livery barn.

Ben Fry likewise got up from where he squatted and, walking over to a bench beside the door, sat down. He selected a clean straw from a pile of hay, thrust it into his mouth and fell to chewing. "Now what do you reckon Doc asked all that for?" mused Ben Fry, staring at the hind quarters of a horse in a stall across the alleyway. "What's got into him? I wonder."

Dr Carey went directly back to his house from the livery barn. He went into the study, sat down at the desk and once more picked up Fritz Zeitletz' diary. Dr Zeitletz had written secrets there, things of which he would not speak. But, dead, Fritz Zeitletz had done a thing that, alive, he would have shunned. How well Eliot Carey remembered that night when he had first met John Mason and Sam Thomas and Judge Rutledge and the argument that had raged about the table. No, according to his own words, Dr Zeitletz would have kept the secrets of a murderer if they had been given to him during his practice of medicine.

But here, in this leather-covered book, was written the thing that had killed Dr Zeitletz; the knowledge that Zeitletz had gained while listening to the ravings of Tray Barry. And here, too, plainly was written the name of Fritz Zeitletz' murderer: Sid Raupert. Raupert had the incentive, Raupert had threatened, Raupert had had the opportunity. All unwittingly Ben Fry had told Eliot that last fact. There was no doubt in Eliot's mind: Sid Raupert had killed Fritz Zeitletz. But what should he do about it?

Of course there was an easy way out. He could take this diary and Ben Fry and go to John Mason.

Trigger Vengeance

That was the way of the law. The evidence was there and Eliot could place it in Mason's hands. But should he? Fritz Zeitletz had kept the secret and gone the way that had brought him his death. That was the path Zeitletz had chosen. Once more Eliot Carey opened the diary. In the light from the window, now growing less as dusk came to Soltura, Dr Carey read once more.

"Whatsoever things I see or hear . . ."

There was his answer. He, too, was bound by that oath, just as the man who had written the words was bound.

But he could not let this go, he could not wipe away the things he knew and let Sid Raupert go unpunished. All his years Eliot Carey had worshiped at the shrine of medicine. All his years he had believed that the greatest achievement of a man was to save life, and here he was confronted with a necessity, a condition that demanded that he wipe a life away. It was as though, in an operation, he had laid bare an ugly, livid, cancerous growth. It must be removed. Sid Raupert was the cancer and Soltura the body and he, Eliot Carey, was a physician. Dr Carey got up from the desk and decisively strode across the surgery and down the hall. In Fritz Zeitletz' room he found the instrument he sought: the heavy-barreled Schoyen-Ballard. Its walnut stock was satin smooth to his touch and the barrel was cool blue silk as he loaded the rifle. Then, with the Schuetzen rifle laid across his arm, Dr Carey left the house. He was searching for Sid Raupert.

Kill to Cure

There was another man in Soltura who wanted to find Sid Raupert, a man who had ridden in from the hills and who had tied his horse behind a building at the edge of town. Mark Neville came limping down the street as Eliot Carey walked along it.

And where was Sid Raupert? He sat upon a bench in front of Jack Brannigan's saloon, motionless, unwinking, his coat pulled about him and his shoulders hunched against the nip of the clear air. A sullen rage smoldered in Sid Raupert, a fire that burned slowly and hotly. He had come to the bench when Jack Brannigan began to sweep the saloon. Time had passed since then and Brannigan's lamps were lighted. They sent a bar of brilliance through the windows out into the dusk, stabbing the twilight.

Bitterness filled Raupert, pride and anger and a desire to kill. He was as dangerous, sitting there on Brannigan's bench, as an injured rattlesnake coiled beside a trail. The rattlesnake would strike out blindly to avenge its injury, and so would Sid Raupert. He waited quietly, and to his ears came the sound of footsteps, even, unhurried, striding along the boardwalk. Dr Eliot Carey came into the light that streamed through Brannigan's window and stopped.

"Raupert!" said Dr Carey.

There was a gun in Sid Raupert's hand. He had drawn the weapon when the footsteps came close. He did not move it. In his hand it was advantage enough.

"Yes," said Sid Raupert.

Trigger Vengeance

"You killed Doctor Zeitletz."

Now Sid raised the gun. The Schoyen-Ballard lay across Eliot Carey's arm, heavy, unwieldy, accurate as death itself but not the proper weapon for this occasion.

"Sure," snarled Sid Raupert, "an' I'll kill you, you——"

"Take me instead, Sid." The voice came quietly from the corner of Brannigan's saloon. Mark Neville stepped out into the light.

When Sid Raupert spoke Eliot Carey had lifted the Schuetzen rifle. He could no more have stopped the movement than he could have forestalled Sid Raupert's shot. The Schoyen-Ballard came up and hung poised and belched lead and fire, but before Eliot's finger could touch the trigger another gun had roared and lanced with red across the golden-yellow lamplight. At the side of the saloon Mark Neville collapsed, sliding down against the wall, but from the ground he fired twice. Sid Raupert had started up from the bench but was forced down upon the seat again as though some invisible force had thrust him back. Sid sat upon the bench and then, slowly toppling, sprawled down beside it. Eliot took a step forward, the Schoyen-Ballard still at his shoulder.

Across the street the dimly lighted door of Fry's livery spewed men: Ben Fry and John Mason, Sam Thomas and Laurence Irish. From the blacksmith shop the smith and another came running. Jack Brannigan, white apron flapping, and two men who had

Kill to Cure

been in the bar boiled out through the saloon door. John Mason reached the doctor's side, wrested the Schuetzen rifle from his hands, whirled and, with two long steps, came to where Sid Raupert lay. The blacksmith was bending over Raupert and now he straightened.

"He's dead as hell," announced the blacksmith, scarcely realizing what he said. "Dead as hell."

"You——" Mason turned toward Eliot Carey.

"Not him . . . me." Mark Neville's voice came calmly. "I reckon I'm done, too, John."

Ben Fry and Jack Brannigan picked up Mark Neville and carried him into the saloon. John Mason, his hand on Eliot's arm, the blacksmith, Sam Thomas, all the others came trooping in. There were more now, for the sound of the shots had brought men running. Neville's face was gray when they laid him on a card table, but his eyes were bright and his lips were smiling. "It was Sid an' me," said Mark Neville to Mason, who bent over him. "I came to get him."

"But I——" Eliot, too, was beside the table, his eyes on Neville's face.

Neville looked at the doctor, reading the young earnest face of the man. Mark Neville knew where his shots had gone, knew that he had been too slow, that Sid Raupert had beaten him. But the young doctor's eyes were haunted. Mark Neville owed Dr Carey and Mark Neville paid his debts.

"Not you, Doc," said Neville, lying gallantly. "You shot right down the street. I saw it."

Trigger Vengeance

Relief flooded the doctor's face and beads of sweat stood out upon his forehead. He had come to kill a man and he had not succeeded. Suddenly he was free again, free of the thing that had hung over him since he had read that page in Fritz Zeitletz' diary. It was as though a condemned man had suddenly been given a pardon. He had not killed Raupert. *He had not killed him!* Mark Neville's eyes were fixed on Dr Carey's face and, seeing the flood of relief that swept the doctor's eyes, Neville's graying lips twisted into a smile.

"I ain't got much time, John," Neville said. "You'd better let me tell you."

"Let me see," Dr Carey ordered, recalled to his duty. "Let me——"

"It's no use, Doc." Neville's voice was even. "Sid hit me twice, low down. I don't feel a thing. Let me tell John."

Eliot's hands were already busy with the man's clothing. He was laying bare the chest and abdomen. What he saw there made him wince. Neville had not been struck twice: four of Sid Raupert's shots had gone home. John Mason's eyes met those of the doctor and Eliot shook his head.

"I knew it," Neville said. "Listen, John. Sid killed Wing Lackey but before he done it he told Wing that he was the man that shot Doc Zeitletz. Wing lived long enough to tell me after I got to him."

Neville's eyes were blurring now and the words came thickly. He gathered himself with an effort. "Maybe it would have been better if this had happened a long time ago," he said. "Maybe . . . Doc, my foot got all right. You saved it for me. I——We're kind of even now, ain't . . . ?" The words trailed off. The blue eyes closed. Eliot Carey's hand went out to catch Neville's limp wrist. There was no pulse there but Mark Neville was not quite done. The blue eyes opened once more and Mark Neville said distinctly, "It had to be Sid an' me, didn't it?"

They waited for more, those men around the card table in Brannigan's, but no more came. The sheriff turned his eyes toward Eliot Carey, and, as though at command, the doctor bent down and placed his ear against Neville's chest. He straightened and shook his head. His face was white and he reeled a little on his feet.

"Sam," snapped John Mason, "you and the captain take the doctor home. I'll stay here and look after things."

Eliot Carey felt strong hands grasp his arms and, unresisting, allowed himself to be led away. Outside the door the cool night air struck his cheeks. He heard a little glad cry and then Janice was in his arms.

Captain Irish took the doctor home in his buggy, Janice riding close beside him, and Sam Thomas sitting behind, his plump legs hung over the low tailboard. In the surgery Thomas wanted to ask the doctor questions but Janice forestalled him. She gave the lawyer Dr Zeitletz' diary to read and pushed Thomas and her father out of the room. Eliot Carey sat in the swivel chair before the old roll-top desk, and when the captain and Sam Thomas were gone Janice came to him. She stood before the man, looking down at him, and Eliot, lifting his eyes, met her scrutiny.

"I meant to kill him," the doctor said slowly. "I knew that he had killed Fritz. I meant to kill him, deliberately. I——"

Janice dropped to her knees. Her hands caught and held Eliot's shoulders and her eyes searched into his. "Do you think you have to tell me?" she exclaimed. "Oh, my dear . . ."

The bright hair was against the doctor's chest, the girl's soft arms were about his neck. Slowly Eliot lifted his own arms until that slender, pliant body was clasped within them. His lips touched the hair, and the girl's voice came, a tender murmur.

"I love you."

Captain Irish, puzzled by the German of the diary, as was Sam Thomas, came to the door of the surgery, looked in and then stepped swiftly back into the hall.

"Better leave 'em alone," the captain informed Sam Thomas.

So it was that John Mason and Ben Fry, coming to the doctor's house, were met at the door by Laurence Irish and taken into the living room. In that room they talked, low voiced. Ben Fry spoke of the visit that Eliot had made to him, and Sam Thomas read a passage from Fritz Zeitletz' diary. John Mason, after hearing both Fry and Thomas, nodded his head.

Kill to Cure

"Doc knew all right," he said low voiced. "He went to kill Sid. He had it reasoned."

"But he didn't kill Sid," Sam Thomas announced. "Neville did that; and Sid killed Neville."

Mason turned away and walked to the window. He did not contradict Sam Thomas. There was no need. John Mason saw no reason to tell Thomas and the captain, or even Ben Fry, that the bullet that had killed Sid Raupert had made a little blue hole in Raupert's chest just above his heart, a hole far too small to have been made by a forty-five such as Mark Neville had dropped beside the wall of Brannigan's saloon. There was no use in telling that.

"Mark Neville——" began Thomas once more.

"Mark Neville was a pretty good man," interrupted John Mason, wheeling from the window. "He was an outlaw, all right, but he evened for things that had been done for him. Let it go, Sam. And, Captain, if you think those two could be interrupted a minute, I'd like to ask Doc a few questions."

The following morning brought a fresh shock to Soltura. The clerks, going to Welch's store, found the proprietor sitting at his desk. He was asleep, apparently, but when they tried to waken him he did not rouse. And so Thomas and Mason were called again, and Dr Carey summoned hastily, only to confirm death. There were two sheets of paper before Allan Welch upon the desk. Two sheets, written carefully and completely. Sam Thomas possessed himself of those papers and read them through, with

John Mason reading over his shoulder. When they had finished they looked each other in the eye and nodded, for Welch had written it all before he went to sleep.

"Jacks and Zeitletz and Lackey," said Mason slowly. "Sid killed them."

"Not to mention Barry," supplemented Thomas. "I think, John——"

"Yes?" said John Mason.

"I think I'll agree with you about Mark Neville," Sam Thomas completed. "He was a pretty good man."

CHAPTER XVIII

You'll Always Have to Go

DR ELIOT CAREY swung briskly along the walk toward his house. The May evening was pleasant, and a field lark, finding it so, climbed straight up and voiced his approbation. Dr Carey smiled. He was returning from Con Abeyta's where he had been called because the Abeyta boy had a stomach-ache. The people of Soltura called the doctor now, almost on any pretext. They liked to have him come, they liked the assurance he brought and, in two years, they had not forgotten the grim fight against diphtheria that he had won for them. *"Un buen doctor,"* they said, and a fighting man, *por Dios.*

Soltura was changing gradually. There was more money in the town and less poverty. Wool buyers came now to compete for the wool, and in the fall the sheep buyers came to bargain for the wether lambs. With more money Soltura had picked up. There was less dirt, less superstition, less ignorance.

Trigger Vengeance

And the word of *el doctor nuevo* was the law, not to be disregarded.

Soltura, Eliot Carey thought, as he hurried along the walk, was a pretty good place to live. A young man fresh out of medical school might turn up his nose at Soltura, but Dr Carey would not. Soltura made him a living and he liked the people and——Well, Soltura was just a pretty good place.

As he reached the gate and came up the walk toward the white house, the door opened and Janice stood framed in the opening. She was waiting, smiling quietly at her husband, and from behind Janice a small redheaded toddler made his uncertain way, staggering toward the steps. Fritz Carey was learning to walk but had not as yet achieved sureness. Dr Carey ran the last few yards toward the porch and swept Fritz up just as the baby reached the steps.

"Hullo, young man!" said Dr Carey.

With medicine case in one hand, baby caught by the other arm, kicking and chortling gleefully, Eliot Carey kissed his wife. Janice relieved him of the medicine case and his hat, following him on into the hall.

"How is Con's boy?" she asked.

"All right," Eliot answered briskly. "There isn't much the matter with him. Hey, young fellow, those are my ribs you're kicking!"

He put the baby on the floor and Fritz Carey promptly started toward the kitchen, took three steps and sat down violently. Not a whit disturbed, the small redhead got to his feet and went on. He had a friend in the kitchen.

In the living room Eliot Carey leaned back in a big chair, his legs thrust out before him.

"Do you remember what day this is?" Janice asked, perching on the arm of the chair, her arm about her husband's shoulders.

Eliot nodded. "Fritz's birthday," he answered. "I bought him a wagon. They'll bring it down from the store pretty soon."

"And the captain says that he is going to give Fritz a pony." Janice's eyes danced. "Do you suppose that will be all right?"

"It will go with the spurs that John Mason bought him and the saddle that Sam Thomas bought," Eliot answered comfortably. "He won't use them for a while. I thought those three were up to something. They ought to be coming, Janice. I saw Father Revelet and he said that he would be here by six."

"The captain is already here," Janice announced. "He's in the kitchen talking to María."

Steps sounded on the porch and Janice Carey, rising from the chair arm, went into the hall. Eliot could hear her voice in brief colloquy and then she returned, carrying a folded piece of soiled paper with the tips of her fingers.

Eliot took the paper and unfolded it. Janice settled down on the chair arm once more, reading over her husband's shoulder.

"Dere doctor," Ramón had written laboriously.

Trigger Vengeance

"My wife hes gone have baby. you come please. i no i treet you to ruff but i will pay you back cent by cent. Ramón Archuleta."

Dr Eliot Carey folded the missive and looked up at his wife.

"Ramón owes you for his last baby," Janice reminded. "And the captain is here for supper and Father Revelet is coming, and John Mason and Sam Thomas——"

Eliot Carey smiled and detached his wife's arm from his neck. "I suppose I'll have to go," he said, disregarding her protest.

Janice stood beside him. She tucked her hand under her husband's arm and pressed firmly.

"I suppose you'll have to," agreed Janice Carey, pride in her eyes. "I suppose you'll always have to go."

Out in the kitchen Fritz Carey gurgled gleefully. Grandfather Irish was riding him piggyback.

"When you think of the West, you think of Zane Grey." —*American Cowboy*

ZANE GREY

THE RESTORED, FULL-LENGTH NOVEL,
IN PAPERBACK FOR THE FIRST TIME!

The Great Trek

Sterl Hazelton is no stranger to trouble. But the shooting that made him an outlaw was one he didn't do. Though it was his cousin who pulled the trigger, Sterl took the blame, and now he has to leave the country if he wants to stay healthy. Sterl and his loyal friend, Red Krehl, set out for the greatest adventure of their lives, signing on for a cattle drive across the vast northern desert of Australia to the gold fields of the Kimberley Mountains. But it seems no matter where Sterl goes, trouble is bound to follow!

"Grey stands alone in a class untouched by others." —*Tombstone Epitaph*

ISBN 13: 978-0-8439-6062-4

John D. Nesbitt

"John Nesbitt knows working cowboys and ranch life well enough for you to chew the dirt with his characters." —*True West*

FIRST TIME IN PRINT!

Will Dryden picked the wrong time to ride onto the Redstone Ranch. He was looking for a job...and a missing man. But one of the Redstone's hands was just found killed, so tensions are riding high and not everyone's eager to welcome a stranger. The more questions Dryden asks, the more twisted everything seems, and the more certain he is that someone's got something to hide. Something worth killing for. Dryden just has to make sure he doesn't catch a bullet before he finds out what's behind all the...

TROUBLE AT THE REDSTONE

ISBN 13: 978-0-8439-6055-6

LOUIS L'AMOUR
TRAILING WEST

The Western stories of Louis L'Amour are loved the world over. His name has become synonymous with the West for millions of readers, as no other author has so brilliantly recreated that thrilling and unique era of American history. Here, collected together in paperback for the first time, are one of L'Amour's greatest novellas and three of his finest stories, all carefully restored to their original magazine publication versions.

The keystone of this collection, the novella *The Trail to Crazy Man*, features the courage and honor that characterize so much of L'Amour's best work. In it, Rafe Caradec heads out to Wyoming, determined to keep his word and protect the daughter of a dead friend from the man who wants to take her ranch—whether she wants his help or not. Each classic tale in this volume represents a doorway to the American West, a time of heroism and adventure, brought to life as only Louis L'Amour could do it!

ISBN 13: 978-0-8439-6067-9

COTTON SMITH

"Cotton Smith is one of the finest of a new breed of writers of the American West."

—Don Coldsmith

Return of the Spirit Rider

In the booming town of Denver, saloon owner Vin Lockhart is known as a savvy businessman with a quick gun. But he will never forget that he was raised an Oglala Sioux. So when Vin's Oglala friends needed help dealing with untruthful, encroaching white men, he swore he would do what he could. His dramatic journey will include encounters with Wild Bill Hickok and Buffalo Bill Cody. But when an ambush leaves him on the brink of death, his only hope is what an old Oglala shaman taught him long ago.

"Cotton Smith is one of the best new authors out there."

—Steven Law, Read West

ISBN 13: 978-0-8439-5854-6

ROBERT J. CONLEY

FIRST TIME IN PRINT!

No Need for a Gunfighter

"One of the most underrated and overlooked writers of our time, as well as the most skilled."
—Don Coldsmith, Author of the Spanish Bit Saga

BARJACK VS...EVERYBODY!

The town of Asininity didn't think they needed a tough-as-nails former gunfighter for a lawman anymore, so they tried—as nicely as they could—to fire Barjack. But Barjack likes the job, and he's not about to move on. With the dirt he knows about some pretty influential folks, there's no way he's leaving until he's damn good and ready. So it looks like it's the town versus the marshal in a fight to the finish... and neither side is going to play by the rules!

Conley is "in the ranks of N. Scott Momaday, Louise Erdrich, James Welch or W. P. Kinsella."
—*The Fort Worth Star-Telegram*

ISBN 13: 978-0-8439-6077-8

To order a book or to request a catalog call:
1-800-481-9191
This book is also available at your local bookstore, or you can check out our Web site **www.dorchesterpub.com** where you can look up your favorite authors, read excerpts, or glance at our discussion forum to see what people have to say about your favorite books.

OUTLAWS
PAUL BAGDON

Spur Award Finalist and Author of
Deserter and *Bronc Man*

Pound Taylor has just escaped from jail—and the hangman's noose—and he's eager to get back on the outlaw trail. For his gang he chooses his former cellmate and the father and brothers of his old partner, Zeb Stone. Pound wants to do things right, with lots of planning and minimum gunplay, but the Stone boys figure they can shoot first and worry about the repercussions later. Sure enough, that's just what they do—and they kill a man in the process. With the law breathing down their necks and the whole gang at one another's throats, Pound can see that hangman's noose getting closer all the time. Unless his friends kill him first!

ISBN 13: 978-0-8439-6073-0

LOUIS L'AMOUR

For millions of readers, the name Louis L'Amour is synonymous with the excitement of the Old West. But for too long, many of these tales have only been available in revised, altered versions, often very different from their original form. Here, collected together in paperback for the first time, are four of L'Amour's finest stories, all carefully restored to their initial magazine publication versions.

BIG MEDICINE

This collection includes L'Amour's wonderful short novel *Showdown on the Hogback*, an unforgettable story of ranchers uniting to fight back against the company that's trying to drive them off their land. "Big Medicine" pits a lone prospector against a band of nine Apaches. In "Trail to Pie Town," a man has to get out of town fast after a gunfight leaves his opponent dead on a saloon floor. And the title character in "McQueen of the Tumbling K" is out for revenge after gunmen ambush him and leave him to die.

AVAILABLE JANUARY 2009!

ISBN 13: 978-0-8439-6068-6

The Classic Film Collection

The Searchers by Alan LeMay

Hailed as one of the greatest American films, *The Searchers,* directed by John Ford and starring John Wayne, has had a direct influence on the works of Martin Scorsese, Steven Spielberg, and many others. Its gorgeous cinematic scope and deeply nuanced characters have proven timeless. And now available for the first time in decades is the powerful novel that inspired this iconic movie. (Coming February 2009!)

Destry Rides Again by Max Brand

Made in 1939, the Golden Year of Hollywood, *Destry Rides Again* helped launch Jimmy Stewart's career and made Marlene Dietrich an American icon. Now available for the first time in decades is the novel that inspired this much-loved movie. (Coming March 2009!)

The Man from Laramie by T. T. Flynn

In its original publication, *The Man from Laramie* had more than half a million copies in print. Shortly thereafter, it became one of the most recognized of the Anthony Mann/ Jimmy Stewart collaborations, known for darker films with morally complex characters. Now the novel upon which this classic movie was based is once again available—for the first time in more than fifty years. (Coming April 2009!)

The Unforgiven by Alan LeMay

In this epic American novel, which served as the basis for the classic film directed by John Huston and starring Burt Lancaster and Audrey Hepburn, a family is torn apart when an old enemy starts a vicious rumor that sets the range aflame. Don't miss the powerful novel that inspired the film the *Motion Picture Herald* calls "an absorbing and compelling drama of epic proportions." (Coming May 2009!)

☐ **YES!**

Sign me up for the Leisure Western Book Club and send my FREE BOOKS! If I choose to stay in the club, I will pay only $14.00* each month, a savings of $9.96!

NAME: _____

ADDRESS: _____

TELEPHONE: _____

EMAIL: _____

☐ I want to pay by credit card.

☐ **VISA**   ☐ **MasterCard.**   ☐ **DISCOVER**

ACCOUNT #: _____

EXPIRATION DATE: _____

SIGNATURE: _____

Mail this page along with $2.00 shipping and handling to:
Leisure Western Book Club
PO Box 6640
Wayne, PA 19087
Or fax (must include credit card information) to:
610-995-9274

You can also sign up online at www.dorchesterpub.com.
*Plus $2.00 for shipping. Offer open to residents of the U.S. and Canada only.
Canadian residents please call 1-800-481-9191 for pricing information.
If under 18, a parent or guardian must sign. Terms, prices and conditions subject to change. Subscription subject to acceptance. Dorchester Publishing reserves the right to reject any order or cancel any subscription.